Power Pm
Rom 10:9 38:9
I cry 56:8
Bottle Tears
have
power
Rev. 21:4
36:5
Weeping

Bryan Powell

The Last Magi

Bryan Powell

The Last Magi

Bryan M. Powell

Bryan Powell

Fantasy - Fiction, Christian - Fiction, Young Adult – Fiction, Historical - Fiction, Prophetic – Fiction
Cover design by Graphics_360 Arewa Olanrewaju
Photography by Amy McCarthy –
photographybymccarthy@gmail.com

Manufactured in the United States of America
ISBN- 13- 9781976355493
ISBN- 10 - 1976355494

Endorsements

The Last Magi completes the trilogy series by Author Bryan M. Powell, and will keep you on the edge of your seat from beginning to end. Just when you think you know what will happen next, the author takes you down a different path to entertain and surprise you. It appears no one is truly safe in this epic adventure. One of the main characters, Gasper, is the loveable Last Magi who will steal your heart and quickly become a favorite.

E. Day

Cast of Characters

Gasper – the last of the Magi is once again drawn into circumstances bigger than himself and learns to trust God.

Colt O'Dell – learns the value of standing alone in a crisis when he finds himself behind enemy lines.

Pastor Scott Wyatt – faces the greatest challenge to his ministry when his core beliefs are questioned.

Simon Levi – curator of the Institute in Antiquities would give his life to recover Israel's national treasure and does.

Saul Mueller – Israel's leading archaeologist is on a quest to find Israel's greatest treasure … the Ark, but his plan changes when he finds something greater.

Jacque de Molay St. John – the French Ambassador and the UN's newest General Secretary leads Israel and the PLO to sign the Unity Accord and throws the Christian world into crisis.

Abdullah Grahani Hasad – a Palestinian with dual citizenship happens to be in the right place and sees the greatest heist in the world take place.

Michael the Archangel – ever the guardian angel overseeing Israel during her next crisis, is once again called upon to defend her.

Prince Azrael – though assigned to watch his earthly charges, sometimes goes above and beyond the call of duty.

Prince Argos – His domain covers the southern regions of the United States, commanding over 22 legions of angels.

Prince Selaphiel – Helper of saintly prayers stands guard over the praying church.

Prince Uriel – Protects those under his care from the enemy.

Preface

No sooner had I finished writing the events concerning the lost medallion in my journal, then my wide-eyed granddaughters clamored for one more story. I had one, but I'd not shared it, not with my son and especially not my inquisitive granddaughters Belle and Mel. Who knows what their wild imaginations would have done with it.

As I contemplated adding one last story to my journal, Felicia's shadow crossed over where I was sitting. She took her seat next to me, intertwined her fingers with mine, making my heart flutter. After nearly thirty years, she still liked to lace her fingers into mine.

Turning her rounded eyes in my direction, she asked, "Which one, this time? You've told them all, multiple times."

###

It was true. I had told my children and grandchildren all but one, and it lay dormant in the back of my mind. My secret was known only to one other person, and he guarded it well. Now that I was nearing the end of my earthly pilgrimage, I began to reconsider my decision.

Lifting my pencil, I turned to a blank page and began writing ...

Prologue

Jerusalem, 587 B.C.

The stones lining the tunnel, two hundred feet beneath the temple complex, glowed orange from the light of a dozen torches as a group of priests and rabbis shuffled along the narrow passage. Above them and just outside the city's walls, gathered Nebuchadnezzar II and the Babylon army. After having conquered Pharaoh Necho at the battle of Carchemish, he set his sights on Israel and was now outside their gates. It would only be a matter of time before they breached the walls and flooded the city.

While King Jehoikim frittered away his remaining days, the High Priest and Levites decided, rather than let the Ark of the Covenant fall into enemy hands, they would risk moving it from its resting place where it stood for the last 402 years.

Laboring under the weight of the gold ensconced Ark with its pair of winged cherubim and fearing for their lives, the holy men huffed and puffed along the stone tunnel. With each step, leather sandals slapped against calloused feet in an uneven rhythm. The limestone tunnel, upon which their beloved city was built, was one of many which King Hezekiah's men carved during his reign. It was ideal for such construction and proved stable enough to bear up under years of steady growth.

After treading for nearly an hour, the priests and rabbis found their query. It was a small alcove hidden deep within the tunnel system. It was there they set the Ark on a stone pedestal. The move was successful and after sealing the chamber which would be the Ark's home for who knew how long, the High Priest and Levites retraced their steps. An hour later, Jerusalem fell.

By the time Nebuchadnezzar entered the city, all he found were the vessels of the house of God ... but no Ark. After plundering the city of its wealth, he burnt the temple, razed the city and deported the remaining citizens. Only the poorest of the poor were left, and even some of them scattered to neighboring countries. For the next seventy years, Jerusalem lay desolate, as promised by God because of their disobedience and rebellion.

As the few men who knew the whereabouts of the Ark died, so did the memory of its location. For the next 2600 years, it sat in darkness waiting for the day when it would be found and returned to the world stage.

This is the account of my small role in its discovery.

Gasper, the last Magi.

Chapter One

After saying a tearful good-bye, Simon, Colt and I left the kibbutz and Sasha's mudder. With the chapter of the lost medallion now closed, I could focus my attention on winning Felicia's heart and training my young understudy ... Colt O'Dell.

Rumbling along the highway leading back to Jerusalem, Simon broke the news that he found replacements for us in the Live Nativity display at the Institute in Antiquities. The news came as a great relief as I worried Colt would soon become homesick. It was refreshing to learn our services would only be needed for a few days until our replacements arrived. Using Simon's phone, I dial the O'Dell's phone number, I related the good news that we would soon be home.

As expected, Karen wanted to speak with Colt. Handing the phone to Colt, I smiled as my young charge gave his mother a glorified version of the last several days. It didn't surprise me that Colt embellished the story emphasizing his mysterious friend named Sasha.

By the time Colt finished, it took me another twenty minutes to correct the record as to my role in destroying the medallion. Rather than dampening the O'Dell's spirits, I chose not to mention any of the details related to Balthazar's and Melchior's deaths. That would be a story for later.

"I'm glad that's over," I said, handing the phone back to Simon. "I'm not excited about having to explain what happened to Balthazar and Melchior. I wish there was something I could have done to save them. I know everyone back home will be saddened."

My voice broke, but I couldn't help it. It had only been a day since I saw my friends fall, and already I missed them. Who was going to keep me straight when I stuck my foot in my mouth? Who was going to teach me the wisdom of the ages? Or chide me when I complained? The thought of Felicia's smiling face brightened my flagging spirit.

Holding the steering wheel with one hand, Simon reached across the space between us and patted my shoulder. "You have nothing to be ashamed of, my friend. War is no respecter of persons. It takes the good and the bad. I should know ... I've lost friends and family to a dozen wars and conflicts."

Nodding, I took a halting breath and put on a brave smile. Though he came from a different era entirely, his perspective on life and death was seasoned with a good dose of reality. He had seen both and was the better for it. It was a lesson I was still learning.

Colt reached over the seat and took my hand. "I'm going to need you now more than ever, Mr. Gasper. I've got so much to learn."

"Me? What can I teach you?" I shot back without thinking.

His eyes twinkled mischievously. "Oh, Mr. Gasper, you are the head of our order and are both wise and powerful. There is much I can learn from your example."

I tasseled his hair. "Colt, my boy, your confidence is sorely misplaced, I'm sure, but I will try not to disappoint you."

For the remainder of the trip, we sat in silence. While staring out the rider's side window at the changing desert, I reflected upon my life. Memories of an earlier journey some two-thousand years ago rattled around in the attic of my mind; some bitter sweet, others brought a smile.

Hearing Simon's voice in the background, I stirred from his musings. "You were saying?"

Simon cocked an eyebrow. "I was saying, you guys can stay with me until your replacements arrive. Then I'll crate you up and send you back the way you came. If all goes well, you should be home by week's end."

I glanced over my shoulder to the back seat where Colt lay sleeping. "That's great. At least, he won't fall too far behind in his studies. I'm sure he'll have some story to tell his classmates."

"We all have quite a story to tell."

Shifting, I looked Simon in the face. "Simon, you know we must downplay any news about the medallion or the Endor kibbutz will be overrun with treasure hunters not to mention the media."

After a moment's reflection, Simon nodded. "You're right. It will have to be our little secret." Changing the topic, Simon glanced at the three staves. "Tell me about those staves. Where did you get them?"

Fingering them, I inspected their smooth surfaces. "I can't speak to how Balthazar and Melchior came into possession of theirs. I assume they were passed down to them from their fathers. Mine, however, was given to me by my father. He often joked about it being Moses' rod used to part the Red Sea, but we both know, that one was buried with Moses somewhere on Mt. Horeb."

"Oy vey, with those being over a couple of thousand years old, they would make a great addition to my antiquity display." Simon gave me a wan smile and drove in silence.

His materialistic interest in the staves left me feeling unsettled. They were not designed to show off; neither was their power to be exploited. I hoped the matter would pass as soon as we got started with the Live Nativity Display.

The Judean sun hung tenaciously to the western horizon. Its golden rays, like fingers of shimmering light, clutched at the cumulous clouds like a drowning man a piece of wood. Finally, they released their hold allowing it to slip silently into the night. By the time we arrived at Simon Levi's home, Colt and I were ready for bed. Like a good host, Simon directed us to the two guest bedrooms where we would spend our remaining time in Israel. While we settled in and washed up, he busied himself in the kitchen preparing a meal of fresh fruits, cheeses and breads which he laid out on the table. As hungry as I was, it took little persuasion to fill my plate. Colt was somewhat reticent, but soon figured out if he didn't eat what was before him, he'd probably go hungry.

As we sat and ate, I couldn't help notice Simon kept eyeing the staves. Finally, he broke the silence. "Would you mind if I took a closer look at those staves?" Simon asked in between bites.

After a beat, I asked, "Why the sudden interest?"

His shoulders rose and fell. "Like I said, they would

make a wonderful addition to my display."

As I handed one of the staves to him, his fingers convulsed at his first touch, and he quickly withdrew his hand.

"What?" I asked.

"Oh, nothing, it must have been static."

He tried to act nonchalant, but I knew better. He felt it too. It was the same spine-tingling sensation I felt nearly every time I touched them. These were no ordinary stocks of old wood. Though no one said so, I knew these staves had been used in powerful ways, had wrought mighty works, and had been the instruments of God's power and mercy. But that didn't stop Simon from extending his hand a second time.

Fingering it more carefully, he peered at one through a magnifying glass for a long minute, then at the other two. "Were you aware that two of these have flakes of gold embedded in the fibers of the wood?"

At hearing the mention of gold, Colt's interest piqued. My raised hand stopped the inevitable question I knew was forming in his inquisitive mind.

Turning to our host, I said, "No, I was not aware of that. You weren't looking at mine, were you?"

Shaking his head, Simon handed mine back to me.

"No, yours is different from the other two. Look at these," he said, holding them up, "they are exactly the same length and diameter. Yours, on the other hand, is a little shorter and has an unusual wood grain. It's almost like it has a rod inside a rod. Theirs, however, are made of an entirely different wood. If I had to guess, I'd say it was acacia wood."

"Acacia wood, what kind of tree grows acacia

wood?" Colt blurted.

"An acacia tree," Simon answered, chuckling.

Colt couldn't hide his chagrin, but he had it coming.

Holding my friend's rods felt like I was given a sacred trust. These were the last tangible belongings of Balthazar and Melchior. For the first time, I inspected them with a close eye. "You know, you're right. I just took it for granted that Balthazar and Melchior got theirs from their fathers who passed them down from theirs. But as to leaving them on display, I'll have to think about that, not that I'll be needing them anymore."

Simon took a long swig of tea and cleared his throat thoughtfully. "I understand, but do give it some thought."

After my unsettling conversation with Simon, I returned to my bedroom. Sitting on a rumbled chair, I ran my fingers along the smooth surface of my staff. He was right; the two others seemed to have come from the same piece of wood. While I inspected them, a sense of loss invaded my mind. I missed Balthazar and Melchior. Ever since being awakened in the O'Dell's attic, we'd been inseparable. Even before that, we studied together, traveled together and suffered together. And to learn recently that Balthazar was my grandfather left a gaping hole in my heart. I had so many questions ... questions about my father and why he and Balthazar were estranged. Why had he never mentioned it on our long journey? Or while we sat around the campfire under a blanket of stars waiting for dawn. Why did he wait until his last dying moments to finally tell me? My eyes blurred, and I swept them aside angrily. Alas, those questions would never be answered, at least, not on this side of the grave.

In the short time since being awakened, I had seen too many friends cross over to the other side, and I wondered how many more I would lose.

###

The following morning, after a hearty breakfast, Simon drove us to the Institute in Antiquities fully dressed in our regalia. For me, he provided regal vesture like the kings of old. For Colt, he found a humble shepherd's toga, complete with an old-fashioned sling and stone pouch. Once he'd gotten us settled inside the glass-enclosed display, he went about his duties.

Glancing at the two additional manikins, Colt said, "These guys certainly don't look like Balthazar and Melchior, do they, Mr. Gasper?" Colt's whispered question bounced off the glass, and I feared someone would hear it.

Cocking my head, I stared at the two wax figurines. A fresh sense of guilt scraped over raw memories. "No, they certainly don't. But let's not think about it. Think about the good memories." I said this for my sake as much as his.

As the hours stretched, I heard muttering. "Colt, is that you?"

"Yeah, my back aches and I gotta go to the bathroom."

"I guess you'll learn not to drink so much milk before you come to the job-site."

"Job-site? Are we getting paid?"

Cocking my head slightly, I tried to keep a straight face. "Maybe I used the wrong word. No, we're not getting paid."

"Isn't there an actor's guild or something that governs

the length of time an actor can be on the job?"

It was all I could do to stifle a chuckle. Memories of my own complaining spirit pinched my conscience. "I don't think this would fall under their jurisdiction. Anyway, what are you going to do, stand up and walk off the display while all those adoring eyes are staring at you?"

Colt gulped and stared back at the group of elementary children on the other side of the glass. "I never thought about that. Do you think they'd mind if I took a break?"

By now, I too had felt nature's call, but I wasn't going to start complaining. After all, I was his wise and powerful leader. "Tell you what, next time Mr. Levi comes by, I'll get his attention and ask him to close the display for thirty minutes a day, so we can eat and use the restroom."

The suggestion seemed to mollify my young charge, until I heard him squirming.

"Okay, here comes Mr. Levi. I'll get his attention." Within a few minutes, the curtain was drawn across the Nativity scene, and Colt scampered off in search of the nearest restroom with me close behind.

"You know what they say, you don't buy a cup of coffee, you just lease it," I said.

Colt stared at me. It was obvious; he had never heard the saying. The comment, however, did bring a round of laughter from someone in the stall next to me. Feeling my face redden, I escaped the restroom before the unknown voice discovered my identity.

Retaking our positions, we waited out the rest of the day. By the time the lights flickered off and on, warning the guests that the Institute in Antiquities would soon close, my back ached, and I guessed so did Colt's.

"I am so looking forward to a hot bath," I said, rubbing my neck and back as we left the building.

"How soon will our replacements arrive?" Colt asked as he stretched.

Simon held up two fingers. "Give me a couple of days."

By the time we reached Simon's home that evening, Colt snored softly in the back seat, and I looked forward to doing the same.

Chapter Two

Once called "X City" by its developer, William Zeckendorf, Sr., the United Nations building was designed to rival Rockefeller Center. Occupying over seventeen acres along the East River, on Manhattan Island, the UN is considered an international territory Those entering its property technically leave the United States and are thus exempt from paying sales tax.

Inside, the United Nations General Assembly buzzed with excitement as the Security Council moved forward on a new and bold initiative. The proposal was the brain-child of Jacque de Molay St. John, the French Ambassador. As the son of a diplomat, he was cultured and suave. His square jaw, piercing dark eyes, and strong bearing made him look every bit the ambitious politician he was.

Fluent in three languages, and a Harvard Law School graduate, he not only was prepared to take a strong leadership position in the UN, but he had the drive to become its leader.

Standing behind a granite podium bearing the United Nations emblem, Jacque St. John read some of the details of his proposal. "This historic document will settle, once and for all, the disputes between Israel and her Palestinian neighbors. After months of working behind the scenes, I, and my staff, have hammered out an agreement which is not only fair to both parties, but will bring a lasting peace to the region."

As the lights dimmed, a dozen plasma screens flickered to life, and St. John began detailing the specifics of the agreement called, the Unity Accord. "At this point, let me direct your attention to page 478, paragraph three sub point Q2." He waited for the assembly to find their places. Reading, he continued, "this was the most contentious, but the most gratifying portion of the entire document as I personally worked with Prime Minister David ben Isakson to come to an understanding, which, I might add, has his full support. Once we, as a body, enact this proposal, he has given me assurances that he will lead the Knesset to adopt it. Now, allow me to walk you through it."

For the next thirty minutes, he elaborated on the specifics of the Unity Accord. "In exchange for being granted Permanent Membership on the Security Committee and given permission by the Palestinians to build the Third Temple near the Dome of the Rock, Israel ceded the West Bank and Gaza Strip to the Palestinian Liberation Organization. Except for dividing Jerusalem, the PLO got everything they wanted and it gives the nation of Israel what she has sought ever since Rome destroyed it in A.D. 70 … her beloved temple. It is a bold move for all the parties involved with risks at every turn, but one that they could live with. All we need now is for the UN General Assembly to approve the proposal." He concluded his comments and opened the floor for questions.

Following a contentious discussion in which the Russians and Muslim nations protested by walking out,

Sir Norman Wilcox, Secretary General from Great Britain, moved to bring the proposal to the floor for a vote.

Jacque St. John sat stoically and watched the 'Yea' votes accumulate over the 'Nays. Finally, after the last vote was cast, he stood and announced the verdict. "Ladies and gentlemen of the world, I can say with confidence, we have guaranteed peace in this generation. The Unity Accord has been approved. All that is lacking now is Israel's and the PLO's signatures which I expect will follow soon."

As the assembly concluded its business, Secretary General Wilcox retook his place behind the podium and announced that, due to his failing health, he was stepping down, a move which came as no surprise to some.

"I recommend we install the French Ambassador Jacque de Molay St. John as temporary Secretary General until a permanent replacement can be found."

Once again, the 'yeas' carried the day and Jacque St. John took his place where Sir Norman Wilcox stood minutes before. "Thank you for placing your confidence in me. I will not fail to maintain the vision and goal of this august assembly."

After his concluding remarks, the assembly scattered to green rooms, spin-rooms and press conferences while St. John began making arrangements to solidify his position as permanent head of the UN.

From his vantage point atop Mt. Herman, Michael the Archangel peered at the western horizon. At first, he thought it was just another bank of clouds. But the longer he stared, the more he became convinced, it was no small storm. Above the horizon rose a large, black cumulous convection of churning, swirling currents. The speed at which it traveled told him it was not a weather system, neither was it a dust storm. This was the eastward movement of the evil one, and it was headed directly at Israel.

Summoning his longtime ally, Prince Gabriel, he began to pace the azure corridors. With each stride, a small golden dust-angel curled up in concentric circles. "We have a problem," he began, "I know we are living in the latter days. Ever since Israel became a nation in 1948, the world seems unified in its opposition to her existence, and I have seen a coming storm." His husky voice carried a tone of dread, not for himself, neither for his forces, but for the nation he so cherished.

Israel, the apple of God's eye, was also his nation. Since its inception, Israel was his to protect. There were times, because of their disobedience, the Almighty had to bring severe judgment but he was always there to guard the Lord's elect.

Prince Gabriel crossed his arms and gazed at the gathering storm. "Your instructions, my lord?"

"The Almighty has not revealed to me the future, for I have asked Him. He has, however, assured me all is well in the kingdom of Heaven. I can only assume this is not the time of judgment spoken by the prophets, but is a time of testing. There are several individuals who may be at the center of this tempest, and will be sorely tested. I want you to place a hedge of protection around Gasper, and the young boy named Colt O'Dell."

At the mention of those names, Prince Gabriel cocked an eye. "I thought we were through with them ... that they were on their way home."

"That is the plan, but with this storm coming in their direction at such a rapid pace, I fear it will arrive before they depart. That being the case, they will need your undivided attention."

The two mightiest angels in God's kingdom clasped each other's forearm in a manly grip.

"And you say, all is well in the kingdom of Heaven?"

Michael nodded grimly.

Taking heart, Prince Gabriel hoisted his mighty shield and locked it in place. Then he glanced at the host of heavenly warriors under his command and said, "Forces of light, salute!"

The heavens rang as an innumerable host of celestial beings shouted the unique name by which their creator was known, then, rose to meet the advancing storm.

Chapter Three

The following day, the Knesset, Israel's ruling body consisting of 120 elected officials, gathered to make a historic decision. Seated behind long rows of light paneled wooden desks, the thirteen parties representing the diverse population of Israel took their places. In the upper balcony and in the media center, anxious reporters and their camera crews stood ready to capture the moment as Israel took the greatest leap of faith since following Moses out of Egypt.

Facing in the opposite direction toward the general seating area, was a seven foot high, seventy foot long counter with a menorah embedded on its front. Seated behind it, Prime Minister David ben Isakson eyed the assembly and wondered if his nation had the stomach for such a bold move. After all the fighting, the skirmishes, the bloodshed … was his nation ready to lay down their guns and essentially live in a two-state nation? Yes, they were getting to rebuild their temple, but at what cost? With this vote, they were giving away nearly half their landmass … land many of his countrymen had fought bitterly to gain, only to be handed over to people who neither cared for it, nor belonged on it. He breathed out a prayer and gaveled the assembly to order.

Being a member of the Labor party gave him some advantage, but he still had to do some arm twisting in order to cobble together a coalition large enough to overcome the opposition party. After an afternoon of bickering, the measure passed. In a move which shocked the Christian world, Prime Minister David ben Isakson announced his country's decision to sign the Unity Accord.

###

Within minutes of the vote, the air-waves and newsstands echoed the shocking news. Israel had signed the peace treaty. Prophets and pundits began debating the hallmark decision. Iran's Ayatollah, their leading religious cleric, condemned the action citing Israel was attempting to start a holy war. Even factions within the US government showed concern, albeit, behind closed doors and off the record.

Like many preachers and evangelists across the country, Pastor Wyatt's telephone began a constant drumbeat of calls. His attempt to quell nervous church member's concerns was an uphill battle.

Angela knocked on her husband's office door and entered before he could respond. He was in deep conversation with an elderly church member who insisted this was the beginning of woes. He partly believed it.

Scott finally extracted himself from the phone and leaned back, giving his wife a weary smile. "That was Miss Emma. She thinks we need to pack up and move to the mountains before they fall on us," he said shaking his head.

Angela walked around the desk and perched a hip on the corner. "What do you think? Should we be taking cover in a cave or a cabin in the woods?" Her question was half serious.

Shaking his head, Scott stood and wrapped his arms around Angela and tugged her close. "I think we'll just ride it out right where we are. Remember the Y2K scare? A lot of folks thought it was the end of the world and look at us. Here we are well into the 21st century as healthy as clams."

Patting his belly, she smiled. "A bit too healthy, if you ask me. Maybe we should adhere to a few austerity measures for your waistline's sake."

As she spoke, the phone resumed its jangling. Giving her an apologetic smile, he retook his seat.

"This is Pastor Wyatt, how may I help you?" It was Gasper.

"Oh, hello Gasper. Let me put you on speaker so Angela can hear you." He pressed the button. "Go ahead, what's going on?"

Angela leaned over to speak directly into the phone. As she did, a cascade of golden hair fell forward which she attempted to brush aside. "Hello, Mr. Gasper. How are you and Colt doing?"

A rush of static filled the speaker. "Fine, Mrs. Wyatt. We are having an interesting time here in Israel. So far, we've been able to do a little sightseeing in our free time. We've visited Gethsemane, Gordon's Calvary and of course, the Garden tomb. And would you believe it ... it's empty, just as the angel said." He spoke in a light tone.

Sitting straight, Scott fingered a pencil. "Any news as to your return? The O'Dells are quite anxious to see their son."

"Jacob's uncle, Mr. Simon Levi, is taking good care of us, and he tells me we should be finished by the end of the week. But that's not what I called about."

Scott shot a cautious look at his wife. "So why did you call?"

After a slight pause, Gasper began. "It's about Israel signing the peace agreement. It's crazy over here. Half the Israelis are happy and half are mad as wet bumble bees. Do you have an opinion about that?"

Wiping his brow, Scott released a tired sigh. "I think the saying is, 'mad as a wet hornet.' But as to your question … it's too early to tell. My phone has been ringing incessantly. I have been swamped with concerned church members asking the same question. Honestly, I don't think there is anything to it."

"There might not be on your side of the Atlantic, but over here it's like a mad-house. Riots are breaking out all over the city. The Israeli citizens are up in arms. I can't tell if they are angrier at their government for voting in a two-state nation or giving away half their land. Can you believe it? They have actually started construction on the Third Temple. Simon says the priests and rabbis are planning on killing the red heifer in preparation for anointing a High Priest who will restore the sacrificial system." Gasper paused to catch his breath, giving Scott little chance to respond.

Sitting up straighter, Pastor Wyatt's tone darkened. "For years there have been attempts to divide Israel into two states. Even as recently as a few months ago, there was a meeting of 70 nations in Paris, France. Their sole purpose was to discuss that very issue. On the other hand, I have heard rumors all my adult life about Israel stockpiling building materials in preparation for the construction of the Third Temple … that they even had several red heifers prepared for slaughter, but I'd dismissed it as speculation. I guess now it is a reality."

Gasper let out a nervous chuckle. "Maybe I should have packed for a longer stay."

"Look, Gasper, keep me informed as much as you can until you leave, which, I hope is soon. I wouldn't want you caught up in an international situation."

"You mean, war?"

"Yeah, but I hope it never comes to that. By the way, what do Balthazar and Melchior think of all this? Do they have any ideas?"

At the mention of his two mentors and best friends, Gasper fell silent. After a moment, he found his voice. "Uh, well, actually, Balthazar and Melchior have a much better understanding of the situation than me. I'm still learning."

Scott chuckled. "Well, give them my regards and tell them we are all praying for you and hope you come home soon."

"Thank you, Pastor. That means a lot ... God bless you."

Chapter Four

Swerving wildly, Simon Levi navigated through the confusing Jerusalem traffic with me and Colt gripping the seat and dashboard to keep from getting thrown around the interior of his car. It had been another long day at the Institute in Antiquities. All Simon could talk about was his country's decision.

"Oy, vey, what could this mean in prophecy?" he asked, his hands waving animatedly.

Not being that familiar with the nuances of biblical prophecy, I was at a loss for words. "Frankly, I'm not sure what to think. I'll need to study it."

I could tell my answer didn't satisfy my friend, but it was true. From my understanding of eschatology, the Lord would come before any peace treaty with Israel was signed. This certainly didn't jibe with what I thought I knew. When he mentioned that his government had already begun construction on the Third Temple, my heart stumbled. *Surely we were not living in the Tribulation.* My thoughts crashed like waves against a seawall.

Later that night, after dinner, I excused myself and retreated to my bedroom. I needed time to think, to study ... to pray. From my examination of scripture, I discovered there would be a seven-year peace agreement. Forty-two months later ... halfway through, the

Antichrist would violate its terms by entering the temple, take his place on or somewhere near the Ark and declare himself God. There was just one problem ... no one knew where the Ark of the Covenant was located and hadn't for centuries. That was the good news. The bad news, at least from my perspective was, the nation had become obsessed with finding it.

The following morning, as we finished breakfast, Simon's phone buzzed. Colt and I excused ourselves and began to prepare our lunches while Simon talked. Despite our attempt at giving Simon some privacy, I could hear the caller's booming voice from the other room.

"Have you heard the good news?" the man asked.

"To which good news are you referring, my old friend? That I have the last of the Magi living in my home? Or that Israel is about to start a world war by attempting to rebuild the temple?"

"Simon, Simon, ever the optimist. If we started the next world war, don't you know we are destined to win it? Come now, let us celebrate."

"Celebrate what?" his hands coming up in perpetual question.

The jubilant caller continued speaking. "We have what we have ... peace in our generation."

Nodding, Simon rubbed the palm of his hand across the few straggly hairs which clung tenaciously to his wrinkled forehead like seaweed. "That's what I'm afraid of. Chamberlain's statement still haunts me."

Apparently ignoring his less than stellar enthusiasm, the caller pressed on. "Would you be interested in joining a team I am putting together?"

"For what purpose is this team? I am too old for soccer, and I don't understand rugby."

Belly laughter filled the connection. "For the purpose of finding the Ark of God, you old schmuck."

Upon hearing the caller mention the Ark of God, my ears perked up. The idea of searching for and finding the lost Ark of God more than outweighed my desire to go home, but who was I? The last time I'd set foot in this country was over two thousand years ago. And even then, the Ark of God was only a distant memory, a myth, a legend. No one knew if it still existed let alone, where to look for it.

"Who else is on this team of yours?" I heard Simon ask.

Again, the man's enthusiastic response caught me by surprise.
"Saul Mueller."

Saul Mueller was the country's leading archaeologist. His discoveries made world news as far west as North Hamilton, Georgia. Many of his finds rested within the walls and displays of the very building where Colt and I stood.

"Yes, I would be honored to serve on such a team … with one condition."

"Oh? Only one?" I heard the caller ask.

"Well, maybe more, but for now, only one."

"And that is?"

"That you allow me to introduce my friend and guest, Gasper, the last remaining Magi, to Mr. Mueller. I'm sure the two men would hit it off rather well."

Although I didn't know what we might be hitting off, I felt my face heat at his glowing support. *If only*

Balthazar and Melchior were here. They would have been so pleased.

"Yes, and I would like you to take a look at the three staves he possesses. I'm sure he would be very excited to hear your take on them. I'd heard a rumor that one of them could actually be Moses' rod. It has an unusual wood grain. With the right persuasion, you might even talk him into loaning them to the museum."

At hearing his caviler enthusiasm of my rod, I huffed. "Who was that?" I asked as Simon hung up.

"That was Rabbi Musselmen, Israel's leading Ark-ologist, as he called himself," Simon answered with a chuckle. "He invited me to join his team in search of the Ark. I'm very excited. Maybe you can point us in the right direction, what with you being a two thousand-year-old wise man and all."

I bristled at his comment, but Colt shot me a warning glance. "Well actually, by the time my colleagues and I arrived in Jerusalem; the Ark was long gone. As a matter of fact, when Yeshiva died, the curtain in the Holy of Holies was ripped from top to bottom revealing an empty room."

Simon's cold stare sent a chill down my back.

Hands extended, I asked, "What? You haven't heard that?" forgetting he was a new believer.

"Actually, no ... I haven't. My knowledge of that time frame is quite sketchy."

I nodded and tried to calm my exuberance. "Well, maybe that's the area where we should study together before you start hunting all over the middle-east for something God rendered obsolete."

His chest heaving, Simon's eyes burned. "Obsolete?"

his voice ratcheted up a notch. "That may or may not be so, but as a national treasure, it is very valuable. You, of all people, should know that. Once we find it, and we will, we will reinstate the sacrificial system, and finally show the goy what a righteous nation looks like."

My heart sank. His zeal was without knowledge, but what was I to say? I hoped in the coming days to find time to show him that he was no longer bound by the Law.

Feeling a tug on my coat sleeve, I turned.

"What's a goy?" Colt's innocent question brought Simon to an abrupt halt in his diatribe.

It was obvious he'd forgotten that Colt was not Jewish.

"It is a derogative term for Gentile, but don't take it personally, I'm sure Mr. Levi didn't mean it that way. Did you Simon?" I held my breath, waiting for his answer.

Simon lowered his eyes. "No, sorry if I offended you. Shall we be going?"

Chapter Five

T he Jeep Cherokee, driven by Amber Kline had only 500 miles on its speedometer ... one of the perks which came with her being one of the hottest info babes in the television business. With the new-car smell still fresh in the passenger compartment, Amber rolled down the windows, folded back the top and took off heading north on Highway 9A out of Manhattan.

She had blown it big time, and she knew it. Her boss, Noel Womack, was ticked off at her for getting her story in just after the deadline for the third time in as many weeks. It seemed she could never get a break. Checking out her sources, getting the facts right, editing and re-editing, word sculpturing her piece ... the task seemed overwhelming. Her stuff was good, no, not good ... it was outstanding, but late didn't cut it in the news business.

She needed a break. She needed to get away from the deadlines, the pressure, and the angry looks from her boss. So this afternoon she found herself racing twenty miles an hour over the speed limit, along the Hudson River. Her auburn hair blew in the wind as if she hadn't a care in the world. Were it not for the fact she was rapidly becoming a household name, she might have been looking for a new line of work. Nevertheless, her interview with the French Ambassador to the UN, a man named Jacque de Molay St. John earlier that week kept her hopes alive. Her boss's instructions to do a thorough background check still rang in her ears. *Grill him. If he's got a skeleton in the closet, find it. If he has women on the side, get their sizes. If there are bodies in the cemetery, he put there, dig them up. I want to know everything about him.*

Her Blackberry vibrated angrily ... it was her boss.

"Amber, where in the name of Sam Hill are you? I've been trying to reach you for hours. Don't you ever check your messages?"

"Yes, sir, I check my messages, I knew you wanted to talk to me, but I wasn't so sure I wanted to hear what you had to say."

"How do you know what I was about to say? Are you adding omniscience to your list of abilities?" he huffed angrily.

Noel treated her as if she could walk on water, and she knew it.

"No, sir, but I can read the tea leaves. I can have my stuff packed up and out of the office by tomorrow."

"The only stuff you need to get packed up is the stuff you'll need to take with you on your next assignment."

"You're not firing me?" she stuttered.

"Me? Fire you? Do you think I'm crazy? I wouldn't let the best info babe in the business go because she got her human-interest piece in late. I had a feeling you would and had my own piece ready to take its place."

Hearing him call her an info babe irritated her to no end, but she was in no position to argue. She let the sexist comment slide and focused on the road ahead.

"You mean to say you're not mad?"

"No, Amber, I didn't say that. Of course I'm mad.

I'm mad most of the time and at most of the people who work for me. It's part of my job description," he said with a chuckle. "Now I have noticed your lack of motivation in doing human-interest stories. I know you like the hard-hitting interviews when you rip your subjects apart and leave them in a puddle of tears."

"You got me, guilty as charged. So why the powder-puff stories if you know what makes me tick?"

"Let's just say it was a lack of viable targets and leave it there."

"So why the urgent call? Do you have a *viable target*?"

Womack paused as if shuffling papers. "Yes, you might say so. Now get your tail back here and let's you and I do some serious planning."

An hour later, a rather windblown redhead came strutting through the main lobby of the CCN building in downtown New York City. She approached the elevator and pushed the button for the 10th floor and wondered how many germs she just picked up on her finger. There were three other occupants on the elevator; men whom she had noticed giving her the once over. She smiled and turned her head as if to say, 'I'm not interested in talking to you.'

As she waited for the elevator doors to close, she casually opened her purse, and pulled out a small bottle of hand purifier. Dropping a few drops in her palm, she rubbed them together. Then, after applying a fresh layer of red lipstick, she fluffed her hair and offered the man closest to her a come-hither smile. Before he could react, the doors slid open, and she pranced through. Like a model walking the runway, she strutted a little more than necessary down the hall. *Might as well give 'em something to look at,* she mused.

Entering the CCN war room, she greeted the secretary with a wave.

"Hello Miss Kline. You're looking refreshed, this morning."

Amber paused long enough to assess the woman's professional attire. It was a bit pinched in all the wrong places, but there again, the woman had been with the company longer than she could remember. "It's amazing what a 70 mile an hour drive will do for you. You should try it sometime."

Seemingly ignoring the catty comment, the secretary stood and opened the door to Noel's office. "Caution, he's in a bad mood," she whispered as Amber brushed past.

Amber nodded knowingly. "Yes, I know. He's always in a bad mood. It's part of his job description, he tells me." She turned to face her boss.

His eyes glinted with a strange look of amusement and appreciation, "What took ya?"

"Traffic—"

"Not interested." He waved aside her lame excuse. "Let's get one thing straight. No more late entries. I'm fed up with covering your tail. You got that?" The comment seemed as much for his secretary's information as it was hers.

"Oh, absolutely, sir. No more late stuff from me." She lied. She had no intention of working any harder than she had to.

Besides, you need me.

It was clear he didn't believe a word she said.

As the secretary closed the door, Amber took a seat, crossed one leg over the other knee and sat up straight. "I'm sure you didn't have me rush back here to lecture me about my tardiness. Do you have an assignment for me or not?"

"Yeah, I got an assignment for you, but not like the one with some old movie celebrity. That interview with Jacque St. whatever was outstanding. I want you to do a follow-up on him. My sources tell me he's about to be named the permanent Secretary General of the United Nations."

"Why the anal exam? I thought CCN supported the UN and all things global?"

Standing, Womack crossed his arms over his broad girth. "I do. I just don't want any surprises. If what I've heard about him turns out to be true, then I want to know it first. If, on the other hand, he turns out to be some religious nut case, well ..."

"Nut case? I'm not following you, sir."

Womack chuckled. "No, I don't suppose you would. Suffice it to say, I've grown up with certain *biblical teaching.*" He offered her a pair of air quotes and continued. "This Unity treaty ... accord ... whatever they call it, well, frankly, it's got me wondering. Heck, it's got a lot of people wondering."

"Wondering? Sir, I still don't get it. Do you mind explaining?"

Womack came around and plopped down in a chair next to Amber. "You ever heard of the Antichrist?"

Feeling the blood drain from her face, Amber took a dry swallow. "Hasn't everybody? You know, six, six, six, the whole rapture thing. There's been scores of movies made on the end of the world scenario, so yeah, I've got an idea."

"Good, keep it between you and me, but watch your back. Now get out of here. Do your homework, get an interview and let's put this Antichrist fear to bed."

"Oh, absolutely, with pleasure." Standing, she strutted toward the door, but paused, hand on the knob. With a quick glance over her shoulder, she caught her boss watching her admiringly. Smiling to herself, she swung the door open and stepped out leaving the door hanging like a kid with a goofy grin.

Chapter Six

It had taken Amber two long days to research the history of the United Nations. Following the evidence, she dug deeper. Her investigation took her to the League of Nations and beyond. One thing was common; there was always someone or some group behind the global movements pulling the strings of power. More questions arose. Late one afternoon she stumbled over the name Knight Templars. Their movement over several hundred years led to much bloodshed. She did, however, discover one interesting fact. The name Jacque de Molay wasn't the first time it had been used. During the dark ages, King Philip IV of France owed the Knight Templars and their militant wing, The Order of Hospitallers, a vast sum of money. He appealed to the Pope and had the Knight Templars declared heretics. The Pope also gave him license to arrest, torture and kill those who refused to accept his terms. Their Grand Master, Sir Jacque de Molay was burned at the stake in 1314. By then, the Order had morphed and became known as The Order of St. John the Beloved of Jerusalem. Though interesting, Amber didn't see the relevance, and decided to go with her gut. It had not failed her in the past, it wouldn't fail her now.

Smartly dressed in a hot pink blouse over cream colored form fitting slacks, Amber stepped out of her

Jeep Cherokee and made her way into the United Nations building. She hoped her last interview with Mr. St. John would lead to a second, especially with his newly appointed position. Her heels clicked sharply on the terrazzo floor as she crossed the spacious lobby and approached the receptionist's desk.

"Hello, I'm Amber Kline with CCN. I have an appointment with Mr. St. John. Could you tell him I am here?"

A look of concern swept over the receptionist's face, and Amber couldn't tell if she was stalling or irritated.

"I'm sorry Miss—"

"Miss Kline," she repeated, "I'm here to do a follow-up with Mr. St. John," she added confidently.

The receptionist pulled a temporary guest badge attached to a lanyard from her desk and handed it to her. "Go to the 38th floor and speak to his secretary. I'm sure she can help you get an appointment."

Being semi-familiar with the layout of the UN buildings, Amber followed her instructions and found her way to the right location where she repeated her request.

"Hmm, I don't seem to have you down for an appointment," she said, looking at his itinerary. "As a matter of fact, he is currently out of the country. I don't expect him back until tomorrow."

"Oh, I'm sorry, my news director, Mr. Womack, must have gotten the dates mixed up when he set up the appointment. Could you pencil me in for an interview at Mr. St. John's earliest convenience?"

After rechecking his itinerary, the woman nodded. "Oh, yes, he has an opening tomorrow at 1:45 p.m. Would that work for you?"

"That works perfectly. Thank you." She turned and retraced her steps.

The ruse worked like a charm. It almost always does. It got me an unscheduled appointment with one of the most powerful men in the world. Smiling to herself, she jotted down the date and time in her appointment book. After thanking the receptionist in the lobby, she pranced out into the bright afternoon sun.

###

The following day, Amber Kline sat in the waiting area counting the minutes before her appointment with the newly appointed UN Secretary General. Having met with him a few weeks ago only heightened her sense of anticipation. She was drawn to his strong personality, to his power. Being a single woman and him being unattached, was an extra perk ... an angle she hoped to use to her advantage.

###

Across the hall, in a large, well-appointed corner office overlooking the East River, sat Jacque de Molay St. John. Having quietly eliminated any opposition to his permanent appointment as Secretary General, he now held the position of power his ancestors had only imagined. It had always been his dream to have power, however, he had never expected so much in so short a time, and at such little bloodshed. "One must crack a few eggs if one is to make an omelet," his father oft reminded him; a metaphor he'd not squandered on mere culinary advice.

Now on to the real power, he mused. *If my associate in Israel can get his hands on the—*

"Sir, Miss Kline is here," His thoughts were

interrupted by his secretary. "Shall I keep her waiting?"

The muscles in Jacque's strong jawline tightened. His last interview with the pretty reporter didn't go as he'd planned. It was supposed to have been a puff-piece on an obscure French Ambassador who happened to be the most eligible bachelor in the world. As it turned out, she came dangerously close to uncovering his deepest secret. *Beautiful woman, fair reporter.* Her innocent question about how his family prospered during Nazi Germany's occupation of France, irritated him. If she continued that line of questioning, he might be forced to do something she'd regret.

"No, I'll see her now. Send her in." He paused to think. "Oh, and have a couple of my men ready to tail her after she leaves. I want to know where she goes and who she talks to."

"Yes, sir, I'll get right on it."

A moment later, Amber stepped through the door and into Jacque de Molay St. John's office and into his life.

Standing, he greeted the tall, shapely woman. Giving her a slight bow, he took her hand and kissed the back of it. If nothing else, he was the consummate gentleman.

"Please take a seat, Miss Kline." He motioned to the seating area a space apart from his desk.

She licked her lips and followed his lead.

"Care for a drink?" he offered, motioning to a wide bar offering an array of spirits.

"No, thank you," she said as he poured himself a glass of Bourbon.

After taking a sip, he set the tumbler on the end table next to him, and crossed his legs. He wanted to remain in control, so he held her gaze, waiting for the first question.

"Now, Miss Kline, how may I be of service to you?"

Amber fumbled with her notebook as she prepared to begin.

His continued stare had its desired effect. *Good, she's rattled.*

"Mr. Secretary General, may I record this?" she asked laying a small recorder on the edge of the coffee table.

With a wave, he gave her an award-winning smile. "But of course, mademoiselle, I want you to get every word ... and not miss a thing."

Amber's fingers trembled slightly as she pressed the record button. "First, let me congratulate you on your appointment to Secretary General. I'm sure your nation is very proud."

"Permanent appointment," he added.

"Permanent?"

"Yes, Miss Kline, you are getting an exclusive. It seems those who opposed my being appointed as permanent Secretary General have either changed their vote or simply left the scene."

Amber felt her face darkened.

"I can see, Miss Kline, you are not quite up to speed on the ever-changing international landscape." He waved his hand. "That's all right. Recent events have moved at such a rapid pace, even I am taken aback."

Amber's fingers flew over the keys on her iPad. Ignoring any spelling errors, all she wanted to do was capture the moment.

"When will you make an official announcement?"

He took another sip of Bourbon and dabbed his lips with a white napkin before answering. The pause was just enough to cause Amber to lean forward in anticipation.

"Soon. With all that is taking place in the Middle East, I want the world to stay focused on the Unity Accord. Also, I am planning on a summit with the heads of all the major religions. Then, we will have a big celebration, and I'd like to invite you to the occasion as my personal guest."

Amber's heart quickened. This was the opportunity of a lifetime and she was not about to pass it up. Slightly shaken, she said, "Thank you, Mr. Secretary General—"

"Please, call me Jacque. It's much too formal to constantly be referring to me as a position rather than a man." As he spoke, he softened his tone, knowing its soothing effect. It was a practiced skill he had developed over the years, and he used it to get his way on more than one occasion.

Amber, clearly taken aback, glanced at her notes, then back into his eyes. "I had a question about the Unity Accord. Do you have any plans to attend Israel's dedication celebration when they finish building the Third Temple?"

Jacque paused in reflection. "Well, Miss Kline, that is a long way off, and they have not invited me. So, let me say, if invited, I would be honored to attend. Over the last year, I have become a big fan of Mr. Isakson. He and I spend many hours together working out the details of the Unity Accord, not to mention, to consume quite a bit of Bourbon." At that, he lifted his glass and feigned a toast, before taking another sip.

Still holding her gaze, he watched Amber shift uncomfortably.

"What assurances can you give the American people that we have a lasting peace on the global stage?"

What a softball question. Smiling, St. John clearly enjoyed the moment. "Wonderful question Miss Kline. By the way, is that a German last name?"

Flustered, Amber appeared to have been caught off guard. "Yes, I, I think so, why?"

St. John brushed away her question. "I can assure the American people, with Israel and the Palestinian Liberation Organization showing us the way forward, we can blaze a trail into a brave new world of peace and prosperity."

After taking one more glance at her notes, she inhaled before asking her next question. "Mr. Secretary General, there are rumored questions about you being some kind of end of the world tyrant. Can you allay the fears of the American Christian community?"

St. John stood and began to pace in a slow, deliberate manner. "Miss Kline, I can assure you, I am no tyrant, neither am I the antichrist, if that's what you're asking. I am just a humble servant of the people who has been thrust into the limelight by sheer circumstance."

His self-effacing comment didn't do much to calm her anxiety, but that was the best she could do without insulting the man with a follow-up question.

As Amber turned off her recorder and put away her notebook, St. John leaned into her personal space and touched her forearm. "Miss Kline," their eyes met. "I would be honored if you joined my team. That is to say, I'd like you to be my press secretary and spokeswoman."

Putting her hand to her heaving chest, Amber stared into his eyes.

You will accept, he thought.

St. John saw it in her eyes. The idea had taken root. It

would only be a matter of time.

Stepping back, Amber caught her breath. "I'd ... be ... delighted, I think. Let me check with Mr. Womack."

Moving closer, St. John led her to the door. "That's already been handled. Submit your article on time today and after that, you're all mine." His broad grin sent Amber on her way with a skip in her step.

As Amber walked to her jeep, a pair of claws tried to penetrate her skull. The spirits of pride, and self-indulgence fought for dominance in her mind. Her desire to become famous had driven her all her life. Despite her father's physical abuse and her mother's subsequent rejection, she determined to make something of herself. This was her chance to make it big, and she wasn't going to miss it. But the further she walked, the more doubts arose in her mind. And then there was that voice she'd heard inside her head. *You will accept.* Was that hers ... or his?

Chapter Seven

The news that the replacements would be delayed, due to the rapidly changing political landscape in the Middle East, hit Colt particularly hard. The country of origin, Saudi Arabia, refused to release their museum pieces thus making their stay indefinite. After a few days, the strain of being away from home and family began to show on Colt's face.

I heard his sniffles during supper, and though he put on a brave front, I knew he was hurting. His appetite had waned and even his interest in sight-seeing had sputtered. When he receded to his bedroom early, I knew something was wrong. I hoped it wasn't the bad dreams again.

"Care to talk about it," I asked, peering around the doorframe, as he slouched on his bed.

"I miss my mom and dad," he said with a trembling chin.

I slid next to him and threw my arm around his shaking shoulders. I knew the pain of being alone in a foreign country. Thinking back over the centuries, the memories of my father packing me up and sending me by caravan to the famous Balthazar, the wise man to become his disciple, were as fresh as yesterday. I never understood why he did it, nor did I understand why he never came to see me. Now I did. The strained relationship between my father and my grandfather,

Balthazar, must have been deep. Neither spoke the others name. I wondered why. Such was not the case with young Master Colt. He didn't deserve this.

Yes, he stowed away. In his boyish enthusiasm, he joined our quest to destroy the medallion. Maybe it was from a sense of guilt for finding it in the first place; maybe he still blamed himself for nearly getting his father killed. Maybe this was his way to atone for himself, but things hadn't turned out like he'd planned. They hadn't turned out like we planned, either. Now he was here, living in a stranger's home, away from his family, away from his church friends, playing a part that was neither glamorous nor glorious and for what? He wasn't even getting paid. He needed something to brighten his dampened spirit.

"Want to call home?"

His face lit up. "Can I? I mean, would Mr. Levi let me use his phone?"

I nodded. "I think so. Let's ask him."

Together, we returned to the living room where Simon sat, reading the paper. "Mr. Simon, would you mind if Colt called home? He's feeling a bit blue." It was a term I'd picked up while living in Georgia, though I hardly understood how color had anything to do with ones emotions.

Simon laid aside his reading and peered at us over his heavy framed glasses. "Oy vey, I thought you'd never ask ... but of course." A moment later, he fished his cell phone from his pocket and handed it to Colt.

"Take as long as you like. Oh, and you, Gasper, if you would like to call someone, feel free to use the phone in the den." An impish twinkle sparkled in his eye.

"Thank you," we said almost in unison.

As I closed the door to the den, I heard Colt's voice crackle with happiness at hearing his mom's greeting. I knew things would improve from here on out.

My own call to Felicia brightened my spirit as well.

"Hello?" her French accent sent my heart atwitter.

"Hello to you. Got a few minutes?"

"Gasper!" Her response was immediate and positive. For the next thirty minutes, we exchanged the news of our lives. The only disappointment I heard was when I told her our stay in Israel was going to last longer than we'd expected.

"I'm sorry to hear that," her tone darkened. "I was so looking forward to having a big celebration when you came home."

I liked the way she said, *home.* It sounded so inviting, so personal, so alluring. Changing the subject, I asked, "How did *Fiddler on the Roof* go?"

Her laughter once again sent my heart skipping, and I wished we were Skyping so I could see her face, enjoy her smile.

"Oh, Gasper, you should have seen them. The kids did great. We played to a packed house both nights. There is even talk about doing another musical in the spring."

I smiled at the prospect. "Have any suggestions?"

Felicia paused in thought. "I'm open to any, but the names *Oklahoma* or *Annie* has been bandied about."

I began humming *Easy Street,* one of the songs in Annie, themes albeit, slightly under pitch, much to Felicia's delight.

"Uh, Gasper, don't quit your day job. You still need

some help with the singing part."

I guffawed her comment.

Hearing someone at the door, I covered the mouthpiece. "Come in." It was Colt. His face was streaked from tears, but his smile told me they were tears of joy, not sorrow.

"Can I say something to Felicia?"

"Now, how did you know I was talking to Felicia?"

He eyed me with a 'you gotta be kidding,' look.

Handing him the phone, I whispered, "Don't say anything about—"

"Hi Miss Felicia, did you know Mr. Gasper talks in his sleep?"

I knew by his laughter, what she said.

"He talks about you," he kidded.

My face superheated.

"I don't know, he just repeats your name and says—"

"Okay, that's enough." I yanked the phone from his small hand. Phone to my ear, I said, "He's making it up, really." I doubted she heard me over her laughter.

"Go to your room," I chuckled as I pointed to the door.

Having gotten me into an embarrassing moment with Felicia, he scampered from the room, giggling. As he did so, he flipped off the light leaving me in total darkness except for the glow coming from the tip of my staff.

Sitting in the dimly lit room, we said our goodbyes with the promise to call again. The following day, we were once again caught in a whirlwind of activity as we divided our time between stints of the Live Nativity and fifteen-minute breaks.

Chapter Eight

The construction on the Third Temple was moving at breakneck speed. Already, the foundation for the Holy of Holies had been laid; an event of historic proportion. Not since the days of King Solomon had there been such a celebration. Once the Holy of Holies was completed, all that remained was for Israel to finish the temple complex, find the Ark of God and the sacrificial system could begin again. Even the brazen altar and bronze basin had been moved to the Temple Mount awaiting their moment when they would be situated in the outer court in front of the gold leafed doors leading into the temple itself.

Simon Levi's attention went from being the curator of the Institute in Antiquities to bounty hunter, to investigator, to treasure hunter. As one of three members of the Ark Commission, it was his and the other's responsibility to locate and restore the Ark of God to its rightful place. The daunting task fell to him, Rabbi Musselmen, and Saul Mueller. The problem they faced was, no one knew where to begin looking. Satellite imagery provided several interesting possibilities as to its location, but upon further investigation, they proved to be dead ends. After pursuing several false leads, the team extended their search to include neighboring countries.

After an exhaustive three week foray into Ethiopia,

Petra, and even the lower levels of the Vatican and coming up empty, Simon returned to the Institute in Antiquities disillusioned.

"Care to talk about it?" I asked him as we rode home.

Simon ran his hand over his broad forehead. "Oy vey, I don't know. If we can't find the Ark soon, we might as well call the temple just another museum. The Ark of the Covenant is the most sacred piece of furniture in the temple, or in all Israel, for that matter. For over four hundred years, it served Israel as the means of connecting us with God." Hands flailing, he continued. "Built under the direct supervision of Moses, the man of God, Israel's greatest and most revered leaders, the Ark of the Covenant conformed to exact specifications given to him by Heshem, himself. There is none like it."

I knew all there was to know about the Ark. I also knew, as a New Testament believer, I had something far better than the Ark with all its rituals. But I was talking to a new believer; one that had not comprehended the book of Hebrews. Silently, I waited for an opportunity to explain New Testament truth.

"Couldn't you just make another?" Colt asked.

"No! It is irreplaceable, and the plans are lost." Simon's voice turned husky with emotion. "All we have is a vague description. It measures eighteen inches by fifty two inches and is a rectangular wooden box made from acacia wood and overlaid with pure gold. Above it is the Mercy Seat with two golden cherubim, which look down upon it. It represented God's Holiness. Inside it are the two stone tablets on which are written the Ten Commandments, a jar of Manna and Aaron's rod which budded. For Israel not to have the Ark of God means there would be no Israel. Since its disappearance, there was always the hope that one day the Temple would be rebuilt, and the Ark of God would reemerge and be placed back in the Holy of Holies. Now, as news spreads that our treasure is missing, I fear our national hope will soon be dashed in pieces like a challis of fine wine, and its contents spilled across the Judean sand."

I had never heard my friend speak so eloquently, nor so downheartedly.

Leaning forward, Colt patted the older man's shoulder. "Could you show us how they are going to build the temple without using even a hammer?" It was obvious Colt had been listening to the adult conversations more than we'd given him credit.

Simon glanced into the rearview mirror and gave him a weary smile. "Well, we can't tomorrow because it's the Sabbath, but we can on Sunday. We'll make a day of it, but no pictures, mind you."

I could see the idea pleased Colt. I liked to too. After having seen Herod's magnificent temple in all its splendor, I could only imagine what this one would look like with all the modern conveniences of air conditioning, defused lighting and special effects. This would, no doubt, be the most spectacular building on the planet. Was it any wonder the Antichrist would want to use that place as his seat of power? It suddenly occurred to me ... *Antichrist? The Temple? Seat of power? Wait a minute. Had I missed something?*

Chapter Nine

C olt's excitement grew throughout the rest of Friday and Saturday as he anticipated our excursion to the temple construction staging site. Finally, the day arrived and the three of us packed a light lunch and headed to the east side of the Old City. After passing through the Damascus Gate, we descended several hundred meters down to the Kedron Valley. Rounding a corner, we entered the mouth of a ragged cave situated on a rocky cliff which served as part of the foundation for the Old City wall.

"Why are we going to a cave? I thought we'd be going to some warehouse or some big field?" Colt asked as we turned off the road and entered a large cave complex with heavily armed IDF guards stationed all around.

Smiling, Simon parked the car and got out. "This is Zedekiah's Cave, built by one of Israel's mightiest kings. It has been said it once housed the Ark, but that's just speculation," waving the comment aside like a gnat.

His eyes rounding, Colt couldn't hide his surprise. "This place is humongous."

"Yes, it's big all right, you schmuck. It goes back about a thousand feet. Part of it is actually under the Muslim quarter of the Old City."

"But why are you storing all the building material

here?" I couldn't hide my interest.

"Because, for years my government has been secretly preparing to rebuild the Third Temple. We possess all but one of the pieces of furniture for the temple. We have recreated the priestly garments and even have several red heifers ready for the first sacrifice."

"Don't you need the altar to perform a sacrifice?" I was incredulous.

"Already taken care of, my good friend. All we lack is the Ark. If the Palestinians or Arab nations knew we were this far along in the construction process, they would have invaded us long ago. As it is, there are many who would love nothing more than to stop us, and they will go to any length to do it. It's very much like the days of Nehemiah when Sanballat and Tobiah tried to stop the rebuilding of Jerusalem's walls. They failed and so will those who oppose us now."

I'd learned Israel's history from my father, but it was refreshing to hear Simon rehearse it in modern terms.

Like two kids in a toy store, Colt and I walked wide-eyed around columns of marble, pre-cut slabs of granite, stacks of pink limestone, which gave Jerusalem's walls a golden-hue in the setting sun, and reams of purple, gold and blue fabric.

"What's in there?" I asked, pointing at a large, sealed vault flanked by a dozen heavily armed guards.

"Oh, that." Simon said, rubbing beads of sweat from his forehead. "That's classified."

Smiling, he gave me a knowing look.

"Got any vague ideas?"

Keeping his voice low, Simon whispered, "Let's just say, they are rare artifacts."

After a full day of exploring, the three of us headed to Simon's car, when a voice called out, "Shalom, my friends."

Turning, I saw a bull-like figure of a man sporting a pair of bushy eyebrows and a straggly beard approaching. It was Saul Mueller.

I had heard Simon speak of him, but had not had the pleasure of meeting him.

Skipping to catch up, he drew closer. "Gentlemen, what brings you out to this dusty cave?" He waved his hand, eyeing us with interest.

"Shalom, Saul." Simon said, "I was hoping to find you here. Allow me to introduce my friends, they are from America."

Looking at me, Simon continued, "This is Mr. Gasper, the last of the Magi."

Saul eyed me with some suspicion before asking, "Hmm, and who is this?" taking a sideways glance at Colt. "None other than the noted shepherd boy made famous by your *Christian* tradition?" His emphasis on the name *Christian,* irritated me, but I refused to give in to the temptation to get into an argument over the commercialization of the holiday.

"Yes, this is his young understudy, Master Colt O'Dell." Simon intervened before I had a chance to speak out of turn.

As we exchanged handshakes, I said, "Good to meet you, Mr. Mueller, I've heard so much about you. How is your search for the Ark coming?" My question brought a soft cough from Simon. I grimaced, knowing I'd brought up a sensitive subject.

Shifting to face me, Saul appraised me thoughtfully.

"It's only a matter of time. We'll find it and when we do, well—" he let his statement dangle. "I understand your claim to being the last of the Magi is authenticated by my friend's personal testimony, but do you have any other confirmation? You know … two or three witnesses."

His question reminded me of the type of question posed by the Pharisees in Jesus' day.

Taking a calculated pause, I thought a moment before speaking. "Well, my advice has been sought by many and has saved them from a lot of heartache."

Straightening, Saul stroked his chin thoughtfully. "Not bad … humble, deflecting praise, but vague, a typical guru type answer. I've read better from a Fortune Cookie."

"Hey, that's no way to speak to—" I cut off Colt's protestations with a wave.

"Do you think you could do better?" He challenged.

I felt my pulse quicken. *This man was daring me to do something spectacular. It was a direct violation of my oath as a Magi to never use my skills for personal ingratiation. Even so, I had a reputation to uphold.*

All at once, a forklift, driven by a potbellied man, rounded a stack of limestone blocks and clipped the corner. In a flash, they tilted, threatening to crush a handful of hard hat clad workmen. Clutching my staff with two hands, I pointed it at the threatening danger, closed my eyes, and guided the limestone blocks back into place. By then, I had a crowd of gawking onlookers.

Relieved, the endangered workmen gathered around me as I stood like Moses pointing my staff at the Red Sea. "Sir, thank you for saving our lives," the astonished men said.

Lowering my staff, I tried to maintain my composure. "Well, I'm just glad I was in the right place at the right time." As I spoke, Colt gave me a wink.

Colt stepped forward. "Don't believe him, he's just being humble, deflecting praise ... vague. You can see that kind of stuff done by any old guru."

"Ah um," I cleared my throat. "You were saying, Mr. Mueller?"

Saul, clearly not comfortable having been put in his place by an adolescent, huffed and stomped away.

Patting him on the shoulder, I smiled. "Well spoken, my young charge ... well spoken."

I cocked my head and watched the man stalk around the corner. "Why is it I got the distinct impression he isn't really interested in finding the Ark?"

"You'll have to excuse my colleague. He's rather skeptical of everything. That's what makes him so good at his job, but I have to tell ya, he can be a real pain in the keister, sometimes. I fear, once we find the Ark of God, we may have two different visions as to how it is to be used."

Prince Gabriel nodded to his underling, Prince Azrael. "Well timed, my prince. How did you know that forklift driver would hit that corner?"

Prince Azrael tucked his hard hat behind his back and knocked a clod of Judean dust from his foot. "Let's just say, I was in the right place at the right time."

"Well, since you have taken such an interest in our earthly friends, why don't you shadow them and keep them from getting into trouble. I'd like to see them get home in one piece, if you catch my meaning."

Prince Azrael, a stocky, muscular angel fingered his broad ax. "I would count it an honor, my lord." Giving him a quick nod, he disappeared, leaving a dusty footprint behind.

Chapter Ten

It had been a grueling three weeks for Rabbi Musselmen. More used to standing behind a lectern or better yet, leading an archaeological dig, Rabbi Musselmen spent his life pursuing anything and everything related to the Temple, especially, the Ark of the Covenant. Had it not been for his relentless searching, many of the articles from Herod's Temple would have never been discovered. Despite his fifty years in the field and in the classroom, however, the rabbi retained much of his youthful exuberance. But these last three weeks left him exhausted.

Dealing with the slippery side of diplomacy was never his forte. He was a man of the earth; of rock, of stone, of parchment and papyrus ... not of words which could mean one thing today and another thing the next. His goal, all he ever wanted for his beleaguered nation, was to find the Ark of God, place it back where it belonged and Israel to assume its rightful place as leader of the nations. *Was that too much to ask, God?* Apparently, it was.

He leaned heavily against the Wailing Wall and poured out his heart. Its rugged surface made smooth by the thousands of hands and foreheads touching it, was littered with small, rolled up pieces of paper tucked in its crevices. Prayers, petitions, demands ... mostly unanswered or worse … ignored.

Had Heshem abandoned them? Had He forgotten His beloved nation? Were all the promises of national restoration just empty words? Was He still angry? Doubts plagued the rabbi's mind even as he tucked his own prayer into a crack in the wall. *After all his years of study, could it be that the Ark was gone? Could the Ark of God really have passed into obscurity like their alleged Messiah?*

Despite his fears, he'd planned a big celebration for the day when he and his colleagues would find their national treasure. Turning, he trudged back to his car where his driver stood. "Take me home, Yani. No ... better yet, take me to the Institute in Antiquities. I would like to schmooze with my old friend Simon without that schmuck, Saul, butting in."

Yani, was not only his personal valet and man-servant, he had been his confidant for longer than either of the two men could remember. Nodding, Yani waited for the rabbi to get comfortable before closing the car door.

Weaving through the narrow streets of Jerusalem was a skill reserved only for the bravest of heart, but one Yani prided himself for having mastered. Fourteen minutes to the second, he delivered his friend and mentor to the side entrance of the institute, just as Simon stepped out.

Seeing Simon next to a man dressed in regal apparel and a young boy dressed like a shepherd, took the older rabbi by surprise. "My, my, when did you begin stealing artifacts from your own Institute?"

For a rear moment, Simon stood, unable to speak. "I'm afraid you caught me, red handed, my old friend."

he quipped. While the two men exchanged the traditional greeting, Gasper and Colt stood as still as wooden Indians. Finally, Simon turned to his two guests. "This is one of the magi and the shepherd boy I brought in to serve as figurines in the Live Nativity display. I told you about them."

Giving the rabbi a rather exaggerated bow, Gasper said. "Gasper the Magi at your service, and this is Master Colt O'Dell, my understudy."

The elderly rabbi ran his fingers through his flowing, grey beard. "Hmm, I see. Well, you certainly look the part, any words of wisdom? You wouldn't happen to know the whereabouts of the Ark of God, now would you?" he asked conspiratorially.

Gasper fingered his staff for a moment. His question was the nation's question. It seemed everyone was looking for the Ark, and yet—.

"Rabbi Musselmen, I see you have recently been to the Wailing Wall. Let me assure you, your prayers have been heard and in time, Heshem will answer them."

Taken aback, Musselmen lowered his gaze. "And how did you know I was at the wall?"

Gasper folded his hands behind his back. "Your forehead, it has dust on it. Your knees also have dust on them. Where else would you find a holy man kneeling and praying but at the Wailing Wall?"

Nodding, Reuben Musselmen smiled. "You are quite observant. It is as you said, but how would you know about my prayers?"

"Is it not the prayer of every devout Jew that Yisrael come to birth among the nations? I share your prayer my friend, and feel I may play some small part on that day."

Patting him on the shoulder, Rabbi Musselmen guided Gasper and the others to his car. "Come, be my guest for dinner. I have many questions."

As Gasper allowed himself to be led to the car, he cocked his head and peered over his shoulder. "Master Colt, let not one word fall to the ground. You might learn something."

Playing his part as understudy, Colt lowered his forehead. "Yes, my teacher."

We followed the rabbi to his residence, all the while, listening to Simon give us instructions as to what to do and not do.

"Master Colt, you are a youth, please do not insult the rabbi by asking a question. If he asks you a question, you may answer it, but only in the simplest terms. Understand?"

Colt's forehead wrinkled, but he answered respectfully, "Yes, sir."

"Good, and Gasper, I know you are given to speaking before you think, so be careful. The rabbi is very orthodox and set in his ways. He may not take to thinking outside the box, if you get my meaning. Oh, and be sure to wash your hands as often as possible. He is a real stickler for cleanliness."

"Well, you know what they say, 'Cleanliness is close to Godliness,'" I said in a humorous tone.

Simon smirked. "Then when it comes to us being Godly, we Jews have a corner on the cleanliness market. All we do is wash something. Humph, I've got soap burns from washing so much." Simon extended his wrinkled hands, and I saw what he meant.

After arriving at the Rabbi's home, we were immediately offered a bowl of soapy water and a clean towel which we used without question.

"There, isn't that better?" the elderly rabbi asked.

I handed his servant my towel and rubbed my hands together. "Much better, I feel clean all over."

He offered me a wry smile. "I see my friend Simon has given you the usual shtick. Something like, all we Jews do is wash our hands."

Simon elbowed me in the ribs. "Yes, something like that. Now tell me about your progress with the temple."

The schmoozing lasted throughout the meal and deep into the night. By the time he'd finished, we were all yawning.

Finally, Rabbi Musselmen turned his attention to my staff. "Tell me, Mr. Gasper, is that the same rod used by Moses, the servant of Jehovah?"

I felt my pulse quicken. I knew it was old, but as to how old and who besides my father owned it was a mystery to me. "Actually, this rod has been in my family for a very long time, but whether or not it was owned by Moses, I cannot say."

The rabbi extended his hand indicating he wanted to hold it. I was reluctant to comply as I knew the power it wielded. With Simon's nudge to encourage me, I handed it to him. His widening eyes told me I was correct. Apparently, he felt the surge of energy I often felt when I handled it.

"And the others ... where did they come from?"

By now, I was sweating despite the air-conditioning. I didn't want to talk about Balthazar and Melchior, but it appeared I couldn't avoid the conversation. "I had two colleagues who gave them to me, sort of as a way to remember them." To say more was too painful and would lead to a lot of questions, ones I couldn't answer.

Finally, Colt, who had been sitting quietly, broke the tense moment. "Mr. Musselmen, when you find the Ark of the Covenant, how will you carry it to the temple site?"

The question seemed to take the elderly rabbi by surprise. He obviously forgot it came from a child.

"I, I haven't thought of that. I am a Levite, but my age disqualifies me. We would have to wait until younger, more qualified men arrived to carry it to a vehicle."

Not satisfied, Colt pressed ahead despite Simon's insistence that he remain quiet. "But sir, I read in the Old Testament when King David brought the Ark back from the Philistines, the oxen pulling the cart stumbled and Uzzah reached out to stabilize the Ark and was struck dead."

Rabbi Musselmen sat upright and stroked his beard. "My son, you are very wise. You honor your master by offering such godly counsel. The Ark of God is to be carried by priests, not on a cart or a truck bed. I will be sure to include several four-man teams of priests on our next expedition to carry the Holy Ark."

With that, he stood, indication the evening was over. As we bid adieu to our host, I couldn't help patting my young understudy on the back. "I think you saved the day on that one, Master Colt."

"Yes, and you may have saved Rabbi Musselmen's life as well," Simon added as his driver started the car.

On the ride home, we all sat in silence taking in the

vacant city streets. Jerusalem was indeed a beautiful city. Its palm trees, illuminated with decorative lights, swayed gently in the night breeze. The old city walls glowed with a soft golden hue while above them hung myriads of stars which sparkled like diamonds ... the same ones which guided my friends and me to this place over two thousand years ago. The memory, as fresh as yesterday, was both painful and exhilarating. To think, the God of the ages who controlled the times and seasons of our fleeting lives, knew exactly where the Ark of the Covenant was located, and just when to reveal it.

Chapter Eleven

"Of course he'll never find it. That's why I chose the bumbling imbecile to be on my team. He has been following every false lead I send him. If he keeps up this pace, the dumb schlep will keel over before he gets anywhere close to it." Saul Mueller drummed his fingers on his desk while Jacque St. John vented. Apparently, the man had his own troubles ... none of which concerned Saul.

Saul Mueller, if nothing else, was a survivor. As a young child, he endured the atrocities of a Nazi death camp. After the liberation of France and the fall of Germany, he subsisted on the kindness of strangers, and scraps retrieved from trash cans until he immigrated to Israel.

Life for him in Israel, however, wasn't much better. As a young man, he joined a group called the United Socialist Society and worked for Israel's independence. In 1948, Israel's fortunes changed when it became a nation and so did Saul's, but he never forgot his roots. By the time he'd reached thirty, he was not only street smart, he was corporate-boardroom smart.

After graduating from Tel Aviv University International with an MA degree in archeology, he went on to establish himself as the nation's leading archaeologist.

His history with the St. John family, however, ran deep. It was Jacque's father, Louis de Molay St. John, who turned his family over to the Nazis after the fall of Paris. It was his father's actions, which took the lives of his parents and older siblings. Jacque couldn't have known these details, but Saul did, and he lived for the day when he could set the record straight.

The two men's paths crossed when one of Saul's expeditions led him to France where he discovered a rare artifice which the Catholic Church claimed to have been stolen by the Templars. It was of particular interest to St. John and after that, it was only a matter of time before the two men formed an alliance.

Ever the archaeologist, Saul never lost sight of his prime objective ... to find the Ark of God, thus, his association with Rabbi Musselmen. He made it his mission to shadow the elderly man, knowing one day his services would be needed. That day had now arrived.

Saul's secret alliance with Secretary General St. John was just one of many he held. Whereas St. John was motivated by his thirst for power, Saul's motivation was much simpler ... revenge.

After his testy conversation with the leader of the world, Saul set his plan in motion. If all went according to schedule, within 48 hours, he would possess one of the world's greatest treasures. He just needed to make a few more arrangements.

Standing in the glass-enclosed Nativity display, Colt and I held our positions for four-hour sessions while adoring eyes gazed on the Madonna and Child. Much to our relief, Simon or one of his associates would come along and shut down the display for fifteen minutes, so we could take a break. It was a lot better than standing outside in Glenn's Christmas display for hours in the cold. Still, Colt's repeated complaints about his back aching or having an itch and not being able to scratch it caused me to chuckle.

"I wish some of those people would notice me," Colt muttered under his breath.

"Don't worry, my young friend. If you weren't there, all the stories and Christmas songs would just not be the same."

All at once, Colt began singing the *Little Drummer Boy* under his breath. His 'Pa rum pum, pum pum,' nearly drove me nuts.

With only thirty minutes left before the last group of children left and the lights were turned out, we started glancing at the clock. All at once, a cell phone buzzed, and we froze.

"I just checked. Everything is in place. The damage from arson will be minimal, especially to your precious relics."

The voice paused. "Sorry, sir. I meant no disrespect to your precious—"

Another long pause.

"Yes, the charges will produce mostly smoke, little fire and even that will be contained to the Egyptian Exhibit. The sprinkler system will trigger an alarm, and the authorities should arrive within minutes, just long enough for you to—"

Colt stiffened knocking over a stuffed lamb. I sucked in a breath, as the man clamped his mouth shut and looked around.

Colt's eyes grew round. "Did he see me?"

I prayed he didn't. "I don't think so. Keep your voice down."

"Who is he talking to?" he asked through pinched lips.

"I don't know. Can you get a look at the guy?"

Straining his eyes, he shook his head slightly. "I can't see his face. He's too far around the corner. Is he talking about what I think he is?"

I leaned closer. "I wonder whose son he is talking about."

Colt stifled a chuckle. "He's not talking about someone's son. He said something about arson."

Confused, I said, "That's what I said ... our son, but whose son is he talking about?"

Shaking his head ever so slightly, Colt muttered, "For a wise man, you sure are dense."

Ignoring his comment, I glanced at my watch; it read a quarter to five. *Good, Simon should be coming by any minute.*

Colt whispered. "I hope Mr. Levi hurries; I gotta go, real bad."

Fifteen minutes stretched into twenty, then thirty. Suddenly, the lights went out signaling the end of the day, but still, no Simon. Colt could wait no longer. He broke character and scampered from the Live Nativity scene to the closest restroom which happened to be near the Egyptian Exhibit.

I had just finished working out the kink in my neck when a loud pop echoed down the corridor followed by several more. All at once, an alarm sounded followed by billows of acrid smoke, which quickly filled the area.

With my eyes stinging, and barely able to breathe, my thoughts turned to Colt.

"Colt!" I choked out his name.

My muffled cries went unanswered as I dashed down the blackened halls calling his name. It was obvious whoever I'd overheard earlier followed through on his plan. This was no fire drill or practice. This was the real thing, and it had turned deadly.

By the time I'd reached the Egyptian Exhibit, I was crawling on my belly. Disoriented, I couldn't tell where the restrooms were located. I felt my way along the wall, calling Colt's name.

No answer came.

Taking my life in my hands, I stood and began to run. That was a big mistake. A bone-shattering crash caught my attention moments before a concrete wall collapsed. I felt a blinding jolt of pain flash across my eyes, then everything went black.

Chapter Twelve

While fire and rescue units responded to the three alarm fire at the Institute in Antiquities, eight men, dressed in black, followed Saul Mueller into a darkened tunnel. It led from the Muslim Quarter through the heart of Jerusalem and ended at an intersection. To their left, the tunnel continued further into the city; to their right, it opened into the Rabbi's Tunnel which led to the Wailing Wall.

Checking his map, Saul calculated that somewhere along the dark passage, a branch would veer off leading to a hidden chamber. He had long suspected its existence … even tested his theory using a GPR device or ground penetrating radar device. The technique was once used to recover over a million dollars in ransom money buried by kidnapper Michael Sams. Today, it is used extensively by archeologists. The devise sends out an electromagnetic pulse which maps the subterranean strata and sends it back to a computer screen which then color codes the information. If it proved accurate, they would find the Ark exactly where the priests had placed it over 2500 years ago … directly under the Holy of Holies.

As the huddled men crept along the narrow corridor, the light from their LED flashlights reflected an eerie green off the slick walls. Silently, without a word, they passed the foundation stone upon which the temple mount stood. 200 feet above them the Dome of the Rock gleamed gold under hundreds of halogen lights. Surrounding it were scores of heavily armed Palestinian guards. Any amount of noise would bring them down there and spell certain death to Saul and his men.

After finding the chamber, the men took up guarding positions while others began their work. Saul held his breath every time one of his men, using rubber tipped picks, struck the plaster covered wall. He hoped the diversion at the Institute in Antiquities would be enough to keep everyone's attention pointed in the other direction. All they needed was ten minutes, fifteen tops, and they would be gone.

Suddenly, the pick struck solid rock. Kneeling, Saul inspected the mortar holding them in place.

"Proceed," he whispered.

Wiping the sweat from his upper lip, the worker began to chisel away the porous mortar. The work went quicker than expected and within a few minutes, he'd loosened the first stone. It was the last barrier between him and Israel's greatest treasure ... the Ark of God.

"Here, you do it," the workman said, keeping his voice low.

Carefully, Saul grabbed the stone and eased it from its resting place. Using a fiber optic "snake" attached to a handheld display, he inserted the cable. Its tiny LED lights brightened the space which had been dark for the last two thousand years. All at once, the screen lit up and Saul clapped his hand over the display. Like a child peeking at a forbidden picture, he separated his fingers enough to see. There, resting on a pedestal, sat the Ark of the Covenant. Fearing he'd be struck dead for looking upon it, he quickly shut off the camera and backed up.

After waiting a minute for his heart and lungs to return to normal, he disregarded all archeological protocols and instructed his men to remove the remaining stones as quietly as possible until the hole was large enough to pass through. Then, he blindfolded the youngest and smallest of his crew and sent him into the chamber.

"No matter what you do, don't touch it. Do you understand?"

The shaken man nodded and forced a hard swallow.

"As soon as you're in, throw this tarp over it and secure it at the bottom. No part of the Ark must be visible."

Again, the younger man nodded, then disappeared through the opening.

Minutes stretched, and Saul began to wonder if the man succeeded. Sweat rolled down his face, stinging his eyes and soaking his dirty shirt. Scuffling brought his eyes to the opening and the man's head reappeared in the dim illumination.

"It is safe to enter," he said with a broad smile.

Saul and his men wasted no time in placing two wooden handles through the vacant rings. Standing, they wobbled under its weight. Being careful not to damage the Ark, they eased it through the narrow entrance and down the corridor. Within minutes, they carried the Ark back to the intersection and across the city. Retracing their steps, the men entered an empty double car garage huffing from exertion.

Outside, the slums of the Muslim Quarter and its urban sprawl slept ... oblivious to the danger which had just befallen them. Under the cover of darkness, the anxious men loaded their treasure onto a truck, tugged a canvas tarp over its bed, and climbed aboard ... unaware of a man and boy watching from the shadow of a door frame.

Once they were loaded, the driver turned the key, and the engine sputtered to life. Putting the truck in gear, the driver released the brake and the truck jerked forward. A minute later, it disappeared into the night. Maintaining a slow speed, the driver navigated the narrow streets through the Muslim Quarter until he reached the main highway heading south. Increasing his speed, he followed the marked map leading from Jerusalem to the Gaza Strip boundary.

Having completed the first phase of his plan, Saul strode to his Mercedes. His personal bodyguard, who also served as his driver, stood nearby smoking a cigarette. The man dropped the butt on the dusty road and ground it with the heel of his shoe before opening the car door. Saul gave the man a satisfied nod and slid inside. A moment later, they left and the darkness reclaimed its domain.

As Saul road through the Muslim Quarter, he recited his favorite passage from the Talmud. "As the navel is set in the center of the human body, so is the land of Israel the navel of the world ... situated in the center of the world, and Jerusalem in the center of the land of Israel, and the sanctuary in the center of Jerusalem, and the holy place in the center of the sanctuary, and the ark in the center of the holy place, and the foundation stone before the holy place, because from it, the world was founded."

"Should I stop them?" Prince Gabriel asked his commander and friend.

Michael the Archangel considered the question for a moment. They had watched in silence as the scheme was played out ... the fire, the theft of the Ark, the escape. It disturbed him greatly to see Israel's national treasure treated so cavalierly. Nevertheless, he knew the Almighty had a purpose in letting the plan unfold.

"No, in this case, we must stand by and allow wicked men to have their way. As the Holy Scripture says, 'evil men and deceivers will become worse, deceiving and being deceived, yet they shall proceed no further.' Their evil devices will be revealed to the world for all to see. Until then, you must guard your charges."

Prince Gabriel summoned his forces with a nod and flew in the direction of the Institute in Antiquities, while Michael held his gaze on the truck cutting its way across the Israeli countryside.

Summoning one of the dark angels, he gave his command. "Touch only those whom I have marked and none other."

"But my lord, there are so many more. Don't they deserve to die also? I would only be doing what I was created to do." The words flowed from his silver tongue like crystal-clear water, yet they carried a deadly bite.

"You will submit to my will or suffer the consequences."

The dark angel snarled, then bowed. "Yes, my lord, but I will be back for more." He sped away, leaving a foul odor ... the stench of death.

Chapter Thirteen

Earlier that day, the usual line of dusty Volvos, Volkswagens and an odd collection of other vehicles congested the highway connecting the West Bank to Jerusalem. At the head of the procession was the Israeli border crossing. Among the frustrated drivers sat Abdullah Grahani Hasad, a Palestinian with dual citizenship. Like hundreds of other Palestinians who routinely made the journey across the border to find work, he considered it a highway out of poverty. As an independent contractor, he'd spent the last 20 years working with the Israelis. Over time, he'd developed a deep respect for the Jewish people. In many cases, they were among his closest friends. Words couldn't express his excitement when he found his company had landed a contract with the General Contractor to provide the concrete for the Third Temple.

It wasn't unusual for Kamil, his thirteen-year-old son, to accompany him across the border to the job site. Since no electrical or power tools were permitted on the Temple Mount for the temple's construction, it was Abdullah's job to provide high-quality concrete from his portable unit and pump it hundreds of feet to where it was needed.

By design, the concrete for the Temple had to be of a certain texture and color. This presented Abdullah with a problem. In order to meet the demands of his employer, he had to use rock quarried from a Palestinian owned cave. If he disclosed to either the contractor or the cave owner his secret, it would end his contract and probably get him barred from doing any more work for the Israelis, but the pay outweighed the risks.

The color and texture of the rock were perfect for the job, and because of the urgency of the Israelis, Abdullah was forced to hire more trucks and drivers. The loads of rock needed to fill the daily requirements meant he had to make the risky journey several times a day between Israel and the West Bank. Many times it was an all-night affair.

Having already made four trips, Abdullah stared ahead through bleary eyes at the line of vehicles. By now, all he wanted to do was finish the run and get home. With the line backed up for a mile, he decided to try another border crossing. After making a sharp turn, he began to maneuver the maze of side roads through the all-too-familiar cityscape.

Suddenly, his truck sputtered and rolled to a stop. In his haste, he'd forgotten to get fuel before he left. By now, his cell phone had fizzled, and he was a long way from his office.

"Well, son, it looks like we'll have to walk home," he said as he swung his door open.

Always ready for an adventure, Kamil jumped out and adjusted his keffiyeh. Five blocks from his truck, Abdullah stopped abruptly and shoved his son into the shadow of an inset door. Ahead, eight heavily armed men dressed in black, struggled with an odd-shaped object covered with a tarp. Something about their movements told him these were not men to be trifled with. As he watched from the shadows, he recognized one of the men smoking a cigarette and walking with an unusual gait.

Why would he be out at this late hour? Abdullah mused. Keeping his concerns to himself, he tried to control his breathing and not get caught.

As the large truck rumbled to a start and pulled away, Abdullah and Kamil held their position, unmoving. Still watching, he noticed a man standing next to an expensive car smoking a cigarette. A shadow moved, and a well-dressed man stepped into the glow of a street light. He was talking to someone on his cell phone.

"It's done," the man said, then waited.

"As secure as can be expected."

Another pause.

"Yes, on its way to the Gaza Strip as we speak."

A dog began barking somewhere down the street making it impossible for Abdullah to hear anything. After scanning to see if they'd been observed, the man slid inside the car and the driver limped over and closed the door.

Abdullah held his breath and pulled his girth deeper into the shadow as the beams of the headlight cut across his body ... only breathing again when the car was well past them. If the radical Muslim elements within his community ever found out what he saw, he knew he and his son would be dead.

"Father?"

"Yes my son, what is it?"

"What do we do? We can't tell anyone what we saw, can we?"

Pulling his son close, he shook his head. "No, son. It will have to be our little secret. That garage is the storefront for a tunnel leading into Jerusalem. Whatever they removed had to be of great value, or they would never have had such an armed presence. For the time being, we need to keep our mouths shut and act as if we saw nothing. Do you understand Kamil? Nothing!"

"Yes, father, but what if the authorities ask? What should we tell them?"

"I don't know yet," he said as sweat gathered on his upper lip. He smiled nervously. "We will worry about it when the time comes."

"I recognized one of the men."

Abdullah's heart skipped a beat.

"So did I, but it was dark and a lot of men walk with a limp. It could have been anybody."

"It wasn't that dark. It was Uncle Mohan, wasn't it? He walks with a limp because a suicide bomb he was working on blew up too soon, right?"

Feeling the wind leave his lungs, Abdullah knelt and looked his son directly in the eyes. "Yes, it is true. In a way, I wish he'd died when it exploded for all the trouble he has caused our family. I hope you never get caught up in the stupid blood feud between the Jews and the Palestinians. If I had to choose sides right now, I would be tempted to go with my friends the Israelis. They have been better to me than some of the people I grew up with, especially my own brother." He eyed the place where his brother stood. A wisp of smoke ascended like a sleepless spirit from the discarded cigarette butt.

Abdullah couldn't help the bitterness that seeped into his raspy voice. He already lost one son to the radical Muslim cause. He would rather die than let his remaining son blow himself up for such foolishness. He didn't believe in Jihad anymore and doubted Allah was behind the political mess they were in.

Chapter Fourteen

oices echoed in the distance, calling to me, but I was in no condition to respond. Movement surrounded me, and I felt strong hands grab my arms and lift me in a fireman's carry. With my head lolling back and forth, I felt a rush of hot air. Heat scorched the hair on the back of my neck and the stench of burning carpet attacked my nostrils. Moments refused to pass as the man carrying me forced his way through a wall of smoke and flames. One minute I was encased in death, the next, I was being laid down on the cool concrete. Glancing around through bleary eyes, I saw flashing red and white lights and men in fire retardant outfits scurrying about. Someone placed an oxygen mask over my mouth and nose, and told me to breathe, which I gladly did.

After a few minutes, my head cleared, and I tried to sit, but a paramedic pushed me back down. "But there is a young boy still in the building." My muffled protest went unnoticed as the man applied cold packs on my scorched flesh. I winched, but let him continue.

"We've searched the building. If he's in there, we'll find him," he said in a grim tone.

My heart sank. *If he is in there? Where else could he be? Could he have gotten out? If so, where was he?* I tried to pray, but with all the commotion, I could barely keep my focus.

Simon Levi's face appeared above the oxygen mask, and I yanked it off. "Simon, have you seen Colt?" It hurt my throat to speak, but I had to know.

His face grew somber. "Oy vey, I thought he was with you." The lines on his face deepened.

"No, I lost him in the smoke, I gotta go back inside." I pushed up on an elbow, but gentle hands pushed me back down.

"Don't be a schmuck. You'll die if you go back in there. It's an inferno."

"But what about Colt? We can't just leave him." By then, I was in a near panic mode.

"Look, they have searched the entire building and not found him. Someone reported seeing a black van pulling out from the delivery zone. Maybe who ever set the fire saw him and took him with them. That would be the logical thing, but whoever said arsonists were logical."

"Are the police looking for a black van? Is there an APB out?"

Simon shook his head. "This is not America. It doesn't work like your made-for-television shows. It will take time, but we will find who did this and also your friend." Looking down, he said, "I see you made it out with your staff."

I glanced around. How I made it out was a mystery to me. The last thing I remembered was getting struck on the head. "I guess one of the firemen must have brought it out as they rescued me."

The attending paramedic returned and looked into my eyes and patted me on the chest. "I think you'll live. Keep fresh gauze and this ointment on your neck and the back of your hands for the next few days."

"That's it? Are you releasing me?"

Looking at Simon, who nodded to him, he returned his gaze to me. "Yes, you're free to go."

Still shaken, I stood on wobbly legs.

"Shall we?" Simon asked, directing me toward his car.

"Aren't the police going to question me to see if I have any pertinent information?"

"Nope! Technically, you aren't in our country. If I allowed the officials to speak with you, we both might be spending the night behind bars. Besides, they got most of what they need off the security cameras. We even got the plates of that black van. If it's not stolen, we should be able to track it down pretty quickly. Then we'll know all there is to know."

On the way to Simon's home, my mind began to clear. "You know, earlier in the day, I heard a man on the phone talking about their son setting fire to the building."

Simon nearly swerved off the road. "Oy vey! Whose son?" His hands waved animatedly.

"I don't know, he said something about our son."

"You mean arson?"

"Yeah, that's what Colt tried to tell me, but somehow, I misunderstood, but that's what he said. It was about 4:45 and I was going to alert you. We waited, but you never came around."

Simon stared ahead. "Yes, I was delayed about that same time. I got a weird phone call, and it kept me occupied. I wonder if their intention was for me to die in the blaze as well. By the time I got off the phone, the alarms were blaring."

I shifted uncomfortably to face Simon. "And another thing ... why didn't the sprinkler system come on? I thought this facility had the state-of-the-art fire suppression system."

The whites of his eyes flashed fear. "I, I don't know. It was inspected just last week, and we got a clean bill-of-health."

"Who did the inspection?"

Simon's shoulders rose and fell. "It was a private company. We subcontract out those sorts of things." Turning to face me, he sucked in a sharp breath. "You're not suggesting someone intentionally sabotaged the sprinkler system in advance of the fire, are you?"

I felt a cold knot form in the pit of my stomach. "It's not out of the question."

Chapter Fifteen

No sooner had Colt finished using the restroom, than an explosion shook the building knocking him off his feet. The alarm sounded, and the sprinkler system sputtered to life. A moment later, it fizzled, then quit. Dazed, he scrambled up one flight of stairs to the Nativity Display, and was met with a wall of smoke and fire. Forced to retrace his steps, he dashed down the stairs in search of the exit, but it was blocked by a fallen column from the Egyptian display.

By now, the wax manikins had burst into flames sending the burning liquid his direction like a lava flow from Mt. Vesuvius down the streets of Pompeii. Hearing voices, he turned and ran in toward the sound. As he rounded the corner, he stumbled to a halt. Peering through the smoke, he saw two burly men struggling with a locked door. Clearly, they were not the custodial help.

Their black masks kept him from seeing their faces, but also kept them from seeing him. As they struggled to open the door, it was apparent they had miscalculated the effects of their arsonist activity. Now, all of them were caught behind a wall of flames.

Knowing he only had minutes to act before the room filled with smoke, his only way out was to follow the men, so he stayed low and waited. The floor rumbled, sending a large support beam crashing down. It struck the wall next to the door sending sparks in all directions. The men cursed and flung themselves through a small opening which appeared when the wall collapsed. Gulping acrid smoke, Colt clambered forward and dove through the opening. He landed next to a wooden crate and climbed in before the men saw him. The men feverishly loaded their equipment in the rear of a black van and failed to notice his movements. Fearing they'd kill him if they discovered his hiding place, Colt held his breath as the men grabbed the crate and tossed it into the van and slammed the doors.

"Get outta here," one man hollered over the crash of glass and crunch of metal.

Too afraid to move, Colt tucked himself into a tight ball and hoped wherever the men went wouldn't be so far that he couldn't find his way back.

All at once, he remembered Gasper. He left him to go upstairs to go to the restroom. His breathing shallowed and he felt sick. *What have I done? Gasper will be so worried.* Colt chided himself for once again acting before he thought. But what was he to do? It was too late. If he revealed his position, the men would surely kill him. His best chance of survival was to stay hidden and wait for an opportunity to escape.

As the van swerved through the streets of Jerusalem, it was all Colt could do to keep from gagging. The stench of smoke, mixed with sweat and the astringent odor of gasoline, nearly overcame him. Forcing down his lunch, he tried to think of more pleasant things. He thought about his mom and dad and knew they'd be so worried when they learned what had happened to him. Shoving aside his concerns, Sasha's angelic face came to mind.

How could an angel join the human race? She seemed so real. He wondered. *I sure wish she was here now. She would know what to do.*

Pinching his eyes shut, he tried to pray, but the next thing he knew, the van lurched to the right and began to bounce down what felt like a washboard road. Peeking through a slit, he could tell darkness had enclosed them like a burlap sack. He dared not poke his head up for fear of being discovered. From where he hid, he wasn't able to hear the men's conversations very well, and even if he could, the snatches he did hear before leaping into the crate were in another language.

Finally, the van bumped to a halt, and the men climbed out leaving the doors open. Fresh cool air rushed in to the rear compartment quickening Colt's dampened spirit. All at once, the voices of other men approaching the vehicle made Colt's muscles tighten. The men who drove him to this location were joined by others and a round of laughter broke the tense moment. It seemed these men knew each other, possibly were part of a fire-starting gang. Someone yanked the rear tailgate open and began to drag out the equipment except for the box where he hid.

As the hours lengthened, it became obvious the men were not coming back for the last box. Colt hoped they'd completely forgotten about it. Peeking over the edge of the box, Colt saw men sitting around a fire in front of what appeared to be a large airplane hangar similar to the one his dad used for his plane. *Somehow I've got to let mom and dad or Mr. Gasper know where I am, but how? I don't have a cell phone and I can't just walk up to those men and ask to use theirs.* He choked back a sob. Crying was for sissies, he chided himself ... not for the Magi, and he was one of them. He had to be tough, not just for himself, but for Gasper.

Laughter brought his thoughts back as the men continued to drink the night away. From time to time, one soldier would get up and replace the man guarding the gate through which they'd entered. He could see in the flickering light every man was heavily armed. This was no band of fire-starting thugs. These guys were dangerous ... deadly.

In the waning hours, the fire burnt itself out leaving nothing but glowing embers. Wisps of smoke hung low in the cool air reminding him of the promised camping trip he would probably never have with his dad. A single tear coursed down his soot covered face, and he wished he'd never left home.

By now, most of the men had disappeared inside the hangar. It was going to be a cold night outside, and he yearned for the blanket he and Sasha sat on at the picnic. As the last man sauntered off, Colt took a chance. Still dressed as a shepherd boy, he figured he could at least fake being lost if they caught him. The few guards, who were left, gathered around a second fire near the far corner of the building. Being as quiet as possible, he climbed out of the box and after waiting for the moon to hide its face behind a cloud, dashed across the open space. He reached the building without being seen and slipped inside. He found himself inside a large, cavernous building. To one side, was a stack of barrels, in the center, a pile of two by fours which formed a square. Being small had its advantages. With the stealth of a cat, he ducked under the windows and passed the door of a block building inside the hanger. Cautiously, he made his way to the stacks of barrels and squeezed between the narrow rows. Finding a small opening, he crouched down and curled up in a ball. It was not much warmer than the van, but at least he was out of the wind. Plus, if they left, he would not be their unwanted passenger.

He pulled his knees up and wrapped his slender arms around then. Then he tugged his shepherd's cape tighter over himself, propped his head back and drifted to sleep.

While he slept, Prince Azrael held his position on top of the stacks of barrels. From his vantage point, he watched the movements of the men. If anyone came too close to his charge, the last thing he'd feel was an ax coming down upon his head. Fortunately, that wasn't necessary and he was glad as it would have been a bit tricky to hide the body of a beheaded man, not to mention the mess it would have made. Instead, he kept a quiet vigil and waited for the day to arrive.

###

The following morning, Colt awoke to bacon cooking over an open fire. The smell sent his stomach into hyper drive. He wished he'd thought to bring along his stash of granola bars, and vowed not to let that happen again.

Soon, bright sunlight bled in through the grungy windows and lit the oily concrete floor. Peeking between the barrels, Colt watched as the three men holding weapons stood around the canvas covered object. Apparently, they'd arrived in the night while he slept. As he counted the hours, other soldiers came and went at thirty-minute intervals in an organized routine. It was obvious they were waiting for something, but what? And for whom?

Chapter Sixteen

Abdullah and his son trudged home to the sound of sirens as fire and rescue units raced to a large fire. Occasionally, a thin sheet of smoke would drift across their path making him wonder what had happened. Had there been another suicide bombing? Had someone fired a missile into the heart of Jerusalem? Was the city under attack? He prayed it wasn't so.

By the time they'd arrived home, his wife and daughters were safely tucked in bed and had been asleep for hours. Knowing his job depended upon a steady delivery of concrete; he didn't wake them, so he grabbed a couple fuel cans and trudged back to his truck. He'd call her later in the day to explain. By the time they returned to the truck and poured the petrol into the tank, dawn had arrived and with it another day. Soon, they were once again on the road.

As they approached the check point, a border security agent held up his hand for Abdullah to slow his truckload of rock. But as he pressed the brake pedal, he felt something pop, and his truck refused to slow. Suddenly, panic gripped him. If he didn't get the truck under control immediately, the guards would think he was driving a truck bomb and shoot him and his son without giving it another thought.

He swerved left, then right. Out of nowhere, a

Bryan Powell

Volkswagen darted in front of him, but despite his efforts, the two vehicles collided sending his truck careening out of control. Kamil was thrown to the right door panel and screamed in pain as glass shards penetrated his tan flesh. When they stopped sliding; armed guards surrounded them with guns drawn. Abdullah pulled a small white handkerchief from his top pocket and waved it at the IDF officer. The man lowered his weapon and Abdullah offered a weak smile.

It took thirty minutes for him and his son to be extricated from the wreckage and even longer for him to explain how the accident occurred. The agent in command seemed truly concerned for Kamil and asked several times if there was anything he could do to relieve the boy's suffering. Although his wounds were not life threatening, his face and right arm were lacerated badly, and he needed medical attention.

Sensing the timing was right, Abdullah took a chance. "Sir, I want you to know I have a deep respect for your country. I have many friends who are Israeli. You can check me out. I am a contractor, helping to build your temple."

The border agent pushed the computer keyboard back and rubbed his tired eyes. It had been a long night for both men. "Mr. Hasad, I have already completed a background check, and I have given you a clean bill of health. As a matter of fact, it is a good thing you had the collision, or we unknowingly would have had to shoot you. That, unfortunately, would have started a new round of blood-letting."

Abdullah mopped his brow with his white handkerchief. "I thank God for the blessing of accidents."

~ 94 ~

"You speak of God, not Allah, why is that, sir?" The agent asked with growing interest.

After a thought-filled pause, Abdullah continued. "Allah has caused me and my family nothing but trouble. No god or deity should require his children to strap explosives to their bodies, and blow themselves up. And for what … to kill innocent people? It doesn't make any sense. I have rejected the Muslim faith the day my eldest son was recruited against my will, and led as it was to the slaughter to fulfill a blood-curse." Lowering his voice, he continued, "since then, I have sought for peace in my heart and found it."

The border agent straightened in his chair, clearly interested. "Where my friend? Where have you found peace in this troubled, war-torn land?"

"Yeshiva told his disciples, 'Peace I leave with you, my peace I give to you, not as the world gives. So don't let your heart be troubled, neither let be afraid.'" He paused to let those words sink in, and to read his inquisitor's face.

The guard's eyes told him what he looked for. There was a glint of recognition between the two men. The guard looked up at the video camera mounted in the corner of the small room and then down at the floor. Using the toe of his boot, he drew an ichthys in the dust. The sign of the Fish had been used for centuries by the early Christians to identify themselves with other believers.

Abdullah mouthed the words, "He is Lord."

The guard replied by abbreviating the statement, saying only, "Indeed."

"Sir, I do have one confession."

Sitting upright, the IDF officer asked, "Oh, and what would that be?"

"The information I have is of such a delicate nature, I was wondering if there was a place where we could talk privately." As he spoke, he eyed the camera.

"You are as private as you can get."

Giving the border agent a cautious shrug, Abdullah began to unpack the story of his brother and the unusual object he saw him loading on the truck the previous night.

"This information is indeed very sensitive and perilous. You have put your family in great danger. If what you say is true, you may be rewarded a great sum of money."

"What was it that we saw?" Kamil asked, his eyes widening.

The officer leaned closer and spoke in a low tone. "You may have witnessed the theft of the Ark of the Covenant."

Abdullah slumped back in his chair. "And to think, it may have been my own brother who took it."

Eyeing him with renewed interest, the agent pulled a notepad from the desk drawer and prepared to take notes. "How can we find your brother? Do you know where he lives?"

Shaking his head, Abdullah said, "My brother and I have not spoken since the day my son died. I can help you find him, but I fear for my family."

"Who else is in your family?"

Abdullah rubbed the back of his suntanned neck nervously.

"I have my son and three lovely daughters; Sasha,

Isabel and Malanie, and my wife, Sophie."

The agent typed in a few keystrokes on the computer. "We can provide you and your family with new identities and a new home anywhere you like in Israel."

Abdullah's eyes grew distant. Shaking his head, he said, "America, I want to start over in America," he said triumphantly. "As much as I love your country, it is not safe for us here. Could you arrange it?"

The IDF agent lifted the phone to his ear and spoke with his commander. After a few minutes, he placed the phone in its cradle and smiled. "Yes, Mr. Hasad, if you can provide us with information, which will lead to the recovery of the Ark of God, and help us bring your brother to justice. I will see to it that you and your family are allowed to immigrate to America and with a sizable amount of money."

Then he stood and held out his hand. The two men shook hands warmly as the guard tussled Kamil's curly black hair.

Chapter Seventeen

I t had only taken thirty minutes for the driver of the truck carrying the Ark to begin to feel sick. First, his palms grew slick. Then his mouth began to flood as his stomach cramped and sent a wave of bile up his throat. He began to sweat, and his vision became blurred. After swerving several times and throwing everyone in the truck around, the man next to him grabbed the steering wheel.

"What's wrong with you, man?"

The sickened driver slumped over the wheel making it nearly impossible to steer. The man next to him grabbed the door handle and flung it open. Then he unclipped the seatbelt and shoved the driver out. The man tumbled to the road and got caught under the rear wheels causing the truck to bounce violently as it rolled over the man's body.

"What did you do that for?" asked the third man in the cab.

"Ali wanted out, so I let him out. Now shut up and watch for the police."

As he did so, he too began to show signs of the illness. He doubled over, gripping his stomach. "Pull over, I'm sick." His face contorted.

By then, the driver also showed signs of the unknown illness. "We must keep going. It's only a few more kilometers before we reach the border crossing. Once we get into Gaza City, we'll stop and get something." As he spoke, he fought down the bitter taste of bile in his throat.

Within minutes, the driver pulled to a stop and waited for the border guards to inspect the contents of his truck. His papers said he was carrying a load of machine parts. The border guard fingered his weapon and walked around to the rear of the truck. He and another guard grabbed the corner of the tarp and flung it back. Climbing in, they found stacks of boxes with Arabic markings; each matching what was on the manifest. What he didn't see was the false wall blocking his view of the real treasure. Satisfied, the border guards got out and closed the tarp. He returned to the driver and handed him the signed manifest.

"Everything seems to be in order. You may pass."

The driver looked at him not speaking. He was feeling too sick to answer; to do so might jeopardize the mission. He needed to get to Khan Yunis Airfield as quickly as possible.

Taking the clipboard, he nodded and pulled through across the border into the Gaza Strip. Within a few minutes, he'd reached Gaza City, but by then, the other man in the truck had succumbed to the mysterious illness.

He slowed to a stop in front of a convenience store, hoping to get something to drink, but barely made it across the parking lot before collapsing. The other men, who'd helped with the heist, rode in a separate vehicle and had not been affected. Seeing the man fall, they sprang from their car and ran to his side. By then, he too was dead.

"Get him out of sight," the driver of the other vehicle

ordered.

After dragging the dead man into the shadows of the store, he climbed into the cab of the truck and raced off leaving the remaining men to follow.

The journey from Gaza City to Khan Yunis took only forty-five minutes, but already the residents of Gaza City began to feel the effects of the Ark's presence. By the time the truck reached its destination, the hospitals along the way were inundated with patients suffering from a variety of illnesses from sick stomachs, to vomiting, to chills. Those closest to the vehicle carrying the Ark suffered the worst. It wasn't long before death totals began to mount and soon there was panic in the streets.

People demanded to know what was going on. Had they been attacked by a chemical weapon released by the Israelis? Was this a fluke of nature or were the gods angry with them?

Moshe and his sixteen-man team stood guard over an empty airplane hangar surrounded by a tall chain-linked fence. In the distance, he saw the yellow headlights of a truck approaching, but its erratic movements concerned him. It didn't look like the driver was in control of the truck. The vehicle swerved from side to side as it rumbled along at a high rate of speed. Concerned the driver wouldn't stop before hitting the chain-linked fence gate, he ordered his men to take their positions and prepare to fire.

"If the driver doesn't slow by my mark, shoot into the engine block. If that doesn't stop him, go for the tires. If he keeps coming, shoot the driver and anyone in the cab."

It didn't matter if the driver was Palestinian or

Jewish, these men were hired guns and followed orders without question.

The truck failed to slow and barreled through the first set of speed bumps.

"Fire!" Moshe commanded.

The first volley left the engine smoking. Steam from the radiator made it nearly impossible to see the driver, yet the truck rumbled on.

"Take out the tires!"

Again, another volley of bullets ripped the front and rear tires to shreds, but the vehicle kept coming, its speed unhindered.

Fearing the truck carried a load of explosives, Moshe ordered his men to stop the truck at all costs.

Another round of bullets sounded. Unaffected, the truck lumbered forward. Lifting an RPG to his shoulder, Moshe flicked the safety off and squeezed the trigger. The projectile raced from its housing and sped directly into the cab of the truck. The explosion shook the ground. An instant later, the burning hulk rolled to a stop a few meters from the gate.

Breathing a sigh of relief, Moshe ordered his men to surround the truck and shoot anyone who tried to escape. A moment later, the car carrying the remaining men skidded to a stop.

The sick driver got out. Holding his stomach, he approached Moshe, then collapsed.

"What's wrong?" Moshe demanded.

Barely able to speak, the dying man glanced up. "I don't know. The other drivers are all dead, my men and I are sick and will soon be dead too. You must get rid of that thing," indicating the contents of the truck.

Moshe ordered his men to inspect the rear of the truck. After rifling through the assortment of boxes, they pulled back the canvas curtain which blocked the border guard's view.

"Get that thing inside the hangar and make it fast. And don't touch it," he demanded.

Being careful not to uncover the Ark, the men lifted it and carried it the rest of the way to the hangar.

Moshe glanced down at the man who lay at his feet. He was dead. "Get them out of here," he ordered his men.

To his surprise, the men backed away. The smoking vehicle groaned and sagged under its own weight, making the dangerous scene even more apocalyptic.

"I said to move those bodies." Moshe pulled his sidearm from its holster and aimed at the closest man.

The frightened men began dragging their fallen comrades off the road and into the shrubs which dotted the surrounding area. It wouldn't be long before a pack of wild dogs or wolves would find them. By sunrise, there would be nothing left but a few bones.

###

It was a rare occasion when both the death angel and one of God's heavenly servants worked together, but this was one of those times. One by one, the men in the caravan carrying the Ark fell to the death angel's touch while God's servant marked those ordained to death.

With his wings beating the air, the death angel busied himself with his ruthless mission. His blood-lust only restrained by the angel of light who shadowed his every move. Anyone within sight of the Ark was subjected to an unknown disease which ended in their death.

Hospitals rapidly filled and soon turned to morgues.

In desperation, the city authorized its sanitation department to dig mass graves and began the gruesome task of burying the mounting numbers of dead bodies. Riots sprang up across the Gaza Strip and quickly spilled over the border between Gaza and Israel.

Finally, after the Ark found a resting place, the hand of the bright one moved and the death angel stopped his homicidal activity.

Prince Azrael drew his sword and sliced the air between the death angel and his next victim. "You will advance no further," his tone resolute.

Snarling like a rabid dog, the death angel pointed his bony finger. "This one is mine."

"No, the Almighty has set his mercy upon that boy. You shall not touch him." Prince Azrael stated flatly, as he stepped between the death angel and Colt.

"Curses." The death angel blasphemed. "I want that one." He pointed at one of the men who helped carry the Ark.

Prince Azrael nodded. "Then you shall have him, but not the boy."

The death angel offered a ghastly laugh and the man fell prey to his touch.

"Now leave, your services are no longer required." Prince Azrael puffed his chest and fisted his hips.

In a rage, the death angel backed away. His work was done there, but he had other rounds to make.

Chapter Eighteen

It was the one phone call I dreaded most. Calling the O'Dell's to deliver the news about Colt would rip their hearts out, but it had to be done. I looked at the clock and did a quick calculation. They would still be up. Slouching on the bed in my room, I made the call. It took only a second for Karen to realize something was wrong. After giving her and Glenn the details about the fire and my attempts at finding him, they sat in stunned silence. Hearing Karen's sobs broke my heart. I lost all attempts at remaining stoic. Wiping my own tears, I tried to put a positive spin on the news.

"The fact that we haven't received a ransom note or found a body, is good news."

At the mention of a body, Karen broke down again.

"Maybe that wasn't the best choice of words. I'm sorry." I added. "Look, Mr. and Mrs. O'Dell, the Israeli government is doing everything they can to find Colt, but we have to face the reality that we live in a dangerous world. This situation is just one example." I knew my statement held out little assurance, but it was true. "Remember, God knew what was going to happen before it happened. He is still in control, and I can't help but believe He knows exactly where Colt is and right now is bringing him help and comfort. It could very well be, that God will use him to turn this tragedy into good. Will you join me in claiming this promise?"

Glenn and Karen sniffed back their tears and answered in unison. "Yes! We believe."

"Help our unbelief, Lord," Glenn added.

"Mr. Gasper, we trust you, to do your best to find our son, but if God chooses otherwise, well, then—" Karen said through a thickening throat.

"I know, Karen. I know. I will keep you posted as the investigation unfolds. Okay?"

Glenn spoke for his wife. "Yes, thank you."

Just as I prepared to hang up, I paused. "Oh, and there is one other thing, please tell Felicia I love her."

Karen chuckled. "I was wondering if you might say that."

Feeling like a schlep, I rubbed the nap of my neck. "Say what?"

"Never mind. We'll keep praying," she added in a lighter tone.

After hanging up, I sat trying to figure it out. *Why would someone want to set fire to the Institute in Antiquities? And where was Colt when it happened? He had just gone to the restroom when the fire alarm sounded. He couldn't have gone far. And since his body had not been found, he had to have been kidnapped, or he stowed away. There is a chance he climbed in the getaway car without being detected. That being the case, he could be hiding right under their noses, and they don't know it. If he could get his hands on a phone, he might call home.* I prayed that would happen.

I found Simon sitting in his study, hunched over an artifact which had survived the fire. A quizzical expression darkened his face.

"Simon, I think I overheard the man who set fire to the Institute." He remained motionless. "Simon, did you hear me—"

His hand shot up. "I heard you the first time." Lifting the artifact for me to see it, he said, "I had a feeling this would happen. It's all about the insurance."

"The insurance," I blurted. "Why the insurance?" I was incredulous.

Holding the artifact to the light, he continued. "See this? It is a fake, a fabrication. A good one, mind you, but a fake nonetheless."

"And you think the fire was set to get an insurance claim? That's absurd. Who would benefit from that?"

He slouched deeper into his chair. "I don't know. I'm just the curator. The owner of the institute is a man whom I have never met. We communicate through the internet. He hired me to run the facility while he goes on archeological digs. From time to time he and others send me new pieces."

"Who sent you that piece? The one you're holding."

Simon peered at it like it was a snake. "Saul Mueller."

In a van, not far from Simon's house sat a couple of men wearing dark suits and headphones. They had been eavesdropping on all incoming and outgoing phone calls as well as conversations with the Levi household for the last two months. Not much had been learned, not until tonight.

Lifting a phone to his ear, one of the men put in the call. "Sir, I have news."

"Oh?" the man on the other end said. "What have you learned?"

"It's about the artifacts. Mr. Levi suspects they are fakes. He may cause you more trouble than you wish to have. Should we silence him?"

"No, not now, he was supposed to have perished in the fire. If he turns up dead now, I'm sure the authorities will come calling me for answers. No, we must let things play out for a little while longer."

The line went dead before the dark suited man in the van could protest.

###

After my unusual conversation with Simon, I left him sitting in his study and returned to my room. It took all my willpower to fight the urge to slide into a blue-funk. It seemed to me, all he cared about was the artifacts, not Colt. The thought of my young friend suffering at the hands of some thugs, made my blood boil.

All at once, I felt my staff vibrate. A warmth which I'd not experienced since my earliest years crept up my arm. It spread into my chest and filled my entire body. A light-headedness caused me to lean back and close my eyes. As I concentrated, the vision of a large warehouse came into view. Upon closer inspection, it became clear, it wasn't a warehouse … it was an airplane hangar. The vision began to fill in as if a painter were adding details. Armed men moved about in a systematic fashion. Inside the building appeared a canvas-covered object. My staff vibrated as I viewed the sight in my mind's eye, and I tried to focus on the item, but something blocked my view. There was an evil presence preventing me from piercing the veil. Focusing, I tried to see what I was missing. *What was the source of evil? And why couldn't I see through it?* Movement pulled my attention away from the object to a well-dressed man. His back was turned, and he was speaking on a cell phone.

That voice ... I know that voice. But with the man's back turned, I had no way of putting a face with a name. Just as the man turned, a knock on my bedroom door broke the trance.

Chapter Nineteen

S imon poked his head into my bedroom. "Care to go on an excursion?"

Looking up, I kept my thoughts to myself. I was in no mood for sightseeing, and eating out was not on my bucket list. "Where to?"

Simon turned and stomped through the house on his way to the car, speaking over his shoulder. "While you were on the phone, I got an anonymous call."

"What did they say?"

"The caller used an electric voice scrambler, and it was rather garbled, but the message was clear. He said, 'go to the Rabbi's Tunnel, and you will find what you're looking for.'"

I skipped to catch up with him and jumped in the car just as the driver hit the gas pedal. "The Rabbi's Tunnel? Isn't that just off the Wailing Wall?"

"The one and the same. I've called Rabbi Musselmen and Saul to accompany us along with some members of the IDF."

"Any media?"

Simon chuckled. "That goes without saying. If it is what I think it is, this will be the biggest story the world has ever seen."

Jerusalem, at that time of day was a parking lot. People from all over the globe converged on the religious capital of the world for their annual Christmas pilgrimage. It made it nearly impossible to go anywhere, let alone to the Wailing Wall. By the time we'd arrived, a dozen official looking cars sat at odd angles behind a cluster of black robed, grey bearded men. Saul broke from the group and greeted us as we joined them.

"What do you have?" Saul asked, not hiding his enthusiasm.

Simon shifted so he could gaze into the grizzled faces of men he'd known for fifty years. After repeating the cryptic message, the rabbi spun on his heels and marched in the direction of the Wailing Wall, ignoring the purification fountains bubbling with fresh, clean water, past the thin military presence and entered the Rabbi's Tunnel. It was all I could do to keep up.

Striding single file, our sandals slapped in an uneven rhythm as we moved along the narrow corridor. To our right, was the crypt bearing King David's bones. Ahead, the tunnel glowed a soft orange under rows of fluorescent lights. Taking a sharp right, Simon began to descend a flight of worn steps. I followed, nearly slipping on the slick surfaces. With each step, I could hear the echoes of the other men as they shouted orders to light some torches. Soon, the tunnel brightened making our descent less hazardous, but I worried that my heart would leap from my chest.

All at once, Rabbi Musselmen stopped abruptly. As if led by a sixth sense, he turned to his right and plunged into the dark. I caught up to him and thrust the beam of a flashlight ahead of him. Suddenly, he stopped. Hand to his heaving chest, he fell to his knees and began shaking violently.

Pushing past his huddled form, Simon and Saul disappeared down a dark hall. Their light from their flashlights cut thin beams as they pressed into a newly opened chamber. I could hear their gasps followed by stifled cries.

I rushed to help the aging rabbi to his feet. Still shaking, he took a tentative step, followed by another. When he'd reached the jagged entrance of a forgotten chamber, he was barely able to contain himself. He leaned over and stumbled into the chamber where Saul and Simon knelt. I followed.

Looking at the sight, my heart stuttered. All that remained of the Ark of God was the pedestal where it had rested for over two millennium. I couldn't believe my eyes. It had been hidden right under our noses ... directly under its place in the Holy of Holies. Now it was gone. Suddenly, it all came clear; the fire, the failed sprinkler system, maybe even Colt's abduction. It was all a ruse, designed to throw off the authorities while the real target was a small room located along a narrow tunnel beneath the Temple Mount.

The shuffle of feet echoed as a score of reporters rushed the chamber and began snapping pictures.

"Get out of here!" Rabbi Musselmen demanded, his voice laced with emotion.

But it was too late. The media, hungry for the sensational, would broadcast this tragedy as soon as they could. Israel would be thrown into chaos. The Islamic world would rejoice, and the Christian world would breathe a sigh of relief. I could only guess what else would happen. Slumping to the cold, stone floor, I began to weep.

After several minutes, Simon placed his weathered hand on my shoulder and gave it a gentle squeeze. "Let's take a walk down the tunnel, and please, carry your staff." He spoke so quietly, I thought it came from within me, rather than my friend.

I glanced up. "Why?" Taking a halting breath, I stood.

Simon tugged my arm. "Because, whoever did this may have left a clue, and I can't help but believe you, and your staff may shed some light on it."

At that, I waved my hand over its end. A warm glow appeared and grew until it filled the room. Suddenly, I had the attention of every man in the room. In my periphery, I caught movement, and I turned. Saul's angry stare sent a chill down my spine.

"Simon, what do you think you're going to find?" Saul asked with unmitigated contempt.

Simon jolted upright. "I don't know ... footprints, a hand print, something ... anything." He pushed passed the others and reentered the tunnel.

As we made our way along the corridor, I couldn't shake the feeling that I had heard that voice before. "Did you hear Saul's question?" I whispered.

Simon kept moving. "Yes, why?"

"Isn't that the same thing your anonymous caller said?"

Simon paused for a moment. Shaking his head, he looked me in the eyes. "Look, neither of us like Saul. He has an ego the size of Gibraltar, but he knows his stuff."

"If he knew his stuff, why didn't he know that the Ark was hidden right under your noses? Why didn't he know the artifacts in the Institute in Antiquities were fakes?"

Simon shrugged and ran his hand over his forehead. "I don't know, but trust me when I say, he's not our enemy."

I didn't.

Simon and I moved quickly along the corridor and turned to follow one of the branches. Within minutes, we found ourselves standing in a dimly lit double car garage in the middle of the Muslim Quarter. It was obvious someone had been there recently as evidenced by a flashlight which gave off a weak stream of light.

Kneeling, I moved the end of my staff in a circular motion. All at once, the shape of a shoe print came into view. "Simon, take a look at this."

He came closer and knelt down. It was not left by a sandal, or a boot. "Clearly, someone in dress shoes was here," he said.

"If only the dust would speak," I muttered.

He nodded as a team of Mossad soldiers rushed in.

"Stand aside!" Their commander ordered.

We complied, and the soldiers began scanning the room for explosives. Once they gave the all clear, others began taking pictures of shoe and tire prints. It didn't take long for it to become evident. Someone with connections high up in the PLO was deeply involved. An ordinary person couldn't just drive down the street in Muslim Quarter, find a double car garage with a tunnel leading to the heart of Jerusalem and steal the Ark of God. This took planning and money ... lots of it.

By the time we got back to the chamber, only Saul and a few others remained. It was obvious from their faces, they were in shock, albeit Saul hid his feelings behind a wall of arrogant superiority.

"Well, whoever did this, certainly knew what they were doing." Bending over, he lifted a chunk of plaster. "See here? This was chiseled out using a four-inch trowel."

I was sure he spoke from experience, but the man's cool attitude stood in stark contrast to Rabbi Musselmen and the other men in the chamber. Whereas they seemed truly broken over their loss, he seemed to take it all in stride, as if it were just another archaeological dig gone awry.

As we emerged from the tunnel, Saul leaned closer and said. "I'm sorry about your young friend. Any word as to his whereabouts?"

His concern came as a bit of a surprise. He'd shown little interest in the fire, or its effects. As many artifacts as he had in the gallery, he should have been deeply concerned, but instead, the same coolness he showed in the chamber carried over to his attitude toward the Institute in Antiquities.

"No, it's too early to know anything and no one has stepped forward to claim responsibility."

Handing me a slip of paper, he lowered his voice. "I have a contact in the West Bank. He's a man with his finger on the city's pulse, if you get my meaning. Here's the thing, he's very skittish around strangers, especially," he eyed me for a moment, then continued, "particularly an American. I recommend you go alone. He may be able to point you in the right direction."

By now, I was desperate for any information which would get Colt back. "How much will this information cost me?"

Saul stroked his chin. "Well, he is a business man. I'd say a couple thousand should do it, but don't quote me. He may be willing to negotiate."

"Negotiate? What do I have that he would want?"

Saul flicked a glance at my staff, then at me. "Like I said, bring lots of money. Oh, and keep this between us. My contact is a very private man."

Chapter Twenty

L ater that night, after Simon had retired, I changed into street clothes and slipped out into the night. If all went well, I hoped to be back in a few hours. Looking heavenward, I was disappointed. The night sky with its myriads of stars was obscured by the city's lights. Only the brightest of the bright could penetrate the shroud of light pollution, as I learned later it was called. Grudgingly, I walked to the nearest corner, glad I didn't have to depend upon the stars to guide me tonight.

After hailing a cab, I handed the driver the address and sat back. Concern wormed its icy fingers through my stomach, but I quickly dismissed it as excitement over the prospect of finding Colt. As we passed through to the West Bank side of town, I couldn't help notice the stark difference in living conditions. The area surrounding Jerusalem thrived with new buildings and propriety, but these neighborhoods reminded me of Chicago's inner city ... or worse. Boarded-up windows, piles of trash, and deserted streets were the norm. It didn't take long for me to realize I'd made a big mistake, but it was too late to turn back now. I needed to find Colt.

The driver stopped at an intersection and waited nervously for the light to change. As we sat, waiting, a gang of hooded gun toting youths eyed us. His thumbs drumming to the rhythm of the music, the driver and I counted the seconds. Moments before the leader of the gang reached for my door, the light changed and the taxi driver mashed the gas pedal. Tires squealing, we made a hasty escape leaving the gang cursing and shaking their fists at us. After weaving through several more streets and running through another intersection with a red light, the driver let out a relieved breath.

"Here it is," the driver called over his shoulder. "But I can't wait for ya." He added nervously.

It was obvious he didn't like the area and wanted to get out of there as quickly as possible. So did I, but I was desperate. Handing him the fare, I got out and the taxi sped off before I got the door completely closed.

Glancing at the address on the slip of paper, I regretted having come, especially with as much money as I was carrying. After muttering a quick prayer, I took a steadying breath and approached the door bearing the number on the paper. It was clear this home would not appear in Better Homes and Gardens. Peeling paint, rotting wood, loose spackling fit the norm.

I knocked and waited. A flash of movement caught my attention, and I cut my eyes toward the curtain. Someone had glanced out, maybe they were expecting me. Suddenly, the door jerked open and a large man holding an Uzi filled the entrance.

"You got the money?"

Taken aback, I stuttered, "Yes. You got information?"

"I'm asking the questions. Now get your hands up." It was clear, this man was not to be trifled with.

I complied, at least until someone struck me from behind.

When I woke, my head throbbed, my hands were tied behind my back, and I'd lost all sense of time.

"What happened?" I mumbled.

"You slipped on a banana peel and hit your head," Uzi man said. A crooked smile parted his scruffy face. Clearly, he enjoyed seeing other people suffer. "Now, like I said, you got the money?"

Still groggy, I forced my thoughts to congeal and focused. I inhaled. A mixture of sweat, cigarette smoke, and fried food hung in the stale air. "Look, I don't want any trouble. I just want to know where a young boy is."

"No trouble, hmm? You already got that. Now it's just a matter of how much it's gonna cost ya to get outta it."

A baby's cry echoed from a dimly lit room deeper in the house, and the man's eyes cut in that direction. "Shut that kid up or so help me—" his expletive laced statement confirmed whatever doubts I had about this man's nature.

"I got the money, but first—"

Thwack!

A fat fist flew at me like a Mack truck. My head jerked to the side, and the iron-like taste of blood stung my tongue.

This is getting bad.

Another cry from the back and the man stood. "Woman!" he hollered, "can't you see I'm negotiatin'? Now, shut that kid up."

A thought flashed across my mind. "You got a sick kid. I can help."

My statement stopped him mid-stride. He wheeled around, his eyes aflame. "What do you care? You're just another rich American. You don't know a thing about what we suffer at the hands of those *Jews*," he spat the word at me like it left a bad taste in his mouth. I knew about human suffering. I'd lived it, seen it firsthand. Those years after my father fell into disfavor were burned into my memory.

"Believe me, I do care, and I can help."

Getting into my face, he said, "What can you do? My kid has an infection." His alcohol and smoke laced breath assaulted my nostrils causing me to recoil.

Fighting the urge to puke, I tried to keep my voice level. "Untie me, and I promise I'll give you no trouble."

The man eyed me with suspicion, then nodded to someone I'd not seen earlier. Suddenly, the rope binding my hands fell away, and I was jerked to my feet.

"Mind if I carried my staff? You wouldn't deprive a man his walking stick, now would you?"

Uzi man glanced at my staff, then nodded. "Okay, but none of that kung fu stuff."

I couldn't help chuckling to myself, but that lasted only a second as the man behind me shoved me down the hall. Inside the room, a woman covered in a burqa cowered in a corner. It was clear, this woman lived in fear. A single bulb lit the room casting eerie shadows across her face. On the other side of the room, laying on a pallet, was a child. By its red face and swollen cheeks, I knew immediately the child suffered from an ear infection. "May I?" indicating my intention to approach.

"Yousef, let him." The woman's eyes left little doubt she was frightened, but when it came to her child, she had the heart of a lion.

Yousef grunted.

I knelt and laid my staff as close to the child as I

dared. Closing my eyes, I began to pray softly. As I did so, I touched the child's head with one hand and touched my staff with the other. Warmth flowed from it, through me and into the child. All at once, the child's struggling movements slowed, and she opened her eyes. A soft giggle bubbled from her chest and her small fingers wrapped around mine. For a moment in time, I felt the love of a child and wondered what it must be like to have a child of my own. That moment was interrupted as the mother scooped her up.

Jabbering in an unknown language, she indicated to her husband that the child must have been healed.

The tension in the room was palpable. I wasn't sure if he believed her or thought I was playing a cruel trick.

"What did you do to my kid?" he demanded.

I shrugged. "Like I said, I just wanted to help. Now, do you know anything about a young boy?"

Yousef jerked his head indicating he wanted me to leave the small room. Feeling betrayed, I backed out followed by the mother's grateful stare.

Once we entered the front room, shadow man shoved me into the seat where I'd been tied, but this time, he didn't restrain my hands.

"I don't know nothing about your kid brother or whoever he is. I was just told to take your money and ..." he left the rest for my imagination. "Look, you did good back there, and I'm obliged to let you live, but I can't do that without something in return." Lifting my staff in his hand, he eyed it with awe. "I'll take this in exchange for your life ... deal?"

I swallowed.

All of a sudden, the lights inside the house went out.

A red dot appeared in Yousef's black shirt followed by two sharp reports. What happened next unfolded as if it were in slow motion. Yousef's knees buckled, and he hit the floor with a heavy thud. Gasper could see he'd been shot, but by whom? The shadow man?

Ducking, I tried to make myself as small as possible.

Another red dot, another muzzle flash and Yousef's partner slumped to the floor. The last sound he made was his final breath escaping his lungs. Pooling blood, a woman's stifled cry, heavy foot falls, all blurred as another bullet whizzed past my head.

Not knowing if the shooter was friend or foe, I belly crawled along the wall until I found the door. Feeling for the handle, I pushed myself to my feet.

My staff, I thought and grabbed it on my way out the door.

"I'll take that," the shooter said.

"Oh, no you won't." I grabbed the one end as he grabbed the other.

The pain I'd drawn from the child surged from me to my assailant, temporally stunning him. He stumbled backward, while I dashed from the house. Just as I passed the door another shot rang out and ripped through the window. It struck the plaster wall across from me sending a spray of concrete chips in all directions. I ducked to keep from getting hit.

Heavy, uneven footsteps chased me down the street. Not knowing which way to go, I took the first dark alley which offered me asylum. With my heart slamming against my ribs, I gulped air and dove into a black corner. The man's curses followed me, and I knew I couldn't stay there.

Pushing myself away from the wall, I ran from one shadow to another. By then, I had lost count of how many shots he'd fired. Nine, ten, I didn't know, nor did I know how often he'd reloaded as he just kept firing.

Seeing a ladder propped against a wall, I scaled it to the top of the flat roofs. With limited sight, I began leaping from roof to roof in an attempt to elude my would-be killer. Another shot ripped the air apart, barely missing me. I dove over one short wall and rolled to a stop against a door. A sharp pain burned up my arm, the result of my hand striking the doorframe. Ignoring my discomfort, I yanked the door open and started down the stairs, but my staff caught the door and snapped from my injured hand. I stumbled down the stairs while my staff clattered to the gravel surface behind me.

Hitting the hard floor, I watched in horror as a shadow appeared at the top of the stairs. I knew at any moment the man would fire his last shot ending my life. Instead, I heard a voice. The man was speaking to someone on the phone.

"Mr. Saul, this is Mohan Hasad. I took out the guy in the house, but the one with the staff got away."

He paused.

"Yes, I got it. He must have dropped it to save his skin, but I'll find him. He can't be far."

Another pause.

"Yeah, I think that's a great idea. Mr. St. John will be more than happy to pay for it if he wants the entire package … the Ark and the staves all for one low, low price."

I remained motionless as the conversation ended. It

all made sense ... *Saul, the theft, the fire, my staff being stolen. They were all done to serve a greater purpose. But who is St. John?*

As the seconds ticked by, I considered my options. If I blinked, as I had done back in North Hamilton, I could be on the other side of town, or better yet ... home. But I still had to locate Colt. I'd come here to get information about his whereabouts, and I was determined not to leave without finding him. While I laid there counting the seconds, the killer silently disappeared.

As I waited for my heart to climb back into my chest, a foot scraped the floor. Movement behind me sent an icy chill down my spine and I froze. *Had he come back?* I held my breath ... eyes pinched shut, expecting a bullet in the head at any moment. I waited.

None came.

After a long minute, I opened my eyes and saw a pair of brown feet in front of me. They belonged to the mother whose child I healed. Apparently, in my haste and confusion, I had run full circle and ended up where I started. The woman stood over me, baby in hand. She wasn't crying. Rather, she looked like a woman who was relieved and I had to imagine how it must have felt now that her abusive husband was no longer a threat to her.

Pushing myself up, I gave the woman a respectful bow. "Do you know anything about the young boy in my care?"

She shook her head. "I know not'ing.' She said in broken English.

I thanked her, then remembered I carried quite a bit of money in my pocket ... money to buy information. This night, I had gained a lot of information at the expense of a bruised skull and the life of this woman's husband. Without counting it, I handed the woman a wad of money. "Here, take this and start a new life."

In her best broken English, she thanked me, and receded into a shadow while I returned to the street.

Chapter Twenty-One

The cool night prickled my arms as I trudged along the dusty streets. I had no idea where to go next, but I knew I had to keep moving. Coming to the West Bank was dangerous, staying here could be deadly.

After an hour of wandering aimlessly, I was ready for the sun to come up. The knot on my head throbbed, and my stomach gnawed on itself. It suddenly dawned on me that I was complaining. With no one to chide me, I realized how alone I was. *Balthazar, Melchior*. My heart ached for their company, and I slumped to the curb and began to weep.

After some time, the weight of loss lifted, though I didn't know how or why, but my attention shifted from my woes to my blessings. I was alive, and that was saying something. I had faced death on more than one occasion in the last year and lived to tell about it. Then there was Colt. Since coming to life back in his attic, he and I had become fast friends. He looked to me as something like an uncle, a mentor. And I looked to him as the son I'd never have. And then there was Felicia …

Forcing aside romantic thoughts, I began to analyze my situation. *Why would Saul send me into the middle of the West Bank? And why was I dumb enough to go there?* The more I thought about it, the more convinced I was that it was a setup. The rumble of an approaching truck arrested my thoughts. I turned as a set of headlights blinded me.

"Hey mister, need a ride?" a thick, gravelly voice called out. He was obviously a resident of that pathetic city.

"Where are you headed?" I asked.

"Where else? America." His cheery tone brought the lines from *Fiddler on the Roof* to mind, and I almost responded by repeating my line. "But first," he continued, "I must make a delivery to the Temple."

"The Temple as in, the Third Temple? The one spoken of in Ezekiel?"

"But of course, is there no other?"

Chagrined, I offered him a smile. "You are right. I think I'll take you up on your offer."

A moment later, we were rumbling along the narrow streets of the Muslim Quarter.

"My name is Abdullah and this is my son, Kamil. What is your name?" he offered a calloused hand.

I accepted his show of hospitality. "My name is Gasper."

"Humph, funny name. You aren't from here, are you, Mr. Gasper?" Kamil asked, his face bore no hidden agenda, just innocent curiosity.

"No, actually, I'm not. I am from America, but I came here to—" I paused, the story was too complicated. "Let's say, I lost track of something very valuable, and I need to get it back."

The man and boy exchanged questioning glances. "Why would an American be wandering around in the Muslim Quarter? Do you have a death wish?" Abdullah asked.

It was true. This was probably one of the most dangerous places in the world, especially without a weapon. I suddenly felt really dumb.

"I came here to find a friend," I said after a moment.

"Obviously, you didn't find him or her. Now what are you going to do?" Abdullah asked, giving me a mirthless laugh.

"It was a him ... a young boy. He was under my tutelage, and somehow we got separated during the fire in the Institute in Antiquities." It was all true. I simply left out a few details.

"The West Bank is a bad place to be looking for anyone. The chances of finding him are, well ... slim."

I nodded. A sick feeling washed over me.

Once we'd crossed the border, we came to a stop near a part of the city I recognized. "You can drop me off anywhere along here." I told Mr. Abdullah.

As he slowed, Kamil looked at his father. "Should we tell him?"

Abdullah gripped the wheel of his truck in contemplation. Nodding, he looked at his son, then at me. "Can we trust you with a secret?"

I felt the heat of their eyes as they held my gaze. Whatever the secret it was, it must have come to them at a great price.

"Mr. Abdullah, I assure you, I am an honorable man. Your secret is safe with me."

Tugging the steering wheel to the right, Abdullah, slowed his truck and brought it to a halt along the side of the street. He shut off the engine allowing the silence of the hour to close in around us. With the windows open, a light breeze stirred the sullen air and I inhaled. The fragrance of night blooming jasmine tickled my senses, making me want to breathe the more. Glancing up, I saw slender fingers of orange reaching over the eastern horizon tugging the earth in their direction. It wouldn't be long before morning arrived, freeing us from the night with its dangers and memories.

"First off, my full name is Abdullah Grahani Hasad."

At hearing the name Hasad the wind left my lungs. It was all I could do to keep from jerking open the door and running. "I'm listening," barely choking out the words.

"I have a brother. His name is Mohan. He is a very violent man."

I clutched the handle more tightly, but Kamil's small hand gripped mine, halting me.

By now, I was dripping with sweat. I swiped my hand across my face to keep the sweat from stinging my eyes. The name Mohan Hasad caused my heart to sputter. "I think I met your brother a few hours ago, does he walk with a limp?"

Abdullah and Kamil exchanged shocked expressions. "Yes," they answered in unison. "Why?" How?" Abdullah continued.

Taking a dry swallow, I tried to keep my answer simple. "A man named Saul Mueller sent me here with instructions to go to a certain house and the man inside would tell me where to find the young boy for whom I am responsible. Needless to say, I didn't find him, but met your brother instead. I heard him talking on the phone to this man named Saul.

Abdullah ran his hand over the back of his neck. "I have a suspicion that all this involves the Ark everyone is searching for. You see, my son and I also saw something last night. It was a group of men and my brother. They were loading a large, odd shaped object on a truck."

My pulse quickened. "Have you told anyone about this?"

Nodding, he said, "Yes, an Israeli border guard, but I don't think he took me seriously. They promised me a lot of things, if this went right, or if that went right."

"So why are you telling me this?"

Abdullah's shoulders rose and fell. "You wouldn't believe it if I told you."

"Try me."

The man's face contorted into a doubtful expression. "God told me to."

Relieved, I let out a long-held breath. "Oh, well, then if that's true, you have a friend in the information business. I too follow God's voice. It was He who told me to come to Israel in the first place." For the next ten minutes, I gave him the condensed version of my being there.

"And you say, the guy who tried to kill me is your brother?"

He nodded.

I continued, "As I said earlier, I overheard him call a man named Saul, and they talked about selling the Ark to a man named St. John. I wonder if this Saul guy is the same Saul who is the archaeologist."

"Father," Kamil interjected, "isn't Uncle Mohan, Mr. Saul Mueller's driver?"

"Yes, and last night I heard him say something about the Gaza Strip." Looking at me, he asked, "Does that mean anything to you, Mr. Gasper?"

My hands slicked. I had never been to the Gaza Strip,

but if it was anything like the West Bank, I had no interest in going there. "No, but I have a friend who may be able to shed some light on this. Could you take me to the Institute in Antiquities ... or what's left of it?"

"Yes, we are not far." Turning the key, Abdullah started the engine and put the truck in gear. He took a quick glance over his shoulder and pulled into traffic. Fifteen minutes later, the truck rumbled to a stop in front of a smoldering shell of a building.

We got out of the truck and gazed at what once was a magnificent structure.

"Thank you my friends. If we never meet again, I'll look for you on the streets of gold." I extended my hand, but instead, Abdullah and his son drew me into a bear hug.

"We will keep listening for the voice of God, for indeed, He may have more work for us to do," he said as he and his son returned to the truck.

We parted having exchanged phone numbers and with the promise to keep in touch.

It was only after the rumble of his engine had faded in the distance that I considered the possibility I might have been entertained by angels. The thought brought a smile to my face, despite the throbbing knot on the back of my head.

One thing I had learned, Saul Mueller was not the man he claimed to be, and he was in cahoots with a man named St. John. It was a mystery who and what this was, but I had to find out. And then there was that statement about the Gaza Strip.

Satisfied his mission to bring Abdullah and Gasper

together was successful; Prince Azrael wished he'd thought of appearing in human flesh. He had done so earlier, but he didn't want to abuse his ability. To do so might compromise his purpose. For the time being, his was to protect the saints. Tonight was no exception. He had guarded Mr. Gasper and brought him in contact with the one person who might be pivotal in getting the Ark of God back.

Chapter Twenty-Two

B y the time I entered the offices of the Institute in Antiquities, the sun had just peeked over the Kidron Valley. A light breeze drifted up its slopes, freshening the air and calling early-risers outside for their morning run.

Seeing me enter, Simon set the phone down and rushed from his office. "Gasper, you schlep, where have you been? I've been so worried."

I took a seat and wiped my brow. "You'd never believe it if I told you, but suffice it to say, it has been a very interesting night. I have uncovered a loose connection between Saul, and a man named St. John."

"Saul Mueller?" he asked, handing me a mug of black coffee.

"The one and the same," I admitted after taking a cautious sip. "It was he who sent me on a false lead to an address in the Muslim Quarter. The guy I met was supposed to have information about Colt. Turned out, he was nothing more than a common thief. After I healed his sick child, he tried to steal my staff."

I could tell I was losing Simon with the details, so I cut to the chase. "As I was trying to leave, the lights went out, and Mohan Hasad came in with blazing guns. He killed the guy who tried to rob me, and I barely escaped. After running for my life, I fell down a flight of stairs, and I lost my staff. The next thing I knew, the guy was on the phone talking with a man named St. John."

Simon slumped to a chair. "Oy vey, Mohan is Saul's driver and St. John is Jacque de Molay St. John, the newly appointed Secretary General of the UN. He is the man who convinced Prime Minister David ben Isakson to sign the Unity Accord in the first place. It is because of his efforts we have peace with our neighbors and can build the Temple."

"But why would this St. John guy be interested in stealing the Ark? Wouldn't that work against all he'd accomplished with the Accord? Wouldn't that destabilize the entire region?"

Stroking his chin, Simon thought a minute. "Yes and no. It depends on what he plans to do with it."

I took another sip. By now, the caffeine had kicked in and I felt a slight buzz. "Well, what does the Gaza Strip have to do with it, other than being a very good place to hide something?"

Standing, Simon walked over to a shelf, pulled a thick roll, and laid it on the table. After spreading it out, he began to study it. "There are several places in the Gaza Strip which would be great for concealing something ... Gaza, Ashkelon, Ashdod, Ekron, and Gath."

I leaned closer. "That's the same territory the Philistines occupied in my day."

"Yes, that's right. During the days of King Saul, the Ark fell into the Philistine's hands and traveled to those same cities."

I felt my heart quicken. "I knew the story and I feared for the people living in its path."

Simon bolted upright, his face flushed and he found it

hard to breathe. "I just heard on the news this morning, there has been a severe outbreak of some kind of virus. It is spreading like a cancer through the center of Gaza." His finger traced a highway through the major cities. "They are having to bury hundreds of bodies in mass graves. The Palestinians think we did it and are ready to storm our borders. The Prime Minister has put the nation on high alert and called up the reserves."

I felt a sick feeling wash over me. For the next few minutes, we sat and stared at the map as if it would give us more information.

"Can you get a live picture of that area?" I asked.

Simon held my gaze. "I might. I have a friend in the Mossad. He just might be able to task a satellite to take a peek in that area, but there's a problem."

"What's that?"

"That's a big area to search in the first place. Secondly, it is blacked out from our satellites and if the PLO discovers we are peeking at them, they could charge us with spying."

I straightened. "Any way to get sandals on the ground?"

"Are you asking if you could go there? Maybe you should have your head examined, you schlep. If you thought the West Bank was dangerous, you've not seen anything. Armed bands of men roam unhindered through the streets of the cities. Any Jew found within their jurisdiction is shot on sight. You might get in, but you won't get out, at least alive."

"Well, what if I went in dressed as an Arab? With me being a Jew from India, I might pass as just another mixed up middle easterner."

Simon stepped back and rubbed his chin. After eyeing me for a minute, he began to nod his head. "You know, it just might work. Just don't talk to anyone. But if you're going to do it, you'll need some muscle backing you. Let me pull a few strings, make a few phone calls. I am not a man without means, you know."

"Good, you do that. Meanwhile, I too have something I need to do."

"What's that?"

"I need to go to New York, to the UN building. I have a hunch the Secretary General isn't what he claims to be."

"That's meshuga ... crazy talk. You can't just fly to—"

By then, I had disappeared, but I heard Simon muttering. "I wish he wouldn't do that."

Sitting in a vehicle outside the smoldering remains of the Institute in Antiquities, two men wearing listening devices exchanged satisfied glances. They were part of Jacque St. John's network of eyes and ears. Their job was to keep him informed of any new developments and report back to him. Lifting the phone to his ear, the lead operative waited for the encrypted phone to sync with St. John's.

"What's the problem?" the second man asked as his conspirator tapped the computer running the system.

"I don't know. There seems to be a glitch in the system. It worked the last time I checked, but this time, all I get is static."

"St. John doesn't like surprises. Do you think we should break protocol and go directly to him?"

The lead operative thought a moment, then shook his

head. "No, there are too many other people out there listening. If we did, we would risk the Israelis or the Americans picking up our signal, and we'd be finished. Let's wait a few minutes and try again."

Satisfied, the two men resumed their surveillance duties while above them, Prince Azrael smiled impishly and continued to suppress the signal with his finger.

Chapter Twenty-Three

" "Thank you Mohan, that will be all for now." As the manservant receded from sight, Saul Mueller took a deep pull from his pipe and tried to relax in his easy chair. The den was his favorite place to muse, and this morning offered him time for such reverie.

He allowed his mind to wander to the many archaeological digs he'd conducted and the many priceless items he'd acquired over the years. The ones destroyed in the fire were only replicas. The real ones were mounted on the walls and stood in glass enclosed displays scattered throughout his lavished house.

Located on the outskirts of Jerusalem in an exclusive community, his home was a sanctuary from the stresses of everyday living. His wealth and notoriety afforded him the best life could offer, including his manservant and driver.

He had discovered Mohan Hasad's particular talents one day when he ran amok with his hired help at a dig. The men he'd employed to do the heavy lifting in an archeological site near the Dead Sea refused to work during their prayer time. It was Mohan who negotiated an arrangement between the men and their employer which satisfied all concerned. Either they worked through their prayer time or they got an early pass to Allah; forty virgins excluded. From then on, Saul used him to carry out special tasks. The false lead he'd sent Gasper on ended up getting a cheap thug named Yousef killed, but it was worth it. *Yousef was undependable, and couldn't be trusted anyway.* Saul mused.

Now that he had possession of all three staves, he was in a position of power. Fingering the staves smooth surfaces, Saul tried to imagine the secrets they held. Then his thoughts turned from their past to their future. If these were the same staves which were used to carry the Ark, then maybe they possessed some of its power. He had already seen what Gasper did when he stopped the stack of marble blocks from falling. Extending the end of the rods toward a 19th century antique Chinese flambé vase, he closed his eyes and concentrated ... nothing happened.

He tried again. This time the vase wobbled a little, then toppled to the floor and smashed into a thousand pieces. A moment later, Mohan reentered the den and surveyed the damage.

"Is there a problem?" Mohan faced his boss who sat with a gaping mouth. Shall I get someone to clean up this mess?"

Saul lowered the staves and nodded, "Yes, then pour yourself a drink. You look thirsty."

Mohan disappeared to find the housekeeper; nearly stumbling into Prince Azrael who'd materialized just enough to topple the vase off its pedestal.

It was a bold act, one that required stealth and timing. It had worked, but nearly got him caught in the process. Fortunately for all concerned, Saul and Mohan's focus was on the staff and broken glass and not on the slightly shimmering presence just around the corner. Having convinced Saul into thinking the staff had power apart from God's power, he let things develop according to plan.

Saul looked at the shattered vase, then back to the staves. *These are real, all right.*

Lifting the phone, he dialed St. John's private number. "Jacque, my old friend, guess what I am holding?"

"Don't tell me, let me guess … it's the staves used to carry the Ark of the Covenant."

Taken aback, Saul asked, "How did you know?"

St. John released a cruel chuckle. "Let's just say I have eyes and ears everywhere. It was my men who discovered your bungling idiots had a kid hiding in their van."

"A child? Who? When?" Saul asked, forgetting his gaff over the staves.

"You fool, by listening in on Simon's conversation between him and some guy named Gasper; they learned the boy's name is Colt. The kid must have climbed into the van during the fire. It's just a small detail, but the kind that gets people killed, if you get my meaning. You need to find the boy and dispose of him."

Saul nodded into the phone. "Yes sir, it will be handled—"

"Now tell me, do the staves offer any promise?" St. John cut him off without acknowledging his acquiescence.

"Promise?" Saul repeated, reclaiming his lost momentum. "They not only hold promise, they hold power, and one of them may be the very rod used by Moses to part the Red Sea."

A mirthless chuckle filled the connection. "And you

are going to tell me how much you want for them, aren't you?"

"On the contrary, I am calling to tell you plans have changed."

"Oh? How so?"

Saul heard a tinge of anxiety form in his question.

"Well, let's just say I am planning to make my own announcement any day now. I can see the headlines in the papers. Noted Archaeologist recovers the stolen Ark. I'll be even more famous than I already am, not to mention the wealth I'd get as a finder's fee."

"You wouldn't." St. John seethed into the phone.

"Try me, or you may want to offer me a better deal. I'd consider something in the ball park of two billion dollars."

Saul waited as St. John vented. Finally, after he'd exhausted his limited supply of expletives, he regained control of himself.

"All right, I'll pay what you're asking. Where should we meet?"

"Ah, ah, ah, not so fast. First, I'll send you an account number. After you've deposited the money into an offshore bank account and the money has cleared, I'll send you the coordinates where you can find the Ark."

"Don't get cute with me. I want to know where the Ark is located before I send you a dime." St. John demanded.

Saul knew they were at an impasse. Neither man was going to budge. If he was going to lure St. John into the trap, he needed to make the initial move. He had sixteen highly trained operatives ready to kill the first person to step within a mile of the Ark. "It is of utmost importance we keep its location under wraps—"

"Tell me where it is or so help me—"

"Now, now, Jacque, don't get in a huff, you know as well as me, I can't ... not just yet. Once I see the money, it's all yours. I will give you a hint. It's somewhere in the Middle-East." He laughed victoriously. "I'll take a down payment of half a billion, as a show of good faith. After I confirm the money is securely in my account, I'll send the exact location, but when you come, come with just enough men to load it on your plane and be sure they leave their toys at home."

St. John blasphemed. "You must think me a fool. When I come, it will be with the full force of UN backing. I am planning a global summit with the religious leaders of the world at that time. Once I am sure of its authenticity, I will make my demands known."

"You do that, sir and you'll have a world war on your hands. You know how fanatical some of the religious leaders are."

"I don't think so. Once they see the power I possess, they will be putty in my hands."

Saul wasn't as interested in the money or the power as he was evening a long overdue score, but he had to make it look like it was St. John's idea. Planting an idea in someone else's mind was one of those tricks he'd learned on the street. His sleight of hand had grown into a full-fledged con game ... one with the highest stakes.

"What about the Jews? Don't you think they may have something to say about your little summit?"

"You're a Jew, what do you think?"

Saul tried to contain his mirth. "I think they will treat you like they treated the last man who tried to pull off the

'God with us,' gig."

St. John released another string of expletives. "You leave the Jews to me. If they don't cooperate, I will roll over them like Hitler did the French."

At the mention of Hitler, Saul fell silent.

"What's the matter Saul? Are you offended at my analogy?"

Saul took a controlled breath and let it out slowly. "Look Jacque, let's just get this over with so we can move on."

"Okay, okay, don't be so touchy. Just make sure everything is in place when I get there."

Saul had already hung up. The exchange with St. John left him fuming. His reference to Hitler and France brought back a flood of emotions. It was Jacque's father who was responsible for the deaths of many Jews, including his family. He stood and walked to his private bar and poured Mohan and himself a shot glass of brandy. "What a schmuck. Once I lure that fool to the hangar, I'll take care of Mr. Jacque de Molay St. John myself. I should have killed him years ago, but revenge is a dish, best served cold."

The two men tapped the edges of their tumblers together then downed their drinks.

"Prepare my plane for departure. I don't plan on being in the Gaza Strip for long, but be sure to include plenty of hardware, if you catch my meaning."

Mohan nodded and disappeared to his duties.

Chapter Twenty-Four

Saul's mind turned the young boy's name over and over again. His body hadn't turned up after the fire, and none of his men reported seeing him in the building before or after the blaze started. He could only assume what St. John said was true … the boy must be hiding somewhere in the airplane hangar.

Lifting the phone, he dialed the number for his security team leader. Moshe, the team leader picked up on the first ring. Moshe was Mossad through and through. The fact that he'd been dishonorably discharged for striking an officer only enhanced his resume' as far as Saul was concerned. Now he worked for Saul Mueller as the head of his special protection unit. His team of eight Israeli and eight Palestinian mercenaries provided enough security around the hangar that no one could get in or out without triggering a gunfight.

"Yeah," Moshe answered in a dusty tone.

"Don't use that tone of voice with me, Moshe. You need to show some respect."

"Yes, sir, Mr. Archaeologist, sir. What can I do ya for?"

Saul shoved his disgust for the man aside. He was too critical at this point in the plan to ostracize. "Moshe, do a complete sweep of the compound."

"What am I looking for?" he asked curtly.

"You are looking for a boy possibly dressed as a shepherd."

Moshe smirked. "Sir, there are shepherds roaming all over these hills, which one are you interested in?"

Saul released a string of vulgarity. "I don't care about those rag heads out there on the hills. I'm interested in you finding the boy who stowed away in the van driven by *your* men. I don't need some kid coming along and messing up my plans. So get your tush off the can and find him. When you do, get rid of him. Do you understand?"

"Sure thing boss. My men will find the little rat and when we do, he'll wish he'd never crossed my path."

###

No sooner had Moshe hung up, than he began barking orders for the men to do a complete search of the premises. Grumbling, the soldiers began moving boxes and searching behind the stacks of barrels.

To make things interesting, Prince Azrael materialized and began to play tricks on the frustrated soldiers. He maneuvered around the building allowing just enough of his cape to appear, sending the men on a wild goose chase. First one of them would get a sighting and run into another man coming in the opposite direction. Before long, the men were at each other's throats.

Finally, in frustration, the men stomped to opposite sides of the building and continued to search. As one man began to move an empty barrel to get further back, Azrael caused one of them to tumble over and land on another man's foot. The man danced around cursing his misfortune, then left in search of an ice pack.

After doing an exhaustive search and not finding the boy, the team reassembled only to be chewed out by Moshe, their commander. The dispirited men separated into two camps to warm themselves and eat a scant supper, while Colt and his unseen protector sat, perched on the upper level of the office, smirking.

###

From where Colt hid, he could only hear one side of the phone conversation between the commander of the security team and someone else. What he'd heard sent a shiver of fear down his back.

Since he'd arrived, he'd found ways to meet his basic needs. After waiting until most of the men were asleep, he'd creep from his hiding place and forage for enough food and water to survive. However, with sixteen men doing an inch by inch search for him left him with little options. Going outside would expose him to the brutal heat during the day. At night, he'd be faced with freezing temperatures, and roving packs of wolves. Staying inside limited his exposure, but also gave him few places to hide. He could climb an I-beam, but that had its risks, or he could stay hidden among the barrels hoping to be overlooked. None of his options seemed that good but getting caught was definitely not an option.

The cavernous hangar ticked and moaned with heat expansion as the sun hastened across the arid sky. As the day wore on, most of the guards stayed within the shade of the hanger rather than standing in the sweltering heat. One man tried to lean against the metal wall and yelped as an angry welt formed on his exposed flesh. Others found refuge from the sun and stagnant air by resorting to an air conditioned room on the far side of the hanger.

From his vantage point, Colt spotted a ladder attached to the block wall which formed the only building inside the hangar. Guessing the building to be an office with several rooms, he considered hiding there, but quickly dismissed the idea. However, the ladder intrigued him. The building was two stories with the second floor reserved for storage. It was there the men started their search. Once they cleared that space, it was unlikely they would search it a second time.

Later that night, once the lights were dimmed and most of the men escaped the heat of the building to enjoy the cooler night air, Colt slipped from his hiding place and crept across the floor. As he did so, however, voices spilled from the office and several large men carrying weapons emerged. Caught in the center of the room, Colt had one option. He dove under the tarp which covered the Ark. He pulled himself into a tight ball as heavy booted feet walked around the area.

The oily smell emanating from the tarp made his eyes water and tempted him to sneeze, but he pinched his nose and prayed. Finally, the boots receded. Counting to one-hundred, Colt peeked out from under the tarp. No footsteps. Taking a calming breath, he inched further away from his hiding place. After checking to see if it was a trap and seeing no one, he scampered across the concrete floor and skidded next to the ladder.

Still no one noticed.

Gulping air, he climbed the ladder and ducked behind a crate just as a group of men returned from searching the perimeter. Their laughter echoed throughout the building, covering the rustling sound he made getting situated.

Sweating profusely and panting like a dog, Colt

counted no less than sixteen men coming and going. By their uniforms, he determined there were at least two factions; one Israeli, the other Palestinian. The two groups seemed to get along, but he could tell the heat, and stress of being on constant watch was taking its toll. There had already been one altercation, and by the way the groups often gathered around two separate fires, he knew it would only be a matter of time before tempers flared. As heavily armed as those men were, Colt had no intention of being caught in the middle of the fight.

Fortunately, the last time he'd foraged, he was able to collect several bottles of water and some energy bars. As he settled in, a soldier from the Israeli camp marched across the open space, yelling at a Palestinian soldier. The two men immediately drew their knives and began slashing at each other. It would be a fight to the death, unless someone intervened. Neither their commander, nor anyone else seemed interested in settling the argument peacefully. Rather, the diversion seemed to come as welcomed relief.

In the distance, the drone of a small airplane grew in intensity drawing everyone's attention to it rather than the two men. Minutes later, it touched down at the far end of the runway and began taxing in their direction, interrupting the fight. Taking up defensive positions, the men prepared to fire upon the approaching plane.

"Hold your fire," Moshe ordered as the aircraft slowed to a stop.

As Saul Mueller climbed out and hurried toward the hangar, Moshe stepped from behind his men and approached him. "Mr. Mueller, we didn't expect you until tomorrow," the surprised commander said, giving him a sloppy salute.

Saul stood and surveyed the armed men in the glow of his vehicle's headlights. It was obvious from their torn uniforms and bloody shirts, he had come none too soon.

"Am I interrupting something?"

The commander glanced over his shoulder. "We were just working out a few kinks in the chain of command."

"Chain of command, hmm? Well, I'm here and I'm in command. Now find that stow away kid."

"But sir, we just searched the entire place."

"I don't give a rat's tail what you just did ... do it again, starting with that van." He pointed to the vehicle Colt, and the arsonists had ridden in.

Having been out maneuvered, Moshe stepped back. "Okay, you heard the man," Moshe said, "find the kid."

As the men scattered, Colt prayed they wouldn't climb the ladder and discover his hiding place. He had already seen one man emerge from the place where he first hid. Fortunately, he left nothing to give away his presence.

While the men searched, Saul and Mohan walked to the tarp covered object. It was only then that Colt noticed Saul carrying three familiar objects. *But how could this man get his hands on Balthazar, Melchior, and Gasper's staves? Had Gasper died in the fire? Did this man kill Gasper and steal them?*

A dozen fear-ridden scenarios played themselves out in his mind as he watched the two men walk across the open space. Together they lifted a corner of the tarp and threw it back.

Clapping his hand over his mouth to keep from gasping, Colt stifled a scream. In the defused light, two winged cherubim covered a golden box. From his Sunday School lessons, he'd learned the Ark was approximately fifty-one inches by eighteen by eighteen. For a long moment, the men stood in awe at the sight. Being careful, they took two of the longer staves and inserted them into a set of rings, which hung on either side of the box. No sooner had they finished, than the room burst into a blaze of golden light.

Colt tried to blink away the vision, but couldn't. The building shook and moaned as the force of energy coming from the Ark grew in intensity. Finally, after the initial shock wave subsided, Colt opened his eyes. Despite the grit and dirt, the two men prostrated themselves before the Ark of God. Hands covering their faces, they remained motionless until the brightness dimmed.

Finally, the men inched backwards all the while repeating the words, "The Lord God is one Lord." The moment they reached the exit, they stood and ran from the building.

Chapter Twenty-Five

Jacque St. John rested his hand on the phone. He didn't like Saul, and he trusted him even less. Any man who would sell out his own country was not a man he wanted to depend upon in a fight. And this was a fight he had to win … he would not settle for anything less. Lifting his sat-phone to his ear, he dialed a number he'd committed to memory and waited for the encrypted code to sync.

"Have a team in the air within the hour. They'll know what to do." After a pause, he continued, "I'll have a location by the time they are over the Mediterranean."

The phone clicked off as the team leader of a select group of highly trained operatives responded with a thick throated, "Yes, sir."

His next call went to a paneled truck sitting on a hill facing Saul Mueller's home. Inside it were two technicians and thousands of dollars of high-tech listening equipment. "Yes, sir," the lead tech said in a respectful tone.

"You missed your last check-in. What's the problem?"

The lead tech cleared his throat and began slowly. "Well, sir … we've been having technical difficulties—"

"I don't give a rat's rear end about your problems. I need answers." He raged. "I didn't pay thousands of dollars in listening equipment just to have you two goons sitting in a van eating whatever you Jews eat. Now tell me you have been able to track any of Saul's calls."

"Yes sir, that we have been able to do. He called a man named Moshe."

"Was he on the phone long enough for you to get a location?"

"That is an affirmative. The call went to an airfield called Khan Yunis. It's an abandoned airport in the Gaza Strip."

Narrowing his eyes, St. John tried to picture in his mind the location. *Saul knows how to pick them. Talk about out of the way.* "Okay, now we're getting somewhere. Anything else?"

"Yes sir, his driver put in a call to a private airport and told them to have a plane ready. I'm guessing he's on his way to Kahn Yunis as we speak."

Satisfied he was one step ahead of his coconspirator, he let out a dry chuckle. "All right, keep up your surveillance, and if you pick up anything else, don't hesitate to call, and this time ... no screw ups."

No sooner had St. John ended the conversation, than his phone buzzed.

"Sir," his secretary called over the intercom, "your press secretary is here to see you. Shall I send her in?"

St. John smiled to himself. *Yes, Miss Kline ... Keep your friends close, keep your enemies closer.*

He knew she'd dug up his past and intended to use it to her advantage. That was how his ancestors would have done it; find out the dirt on your enemy and use it against them. That's how he would do it. *Once she had fulfilled her usefulness, well ...*

"Yes, send her in."

A moment later, Amber Kline, his newly appointed press secretary strode in. Since their last meeting in which he offered her the job, and she accepted, a lot had happened. Taking her seat, she opened her iPad and prepared to type verbatim his statement about the mounting tension in the Middle East.

"I am planning on a summit with the PLO and Israelis later this week in which I will unveil a bold new initiative."

Amber's eyes rounded. "Do you think it safe to go now? The Middle-East is a powder-keg, it's about to blow up, what with that deadly virus spreading like the plague."

If I needed your advice I'd have asked for it, but now that you mentioned it, I could use this to my advantage.

"On the contrary, Miss Kline, this is the perfect time to step into the fray. Since I am known as something of a peace maker, I could ride in on my white horse and save the day."

She nodded thoughtfully. "Mr. Secretary, that is absolutely brilliant." Looking at her calendar, she scrolled through his itinerary. "Let's see, Friday is the Muslims holy day, and Saturday is the Jewish Sabbath. So what day are you thinking?"

Not missing a beat, St. John pointed at her calendar. "Saturday, after sundown. That way, I'll catch all those naysayers in churches in the US with their pants down. Tell all the media outlets to cancel their programing and plan on a live, televised broadcast at seven o'clock in the evening." It was a dangerous strategy, one that could backfire if he didn't play his cards right, but one that he could live with ... or die for.

Amber's fingers flew over the keypad trying to keep up as he rambled on about global initiatives and world peace. "They will ask the usual who, what, when and where questions. What should I tell them?"

St. John scribbled himself a note. "Tell them to be ready for anything. In the meantime, I want you to act as my liaison between the Vatican, the major religious institutions in the US, the Ayatollah in Iraq, and the Dalia Lama. Arrange to have them flown to an undisclosed location on Saturday at my expense, of course. I will provide the transportation and accommodations. All they need to do is be ready, I'll do the rest."

"Are you at liberty to share any details at this time?"

"Not at this moment, but I am planning on an intimate dinner party at my home in the Palisades. It is then, I will share my heart. Would you do me the honor of attending?"

He peered into her rounded eyes. *You will come.*

She started to turn him down when the voice in her head convinced her otherwise. Hand to her temple, her forehead wrinkled. "Yes ... I suppose." Her voice wavered, then grew stronger. "Yes, I'd be delighted."

"Splendid, I'll have my driver pick you up around 7:30 this evening. Please be ready."

Amber returned his smile, stood on uncertain legs and prepared to leave when St. John added one other request.

"Oh, and invite all the media outlets to the summit as well. I'll provide the transportation. Tell them to have their passports and visas ready. That should pique their interest. I'm sure your old boss, what's his name?

Womack, yes. Be sure he gets an invitation. It's the least we can do for me stealing you away from him. Tell me, is he still miffed?"

Amber's apple-red lips curled back into a coy smile. "Oh, he'll get over it, I'm confident of that. I'll see you at dinner."

Standing, St. John came around his desk and brushed a few strands of auburn hair from her forehead so he could gaze into her limpid green eyes. "I wouldn't miss it for the world. Arrive a little early as I have a few guests I'd like you to meet."

"Oh, I thought it was just—"

St. John waved off her protest. "It's just a formality. We'll meet and be done with it. Then we can move on to more important things." A wicked grin wrinkled the lines around his eyes.

It took Amber the rest of the day to call the religious leaders around the world. As the voice and face of the UN Secretary General, Amber was quickly given an audience. Through the miracle of modern technology, she was able to look directly into the faces of each man or woman on her list and get their support for St. John's proposed summit and their attendance. Only the Ayatollah offered some resistance, but with her assurance that it was in his best interest to back Jacque St. John, he relented. It was no secret what happened to those who stood in the Secretary General's way, and she knew the Ayatollah, if not anything, was a pragmatist. He had survived thus far by being open to suggestion … she just hoped for his sake, he would continue.

Now all she needed to do was to get Mr. St. John into

a compromising position. If she could do that, she'd have him wrapped around her little finger. She had enough information to sink any plans he might have of becoming a world dictator, but she'd rather get him to bend to her wishes instead. Being the wife, or better yet … mistress, of the world's most powerful man wasn't so bad, just as long as she could be the power behind him.

Chapter Twenty-Six

As the evening formed over the eastern hemisphere and the sun yielded to the growing darkness, four sleek limousines picked their way along the tree lined road leading to Jacque de Molay St. John's estate. Rightly named, Seven Oaks after the massive oaks surrounding the sprawling house, it was set deep in a heavily wooded community of Palisades, New York. Seven Oaks boasted nine bedrooms and six baths, its tiered lawn held a commanding view of the Hudson River while remaining secluded behind several walking gardens.

After delivering their occupants, the limos disappeared around the back of the estate where their drivers were kept sequestered in a separate facility. What purpose their query had in meeting with the most powerful man in the world was of no consequence to them. Theirs's was to drive and ask no questions.

Once inside, the four dark suited men were ushered to a parlor where Jacque waited. Their greeting was as unusual as were the men themselves. The ritual dated back beyond memory; nevertheless, they performed each step keeping to the strictest order. Then they took their seats around a heavy oak table. The four grim faced men waited for Jacque de Molay St. John to speak. When he did, it was in a somber tone. "Gentlemen, as you know, our purpose in meeting here, yea rather, the purpose in our very existence, is to see the Order of St. John and its militant wing, the Order of the Hospitallers reach its full potential." Standing, he began to pace.

"My great-great grandfather, Jacque de Molay, gave his life rather than surrender the secrets he possessed. Your fathers and grandfathers have been privy to such knowledge as well and have suffered the same fate. We have survived these many years because we have used our wealth and influence to keep our foes at bay. Today, we are at the brink of seeing our forefather's dreams come true, but we have a couple of problems. One is Saul Mueller. He made his demands known a few hours ago."

The men he'd known nearly all his life exchanged nervous looks.

"What are his demands?" the eldest of the four asked.

St. John smirked. "Two billion in US currency to be transferred to his off-shore account within 24 hours. Of course, I have no intention of paying it. Nevertheless, I need him to think I will long enough for me to arrange my summit meeting with the religious leaders of the world. Mr. Roche, I need you to use your connections to hack into Saul's bank account. Make him think I transferred the money. Once he's dead, we can back out and leave no trace of ever being there."

While St. John continued, Mr. Roche lifted the phone to his ear and set things in motion.

"The other little problem is Miss Kline. It seems she's been doing some snooping and connected the dots between me and my grand ancestor. Unfortunately, she is in a position to do us great damage if she is allowed to ... shall we say, hang around."

A quartet of grim faced men exchanged nervous looks.

"As the last remaining sons of the Order of

Hospitallers, we are the sworn protectors of the wealth of Jerusalem. Much of it, however, has been reclaimed by the Israeli State over time, but our quest for the greatest treasure has never waned. Now that it is within our grasp, we will not let anything, or anyone stand between it and our goal."

"Sir Jacque," a stoic gentleman with a narrow mustache and steely blue eyes interrupted. "Sir, if I might be so bold as to make a suggestion."

St. John poured himself another tumbler of Magellan or "M". It amused him that a bottle of whiskey, which cost him $630,000 at a Sotherby's auction a few years ago tasted no better than a lesser expensive brand, but such were the times. One must pay to keep up appearances.

"Say on, my good man," he said with a nod.

The man's eyes cut across the faces of his compatriots. "Well, a man in your position can't afford to have a lot of bodies piling up. And, since you are the most sought-after bachelor in the world, why don't you simply marry the woman? You do need an heir and well ..."

Heads began to nod slowly, and wry smiles appeared as the idea settled in.

Stroking his chin, St. John grinned sheepishly. "You devil, you." He patted the man on the shoulder. "No, I have no use for the woman in that way. I have a better, less intrusive idea."

"And if things don't work out, you still could marry her, could you not?" A short, balding man peered at him from behind a pair of thick spectacles.

"Yes, yes I could. One must keep up appearances. On

the other hand, accidents do happen you know. Tragic as they seem." St. John poured another round of drinks, and they toasted the decision. "But first, we have a ceremony to perform. It is with great desire I have waited for this moment to give myself to the cause. Fear not what you must do, but the ultimate sacrifice must be made if we are to fulfill our dream."

For the next three hours, they sat, and focused their collective energies on their familiar spirits. Finally, St. John spoke. "We beseech you oh mighty ones in the name of him who is forever. Give us the wisdom of the ages. Give me the keys to your kingdom, your power, your dominion. I have done all you asked. I have found the Ark of power. Allow me to be your vessel. I give myself to you in exchange for the world." Jacque's voice rose above the others.

As he spoke, the lights inside the room dimmed. The atmosphere became oppressively thick. The other men sat in a trance, their eyes locked straight ahead, unmoving, unblinking. Hovering just on the other side of the thin veil separating the physical from the celestial, was a myriad of dark spirit beings preparing to pounce. Already, some of their talons had penetrated the minds of their hosts. Then, like a giant sumo wrestler taking his place in the center of the ring, a massive demon parted the assembled spirits and glared down upon the mortals. With his breath coming in short, angry puffs, he reached inside St. John's mind and planted a seed ... one that would, when fully mature, control his every thought, words and actions.

Using his powers of mental telepathy, St. John focused his attention on the four men sitting in front of him.

Make the sacrifice ... you must kill me.

Then he took his place on the center of the table. Laying down, he spread his legs and arms so as to touch the points of the pentagram. *Do it*, he commanded.

The men rose to their feet. Their unblinking eyes drawn to a leather box bearing the same markings which were on the table; a five pointed star. The group moved mechanically to the table, and from the eldest to the youngest, took their place as Mr. Roche lifted the lid. Inside, lay four knives. Each handle was ornately decorated with symbols of the zodiac. One by one, the members of the Order of Hospitallers lifted a knife and retook their place around the table where Jacque de Molay St. John, son of the Grand Master of the Order of the Hospitallers waited.

"I do not fear him who can kill the body, nor do I fear him who can kill the soul." St. John uttered. "I fear living without the power ordained to me from the cradle of civilization." His voice resonated throughout the room.

As he spoke, the four men lifted their glistening blades and brought them down. Immediately, the gutter encircling the table began to fill with Jacque St. John's steaming blood. Unaffected by their gruesome deed, they wiped the blood from their knives and returned them to the box.

Turning, they stared in wonder.

Jacque de Molay St. John stood in their midst enshrouded in a black robe. Pulling back his hood, he lifted his arms wide and tilted his head back. His eyes sparked with fire as he spoke in booming tone. "I have come to take what is mine."

Chapter Twenty-Seven

As expected, the limousine arrived exactly on time causing Amber to rush through her last-minute preparations. It didn't matter, however, she looked good on and off camera, and she knew it. But this evening was special … it was the first of what she hoped would be many visits to Jacque's mansion. After running the brush through her hair one last time, she applied a fresh layer of lip-gloss and pranced down stairs. Taking a final look in the mirror which hung next to the front door, she gave herself a once over, smiled with satisfaction and stepped out, leaving behind the aroma of jasmine and vanilla.

The drive through that part of New York was much different from that of city driving. It gave her time to reflect on her journey thus far. Winning homecoming queen her senior year, voted most popular and most likely to succeed was only the beginning. Having won scores of beauty queen pageants enhanced her resume. But she wasn't finished. She set her sights even higher. She aced journalism in college and immediately found herself swimming in lucrative offers from news media outlets. Now that phase of her life was behind her, she set a new goal … one that focused on the most powerful man in the world … Jacque de Molay St. John. For better or for worse, he was all hers.

Dressed in a form-fitting evening gown, with her hair parted in the middle, and cascading loosely over her shoulders, Amber stepped from the limousine and strode up the flag-stoned walk leading to the front of St. John's palatial mansion. *I could get used to this,* she mused. It also gave her time to rehearse her plan. If she could get him alone, *well, maybe ... he is a man and if anything, I know men; I know what they want, what they need.* She let her mind wander until she reached the massive door guarding Jacque de Molay St. John's sanctuary, appropriately named, Seven Oaks.

As the resonant tones of the doorbell faded, Duncan, the manservant swung the door open and gave her an appreciative glance. "You are expected, Miss. Kline, may I take your hand bag and cloak?"

Smiling to herself, Amber handed him the items and followed him deeper into the house. As they passed along the broad hallway lined with hand painted portraits and original works by noted artists, laughter spilled from the formal parlor. Someone mentioned the name Gasper and his mighty staff, followed by a command to hush. Hearing the laughter, she slowed her stride and peered through the open door.

"Ah um." It was Duncan indicating she should keep moving. "That is a private meeting," he said in an aloof tone, then pulled the door closed. "If you will wait in the Library, Mr. St. John will introduce you to the group when he is ready."

Feeling slighted, she jutted her chin, and continued down the hall behind the slender man until they reached a solid oaken door.

"Please, if you will be so kind as to take a seat, he will call for you shortly."

Amber obeyed, but as the door closed, she couldn't help feeling that this was going to be a long evening. Waiting was never her strong suit, and she soon became listless. An antique clock on the mantel of a large fireplace marked the slow passing of time. As the hands dragged themselves around the clock's face, she studied the room's architecture, but that lasted only so long, before boredom set in.

Who is Gasper?

Pulling her ever-present iPad from her bag, she tapped in the name Gasper. A number of entries appeared, but only one interested her. Apparently a few months earlier, his name along with two others made the local news in a north Georgia town for rescuing a child from a cave. She skimmed the details looking for the city and found the name North Hamilton along with the family of the child they'd rescued.

Why would the UN Secretary General be interested in a local hero? Was he the head of an important company? Maybe he had a staff member Jacque was interested in hiring. He has a way of stealing the best of the best from his competitors, she mused.

Hoping Duncan or St. John wouldn't catch her, she reached for her cell phone. *Drats, it's in my handbag.* Without thinking, she jerked the door open and dashed down the hall. Finding the cloak closet where Duncan had stored her belongings, she gulped, and began to fish her cell from her purse and returned to the Library. Still breathing hard, she quickly called up the Yellow pages. "The Glenn O'Dell's, in North Hamilton, Georgia, please." The automated system scrambled for the number. "We have three listings for Glenn O'Dell in north Georgia, which one would you like to call?"

Frustrated, she huffed and clarified her search. "North Hamilton, Glenn O'Dell."

Again, the automated operator checked the listing. "We have found one listing. Would you like me to send the number to your in-box, or dial it?"

"Dial it, please." She wondered why she was being so polite to an automated operator. *It must be my good training, yeah right.*

After three rings, a female voice said, "Hello?"

Brushing a strand of hair behind her ear, Amber continued in a professional tone. "Hello, my name is Amber Kline the UN Secretary General's press secretary."

A sharp intake followed, but Amber pressed ahead. "I am trying to reach a man named, Gasper. I don't know his last name. Do you know him?"

Karen chuckled. "Yes, I know him, but he only has one name."

"Oh, I see. It is extremely urgent I speak with him. Could you provide me a phone number?"

The connection between Amber and the O'Dell's grumbled as Karen handed the phone to her husband. "This is Glenn O'Dell, what's this all about?"

Amber forced aside her frustration and spoke and tried again. After repeating her earlier request, Glenn's tone softened. "Actually, Mr. Gasper is in Israel, but he doesn't have a phone. He is staying with a man named Simon Levi."

Amber scribbled down the number, stuffed it into her

pocket, thanked Mr. O'Dell and ended the call. She had heard Mr. St. John mention the name Simon Levi one time on the phone, but thought nothing of it until now. With this new development, her interest piqued.

Taking a steadying breath, she turned the knob and eased the door open. A quick glance, told her the hall was clear. *What am I thinking? ... If I get caught, my tail is roasted.* Tiptoeing, she made her way to the closed door. Head against the wood, she listened. What she heard chilled her to the bone. She had to leave ... now.

She had barely enough time to make it back to the room before Duncan, the tall lanky manservant, appeared at the door. His expression had changed from a passive stoic, to one of suspicion. *Had he seen her? Did he know of her little escape? Could he be trusted?* Her mind slammed against logic. *Of course he couldn't be trusted. He was one of them.*

"Umm, could I use the ladies room?" It was a lame excuse, but she didn't have time to think of anything better.

He dipped his head. "Yes, of course, we have six bathrooms. Which one would you like to use?"

On a lark, she said, "The one closest to the front door."

The corner of his mouth twitched, and she knew he'd figured out her plan. "I'm afraid that one is not an option. Follow me," he said, turning.

While Amber waited in the other room, Jacque and the four remaining members of the Hospitallers made the final arrangements. Finally, after everything was in place, Jacque stepped over to a velvet shash and gave it a gentle tug. A moment later, Duncan appeared. "Duncan, everything is prepared, send in Miss Kline."

The man tilted his head slightly. "Very good, sir. She is right here."

St. John glanced over his shoulder. Amber, looking rather flustered, still radiated with beauty he'd seen in few women. His hunger for power had always outweighed his desire for female company, but this woman had an intoxicating effect upon him. "Of course, send her in."

Wide-eyed and tentative, Amber followed Duncan into the formal parlor where a quartet of older white men stood behind Jacque St. John.

"Please, take a seat."

The men parted revealing a single chair set in the middle of the room.

Glancing from side to side, she took the proffered seat. "Is this some kind of game?"

As Duncan closed the door leaving her with the stoic looking men, Mr. St. John stepped forward. "I assure you, Miss Kline, this is no game. Would you kindly hand over that piece of paper in your pocket?"

Her hand instinctively touched her pocket. She took a dry swallow. "What piece of—"

Crack!

St. John's hand struck her with such force, she nearly lost her footing. Stumbling backward, she touched her stinging cheek. "Why did you do that?"

"Because, Miss Kline, I know with whom you spoke and why. Now give me that paper or things might turn ugly."

Reluctantly, Amber pulled the paper out and handed

it to him.

"There now, that wasn't so bad. Was it?" He gave her a smug smile.

"What are you going to do with me ... kill me?"

The men exchanged somber glances.

"No Miss Kline, but from now on ... no more snooping around. If you want to know something, simply ask."

Amber took a deep breath and let it out slowly. This was it, if she was going to find what she sought, she had to ask, but even if she did, there was no guarantee he'd tell her the truth. "Okay, in that case, who is Gasper and what does he have to do with Simon Levi?"

St. John's lips curled back into a cruel smile. His eyes cut a line across the faces of the men, then returned to her. "See, it is as I guessed. Give a woman a chance and she'll almost always say too much."

The men nodded. Amber forced her lungs to breath.

"What? I thought you knew I spoke with—"

Hands on her shoulders, St. John pushed her into the chair. "No, I did not, not until you told me. It's unfortunate, but you've been just a little too good at your job."

Taking an amulet attached to a gold chain, he knelt in front of her and began to swing it in front of her. His tone cooled, but his eyes stayed riveted on hers.

"Now Miss Kline, I want you to relax ..."

Amber's eyes followed the movement of the amulet as Jacque St. John spoke in an even tone. "Miss Kline, I want you to return to your office tonight and delete all references to the Order of the Hospitallers and the Knight Templars from your computer files. Any and all references you may have discovered connecting me with my ancestor Jacque de Molay are also to be removed and destroyed from your records. When I snap my fingers you will remember nothing of this conversation and will follow my directives without question."

Straightening, he snapped his fingers and Amber blinked.

Head wobbling, she glanced at the men surrounding her. "Oh, my, I must have drifted off, what were you saying, Mr. St. John?"

"Yes, we were discussing our plans for the summit. Rather boring details, you must have, as you said, drifted off." St. John replied. "Now, shall we get on with the real purpose of our meeting? Miss Kline, if you would be so kind as to take a seat at the table, we shall commence."

Chapter Twenty-Eight

The phone call from Gasper left Glenn and Karen shaken. Not only had the news of their missing son given rise to fears, but the report about Israel signing a peace agreement brought a new wave of concerns. Then, having received a call from Miss Amber Kline, the UN Secretary General's press secretary, Glenn could not dispel the feeling that Gasper was caught up in something really big.

From what Glenn had studied, the rapture, or catching away, was the next event on God's calendar. Following that, the man of sin, also called the Antichrist, would be revealed. It would be through his efforts Israel would sign a peace agreement which would last seven years, triggering the Tribulation. But with the news of Israel signing the Unity Accord and beginning to build the Third Temple, it became clear, he'd missed something.

The following morning, Glenn drove to the church and found Pastor Wyatt hunkered over a tattered Bible. "Good morning, pastor." Glenn handed him a cup of coffee he'd picked up from the local donut shop.

Pastor Wyatt extended his hand and accepted the proffered cup. After setting the cup on his desk, he gave Glenn a warm smile, and the two men shook hands. He loved seeing the changes taking place in Glenn's life. It was like he'd been reborn. Since the ordeal involving the stolen medallion and the attack, Glenn was a new man.

"Good morning to you, brother. Are you as concerned over what's going on in the Middle East as I am?"

Glenn took a seat. "That's kinda why I stopped by."

The Pastor took a sip of the steaming brew and winced. "Oh, that's hot, but good. Got a donut to go along with it?"

Glenn pulled a bag from behind his back. "Thought you'd never ask."

As they munched their first of a dozen glazed donuts, Glenn got down to business. "You know Gasper and the others went to Israel?"

Pastor Wyatt nodded. "Yes, and from what I've heard, Colt stowed away with them. Any word from him or our three friends?"

Glenn nodded sullenly. "As a matter of fact, I have, and the news isn't good."

Forehead wrinkling, the pastor waited for the rest of the story.

"The wise men and Colt were going to return sooner than we thought, but then there was a mix up of some kind. If that wasn't bad enough, there has been a fire at the Institute in Antiquities. Gasper received burns on his hands and neck along with a near concussion."

Glenn paused to fight back a sob, but gave into it. Burying his face in his hands, he released a torrent of emotion. "Colt is missing," he croaked.

"Missing?" Pastor Wyatt repeated. "How? Where?"

Glenn shook his head. After he'd regained his composure, he continued, "The authorities don't know. They think he may have been taken hostage by the arsonists who set the fire, but we've not heard a word from them."

"And Gasper? What does he think?"

Another round of tears flooded Glenn's eyes. "He's as upset as we are. He feels responsible, but it's not his fault. He explained when the fire alarm went off, he began searching for him. He endangered his life trying to find our son. To add to that, last night, I received a call from a woman associated with the UN Secretary General. Her name was Amber Kline, and she started asking me about Gasper."

"What did you tell her?"

Glenn shrugged. "I told her the truth ... that Gasper and his friends were in Israel."

Scott stood and came around his desk and laid his hand on Glenn's heaving shoulder. "Let me pray and ask God to protect him and bring him home safely."

Kneeling, Glenn allowed his pastor carry his burden to the throne of grace on his behalf. "Now Lord, you know our hearts, how we mourn with those who mourn and weep with those who weep and rejoice with those who rejoice. But right now, we carry a heavy burden. Colt O'Dell, one of your precious children, is missing. Send one of Your angels, who beholds Your face continually, to camp a hedge of protection around him. Cause someone to find him and bring him safely home to his parents. We ask this in Jesus' mighty name, amen."

Pushing himself to his feet, Glenn waited for the blood to circulate into his lower extremities. "Thank you, Pastor. Now there is another matter that concerns me."

Scott retook his seat behind his desk and laid his hand on the Bible. "If it's the matter of Israel and the peace treaty, let me say, I am revisiting everything I've studied down through the years. I should have a definite answer to your questions soon. As a matter of fact, I am planning to start a complete study of eschatology in tonight's prayer meeting."

Taking a raggedy breath, Glenn smiled. "I look forward to hearing what you have to say, Pastor. Karen and I will be praying for you. I know it's got to be hard."

As the two men eased toward the door, Glenn shook his head. "I'm certainly glad Cecil Clavender is gone. I can't imagine the mess he would make out of this Unity Accord thing."

Pastor Wyatt gave his friend a rueful smile. "God only knows the sorrow he spared us."

Chapter Twenty-Nine

L ater that evening, Glenn and Karen entered the rapidly filling auditorium. Word of Pastor Wyatt's upcoming series of messages had been sent to the congregation via email, Facebook, and Twitter resulting in a packed house on a Wednesday night.

Seeing Felicia, Karen gave her a quick hug before taking their seats.

"Have you heard from Gasper? I miss him so much," Felicia said, her eyes glistening with expectation.

Glenn leaned over and touched the back of her hand. "We spoke just briefly."

"Did he say anything, I mean ..."

Taking Felicia's hand, Karen gave it a gentle squeeze. "If you're wondering if he mentioned you, the answer is yes."

"And?"

"And he said to give you his love, Karen added with a reassuring smile."

Hand to her chest, Felicia leaned back, a dreamy smile poised on her lips. "I was so worried about him. The last time we talked, he said it would be a few weeks before he would return. Now with all that's going on, I'm beginning to wonder if he'll ever get back." It was clear she let her imagination get the best of her. "If he calls you again, give him my new number. I've been getting some crank calls and had to change numbers."

"I promise, I will," Karen answered, giving her another hug. "Absence makes the heart grow fonder."

Glenn cocked his head. "Yes, and gone too long will make it wander."

"Let's just hope Gasper doesn't stay away too long. I can see a number of eligible bachelors getting out their dance cards even as we speak."

Glenn cast his eyes in the direction of a cluster of millennials who were watching Felicia glide across the auditorium to her seat.

Karen tucked a strand of hair behind her ear. "I don't think he's forgotten about her, but right now, there is a lot going on. She needs to be patient and hope he calls as soon as he gets a chance."

###

As she and Glenn took their seats, the prelude music subsided and the auditorium grew still. An air of expectation spread across the congregation like a low fog.

Pastor Wyatt stepped to the podium. "Folks, we have a lot to cover tonight, so I asked the worship leader to dispense with any music. And, because of the importance of these days, I've also asked the youth director to bring in the teens. So please, be on your best behavior. I wouldn't want you to corrupt our young and impressionable youth." A ripple of nervous laughter scattered across the auditorium.

As the lights dimmed, two large screens flickered to life. After leading the church family in prayer, Pastor Wyatt got down to business.

"There are three primary positions when it comes to Bible prophecy. The first is the post millennial view, the second is the mid-tribulation view, and the third is the pre-millennial. In a nutshell, the post-mill takes the position that Christ's second coming will occur after the Golden Age. Now, before you get too concerned, I will explore all these views in greater depth in the weeks to follow. This is just preliminary. The mid-trib teaches that Christ will return for his church halfway through the seven-year tribulation period." Couples exchanged concerned glances. "The third, and I might add, the one this church espouses, is the pre-millennial, view."

###

Surrounding the platform and scattered throughout the vast auditorium stood a great host of angelic beings. Each one unique from the other ... as different as snowflakes. Their pure white torsos and ethereal wings shimmered in the light. They gathered as a unit against the dark forces of discouragement and doubt, but they couldn't stop the spirits of fear some of the church family brought in with them.

"This is going to be one of Pastor Wyatt's severest tests," Prince Uriel said to his longtime companion.

Prince Selaphiel nodded grimly. "How can we assist these pilgrims on their way to truth?"

A moment passed as the mighty warrior chose his words carefully. "Some battles are given to us to fight ... some are left for the mortals. This is one for them. The Almighty has endowed His servants with all that is necessary for life and godliness. In addition, He has not given them a spirit of fear, but a sound mind. His Word is sufficient for all situations. They just need to be diligent, and rightly divide it in light of context, historical setting, and linguistic accuracy."

"That was a mouthful," Selaphiel said, moving his jaw.

"Yes, but far too often I have seen good men differ over these matters because they approach them with preconceived ideas. There is one thing you can do for this beleaguered pastor."

"And that is?"

"Stand next to the pastor and nudge his mind in the right direction. If necessary, I'll send one of our lesser angels to touch him. I think he may need it before this ordeal is over."

With that, Prince Selaphiel shifted closer and laid his hand on the podium.

Chapter Thirty

Taking a steadying breath, Pastor Wyatt plunged in. "Before we focus in on the mid-tribulation view, I wish to address a few quick but very important points. Let's begin with a familiar scripture, in Mark 13:32. 'But of that day or hour no one knows, not even the angels in heaven, nor the Son, but the Father alone.'

With that verse in mind, look at another scripture that's not quite as familiar, but it will help to give proper balance to the scripture we just read. In 1 Thessalonians 5:1-5 we read, 'Now, brothers, about times and dates we do not need to write to you, for you know very well that the day of the Lord will come like a thief in the night. While people are saying, 'Peace and safety,' destruction will come on them suddenly, as labor pains on a pregnant woman, and they will not escape. But you, brothers, are not in darkness so that this day should surprise you like a thief. You are all sons of the light and sons of the day. We do not belong to the night or to the darkness.'

The obvious points from these two scriptures are clear. No one knows the exact day or hour. For believers, that day should not surprise us. Jesus wants his children to know the general season of His coming, but not the exact day.

That being said, I'd like to open in prayer. Heavenly

Father, in Jesus' name, I ask for your wisdom and understanding to rightly divide Your word. Give me the ability to explain this difficult subject to your children, so they may grow in grace and knowledge, and be found standing, walking by faith in the latter day."

After reading 1 Corinthians 15:51-57, he directed the congregation's attention to verse 51 and 52.

"We see the words Mystery, Last Trump and the word raised. Paul obviously is talking about a resurrection of believers here; otherwise, he would not have used the word *raised* with respect to the dead. He is also talking about the end of the church age. So we are not disputing if the Lord will come, what we are concerned with is the when. When will all these things take place?

A similar question was asked of our Lord by the disciples in Matthew 24, saying, 'Tell us, when will these things happen? And what will be the sign of Your coming? And the sign concerning the end of the world?'

Let me summarize our Lord's answer by saying, Jesus warned them not to be deceived, for many will come in His name and make false claims. There will be wars, and rumors of wars. But the end will not yet come. There will be famines, pestilences, and earthquakes in different places. All these events we have seen in our lifetime, but this is just the beginning. Persecutions will follow, many false prophets will arise and deceive many and because of the wickedness of the day, the love of many shall grow cold, but he who endures until the end, the same shall be saved or delivered.

Only after the kingdom gospel has reached around the world will the end come. It will be announced by this sign; when you see the abomination of desolation, spoken of by Daniel the prophet, that is, the man of sin, standing in the holy place, then the great tribulation, or wrath of God, will be unleashed upon the world. Daniel's week of trouble will be so bad, Jesus said, such time has never been seen since the beginning of the world. And unless those days are lessened, no one would survive. Then shall the sign of the Son of man appear in heaven: and then shall all the tribes of the earth mourn, for they shall see the Son of man coming in the clouds of heaven with power and great glory. He shall send His angels with the sound of a mighty trumpet, and they shall gather together His elect from the four winds, from one end of heaven to the other. The warning which follows that sign is very clear."

Pastor Wyatt mopped his brow, clearly shaken by these revelations in light of the current world situation.

Pressing ahead, he spoke to a dead silent auditorium. "This of course, was a complex answer to three questions posed by Jesus' disciples. They were asked from a Jewish perspective and focused on a Jewish Kingdom ruled by a Jewish king. Jesus answered those questions within that context. Obviously, some of those predictions span our time, but, just like looking across a mountain range; we see the mountain tops, but not the valleys. We have no depth perception … no way of knowing the gap between peeks. So it is in prophecy.

For example, Jesus mentioned in the Olivet Discourse the sounding of a great trumpet and gathering of His elect. Keep in mind, when Jesus speaks of His elect, He is speaking of Israel, predominantly. This is where some of our Mid-Trib brethren get their beliefs."

Revelation 10:7 flashed on the screen, and he continued. "Please bear with me as we get rather technical. We see the word, 'Mystery' and the promise that when the seventh angel sounds his trumpet the Mystery of God would be fulfilled. The seventh angel in Revelation is the same one who blows the seventh trump; the kingdoms of this world have become the kingdom of our Lord, and of His Christ; and He shall reign forever and ever. And the nations will be angry because God's wrath has come.'

According to the Mid-Trib brethren, all the events which occurred before this scripture are called judgments and tribulations, but not wrath. It is only when we get to Revelation 14:13-20, that we see what is called the rapture or catching away. An angel will come from the temple in Heaven, crying with a loud voice to him who sits upon the cloud, insert Rapture here, Thrust in your sickle, and reap: for the time is come for you to reap; for the harvest of the earth is ripe. And He thrusts in His sickle and harvests the elect from the earth. Now is when the wrath of God will be unleashed upon the earth, once the church has been removed. The first sickle is the rapture of Christian believers; the second sickle is God's wrath. This is where the rapture actually takes place ... Revelation 14:14-16 according to the Mid-Trib position."

Matthew 24:30 scrolled across the screen. "He will send His angels with the sound of a great trumpet, and they will gather together His elect from the four winds, from one end of heaven to the other.'

So, according to the Mid-Trib approach, a 'great trumpet' will be sounded, after which the elect will be gathered together, 'from one end of heaven to the other.'

I understand there are many arguments supporting pre-tribulation rapture teaching. Nevertheless, know this, Jesus spoke of tribulation as being a series of tribulations and events.

Again in Matthew 24, Jesus spoke of the Great Tribulation as a different event. This great tribulation is connected to the future desolation of a third rebuilt Jewish Temple. The prophet Ezekiel spoke of this in the 37th chapter of his prophetic book.

The Wrath of God, the seals and trump judgments are three different events. The seals and judgments are given to us as a warning to turn from our sin and repent. They were not the full wrath of God. The wrath of God is His anger poured out upon the nations who have rejected Him and all persons who worshiped, or took the mark of the Antichrist."

When he finished, Pastor Wyatt's color had turned ashen. Shaken, he wobbled to a pew and buried his face in his hands as frustrated church members filed out of the auditorium. Angela took a seat next to her husband, not speaking. Finally, she broke the thick veil of silence between them. "Scott, do you believe what you just taught us?"

He raised his face and met her watering eyes. "Frankly, I am not sure what I believe any more. I need to continue studying, but I just don't know..."

As he spoke, Prince Selaphiel extended his hand and laid it on the pastor's shoulder. Closing his eyes, he sighed. As he did so, a surge of heavenly power seeped from him and into Pastor Wyatt's body and touched his spirit.

Drawing strength from the unseen touch, Scott

inhaled deeply. Standing, he took Angela's hand. "After Daniel confessed his sins and the sins of his fathers, he sought the Lord with prayer and fasting until he heard from him. I think that's a good example for me to follow."

Tears welled in Angela's eyes and coursed down her cheeks. "I'll join you in fasting and praying. Together, we will squeeze heaven for an answer."

Scott liked the way she phrased it and gave her a gentle squeeze.

Chapter Thirty-One

W hen I blinked away from Simon's presence, I wasn't exactly sure where I'd end up. So far, blinking was still a bit new to me. I knew from past experience, I could handle short distances, but leaping over the Atlantic was even more than what I thought possible. What if I missed my mark? I could end up in the middle of the Hudson River, or worse ... in the frigid ocean.

Fortunately, I had done a little research and learned the office of the Secretary General was on the 38th floor of the United Nations building. After checking the time difference, I knew I had to wait until I was sure the building was empty. It was nearly 8:30 in the evening before I thought it safe to make my move. I must say, hanging out in a coffee shop in New York City was a lot more expensive than hanging out at the coffee shop in North Hamilton, but the coffee was far better.

Having finished off my fifth cup and eaten my fill of pastries, I had run out of ways to look inconspicuous, so I stepped to the men's room. After relieving my over-charged kidneys, I blinked.

The next moment, I was standing in a large room with cubicles ... probably a secretarial pool. Taking a quick glance at my watch, I let out a tight breath. *Good, it was 8:30 on a Wednesday, and all the secretaries and pencil pushers had gone home for the day.*

All at once, a door opened on the far end of the room, and someone entered. It was a woman and by her nervous glances over her shoulder, I knew she didn't want to be seen either. Backing around a corner, I peered out, hoping to see which way she might go.

After a quick scan around the room and seeing no one, she tiptoed across the floor, disappeared into an office and closed the door. By the time my breathing slowed, I checked and I couldn't tell which room she entered. Fearing someone else might show up, I began trying door knobs hoping to find an unlocked office where I could hide until later when I could work my way to the Secretary General's office. The information I was looking for had to be there. After taking a glance and not seeing anyone else, I slipped inside the first unlocked office I found.

In the darkness, someone sucked in a sharp breath, and I ducked to the floor.

"Who are you?" It was the woman I'd seen sneak into the building.

She spoke in a whispered tone, and I knew she was as frightened as me. I considered what to tell her? *Should I tell her that I'd come to investigate the most powerful man on the planet?*

Whatever I said would surely bring the police if I didn't blink out in a hurry.

I decided on the truth. It worked in the past, why stop now? "My name is Gasper."

She took another sharp intake.

"Did you say, Gasper?"

"Yes, why? Is that a problem?"

"No, I mean, yes ... I mean. I heard your name before, but I can't remember where I'd heard it."

Standing, I cautiously approached the woman. She was hunkered in a corner, clutching a file in one hand and a laptop in another.

"I'm not here to hurt you. I just came to get a few questions answered."

The woman's face showed a mix of confusion and fear, with a touch of disorientation.

"Are you all right? I mean, you don't look so good." I asked.

Staring ahead, the woman's wrinkled brow told me she was trying to remember something.

I knelt next to her and offered her my hand. She stared at it for a moment. Then, to my surprise, took it. Being careful not to spill the contents of the file, she straightened her legs and wobbled to a chair. "I don't feel so good," she said, placing the file on the desk and rubbing her forehead.

The city lights provided enough illumination for me to get a look at the file. At seeing the name on the top of the stack, I had to admit, I didn't feel so well either.

"My name is Amber Kline. I am the Secretary General's press secretary."

Her name meant nothing to me, but her relationship to him gave me an idea. "Could I ask you a couple of questions?"

Miss Kline held my gaze as if trying to place my name with my face. Suddenly, she slumped forward. In an instant, I was there to catch her before she hit her head. I could see she was a very attractive woman, and I hoped no one stumbled into the room. I was sure if they did, my actions would certainly be misunderstood. Placing my hand on her forehead, I noticed it was cool and clammy. She could have been sick, I couldn't tell, so I closed my eyes and breathed a prayer asking the Great Healer to do for her what I could not.

All at once, Miss Kline perked up. I could tell there was a clarity in her eyes I'd not seen earlier.

Surprised at our closeness, she pulled back, stood and adjusted her blouse. "I know you. I heard my boss talking about you. You're one of the wise men who saved a baby somewhere in the south. But I thought you were in Israel."

I gulped. *How much did this lady know about me?* I could only guess. Even so, the fact that she and her boss even knew my name concerned me greatly. "Why was your boss talking about me?"

She waved her hand. "It's a long story, and I don't have time to tell you, but I think my life is in danger."

The revelation came as a shock. "Why would the Secretary General want to kill you? You're his press secretary."

She pointed at the file on the desk. "I have been doing a lot of digging into Mr. St. John's background and uncovered some very damaging information connecting him with an organization called The Order of Hospitallers and the Knight Templars. That's why I am here. He hypnotized me and told me to destroy it, but now, I don't know. He told me he was planning on a big summit meeting with the major religious leaders of the world to make a very important announcement."

I sensed urgency in her voice, but I knew for her to destroy important evidence would be criminal. "Look, can you make a copy of all this stuff?"

"Yes, why?" Her eyes widening as she spoke.

"Because, if you do that and give them to me, you can destroy the originals and say with a clear conscience that you obeyed his instructions. Then I can take the proper steps to expose this man for the fraud that he is."

Miss Kline's lips trembled. "But what if he presses me? He has a way of knowing things; things inside my head. He will know I'm covering something."

"Look, he needs to think his secret is safe with you. So I will pray for you, that God will strengthen you in your inner man, that you will be able to withstand the wiles of the devil."

Amber's mouth fell open. "People now days don't talk like that."

I felt my face heat. "Yes, I know, but look, make the copies, destroy everything else. Then we'll plan our next move."

Taking an uncertain breath, Amber gathered the file and laptop and began to copy the information to a flash-drive. While the copy machine and the computer were working, she turned to me. "How did you get in here without alerting the guards? Are you some kind of professional burglar?"

Me? A professional burglar? I was flattered. "What's a burglar, anyway?"

The woman offered me an incredulous expression. "since you got in here undetected, can you help me get out of here without being seen?"

That question threw me for a loop. I'd never transported anyone besides myself and doubted I could do it. To even try might turn disastrous. Reflecting on what she'd told me about the summit, I made a decision. "With St. John planning to come to the Gaza Strip this weekend, you need to get ahead of him. Since you're his press secretary, why don't you leave on the next plane to Israel? Tell him you're going to set things up with the Israelis. Which, I might add, is the truth. You can't expect every religious leader in the world, their entourage, their press and security details just to pop into the country without some groundwork being laid. He will appreciate you taking the initiative and probably thank you."

Miss Kline thought about it for a moment. "You know, you are a wise man. That's a great idea."

Again, I felt my face growing hot. I had to guard my mind. She was such a beautiful woman and to have her so close was something I wasn't accustomed to. Taking a deep breath, I backed out of her personal space. The copy machine beeped and laptop finished downloading, suspending the electrically charged moment. My main focus was to get Colt back, not find the Ark or bring down the most powerful man on earth, but if in so doing it brought me one step closer to finding Colt, then it was worth it.

Clutching the flash drive and copies of paper in my hands, I said, "Would you mind closing your eyes?"

This time, it was her turn to blush. "Why Mr. Gasper, I—"

Hands held in mock surrender. "No, no, no, it's not that. I'm about to leave, and I don't want you to know where I went or how I got away. That's all."

Miss Kline fanned herself. "Oh, I thought ... oh, never mind."

"That's okay, it happens all the time. Now, if you'll just close your eyes."

She complied, and I blinked before she had a chance to peek.

###

A moment later, I stood in front of a wide-eyed Simon Levi.

He gasped, "Gasper, where did you go? One minute I'm talking to you and the next, I'm talking to thin air?"

I couldn't help but chuckle. I would have slapped him on the back, and we would have had a big laugh were it not so serious. After handing him the information and filling him in on what I'd learned, he mopped his brow.

"I gotta hand it to you … you've got a lot of moxie."

For a moment, I wondered what he handed me and what I had, but rightly guessed it was one of those phrases people throw around without thinking. *Like something being easier done than said.* "Simon, I need to get to the Gaza Strip, quickly."

He folded his hands behind his back and began to pace. Chin buried in his chest, he said, "I've been working on that, but with Friday being the Muslim's holy day and the Sabbath coming up, it'll be difficult to get a corporal's guard."

The cliché eluded me, and I wisely didn't press the issue. I pulled a wadded paper from my pocket. It was Abdullah's cell number. "Here, call this number. Have him meet us as soon as possible. In the meantime, I'd like to talk with Rabbi Musselmen."

The lines on Simon's face deepened. "I guess you haven't heard."

"Heard what? I've been out of the country for the last

few hours."

Simon stopped pacing; his face was drawn in a pained expression. "Rabbi Musselmen had a heart attack after we left the tunnel. He's in stable condition, but we won't be able to count on him. It's up to you and me, now."

"That's too bad, all the more reason for me to see him. Could you take me to the hospital?"

Simon thought a moment. "We might as well. We are doing no good sitting around here."

Grabbing his keys, Simon trudged through the house heading to his car with me trailing behind him.

Chapter Thirty-Two

It took Simon and Gasper only forty-five minutes to navigate through afternoon traffic and find a parking place at the Hertzog Hospital. With pilgrims from all over the world arriving daily to celebrate the advent season, it was a wonder they made it at all. But with Simon's knowledge of Jerusalem, he took all the back roads, saving them much time. Once they arrived, they were quickly escorted to Rabbi Musselmen's room in ICU.

Entering, Simon halted and gasped. "Rubin, my old friend."

The man stirred, but didn't open his eyes.

"I thought you said he was stable." Gasper whispered, looking at the tubes and electrodes coming out from under the covers.

The nurse, who'd followed them in, gave them a tentative expression. "He had a rough night. He may not even wake up, but you're welcome to stay for a short time."

Gasper glanced at Simon. Lowering his voice, he waited until the nurse finished her duties and left. "Keep a look out for anyone coming. I wouldn't want someone to interrupt me."

"But you don't have your staff. Can you still work miracles or whatever you do without it?"

The question gave Gasper a moment of pause. "I don't know. I know I can move from place to place without my staff, but healing ..." He shrugged his shoulders. "Let's hope so."

Simon took a watchful position while Gasper went to work. First, he laid his hands on the rabbi's head, then suddenly pulled them back.

"What?" Simon asked. "You afraid of germs?"

"I'd better wash first. You know how sensitive the rabbi is about cleanliness."

Simon offered a soft chuckle. "Right now, I don't think he much cares."

Turning, Gasper stepped to a sink and began to wash his hands. After drying them, he returned and placed his hands on Rabbi Musselmen's head. Inhaling, he drew in a deep breath and began to pray. After several minutes, he pulled a small bottle of oil from his pocket and poured a few drops in the palm of his hand. Then he laid his hand on the rabbi's chest and continued to pray, invoking the Lord's name and claiming his healing power.

All at once, Rabbi Musselmen's eyes popped open, and he sucked in a sharp breath. "Oy vey," he said eyeing Gasper. "What are you doing?"

"I'm healing you, you old schmuck. Now hold still."

His eyes widening, the rabbi pulled back. "But you're touching me. You're a goy, how dare you."

Gasper's hand jerked back. "I'll have you know, I am no goy. I am as Jewish as a lamb on Yom Kippur. I just so happen to come from India, so stop your complaining."

Suddenly, the rabbi burst out in laughter. "It has been a long time since anyone had the schmaltz to talk back to me."

Simon glanced at Gasper, then down at the rabbi. "Well, it's long overdue. Now Mr. Gasper has a special message of hope and peace for you. So sit up and listen."

Just then, a dozen nurses and doctors rushed into the room knocking Simon aside and began checking on their patient. Shaking his head, the attending physician looked at the rabbi's vitals, then at his chart. "I can't believe it. The rabbi's blood pressure, EEG, blood gases show no sign of a heart attack." Scratching his forehead, the doctor leaned closer, placed his stethoscope on Rabbi Musselmen's chest and listened. After a few moments, he straightened. "I am recommending an EKG to confirm it, but I think this man has had a miraculous recovery."

Once the room cleared, Rabbi Musselmen pushed himself up in bed and looked at Gasper. "What did you do?"

Gasper shrugged. "I give all the glory to Yeshiva Meshach ben David, the great healer."

"Yeshiva Meshach ben David, hmm?"

"Yes, his name in English is Jesus Christ the Son of David."

"I know to Whom you are referring," his voice, though raspy, carried a bit of an edge.

"Now, now, Rubin, don't use that tone of voice. You and I have had many conversations about who the Messiah could be. And you know as well as me, Jesus of Nazareth fits all that was prophesied of the coming Messiah."

The old rabbi huffed, but continued to listen.

Gasper opened his Bible. Reading from Matthew 1, he listed the generational names of the Anointed one's ancestors. "In verses seventeen, we read, 'so all the generations from Abraham to David are fourteen, and from David to the deportation to Babylon are fourteen generations and from the deportation to the Anointed one, fourteen generations.' Does that mean anything to you?"

"Yes, it means Heshem likes to do things in groups of seven."

Gasper nodded. "Of course he does, and in the fullness of the time, God sent his Son, made of a woman, made under the law, to redeem those who were under the law, that we might receive the adoption of sons. You know the prophecy of the virgin."

Rubin nodded grudgingly and cut his eyes toward Simon. "I hope you didn't bring this man here just to heal me so he could bore me to death."

Simon patted his old friend's shoulder. "Just listen. You might learn something."

Quoting from Isaiah, Gasper began. "'Behold a virgin shall conceive, and shall bear a son and call His name Emmanuel.' Did you know that the Messiah's mother, Mary, was in the direct line of David? We are given the Anointed one's complete genealogy by Dr. Luke from Adam to His mother, meaning, Yeshiva was not only the legal heir to David's throne through His supposed father, Joseph, but His natural mother.

The rabbi cast a fleeting glance at Simon. "And you believe this?" his voice rose in question.

"Believe? What's there to believe? It's a genealogical fact. And when you put all the prophecy, the miracles, the works of Jesus of Nazareth, you must come to one conclusion."

"And that is?"

Simon held his friend's steady gaze. "That we missed Him." The words caught in his throat. He took a dry swallow and continued. "He came unto His own, and we esteemed Him not, but turned our backs to Him who came as our sin bearer."

The news coming from one Jew to another struck the rabbi hard and his lips began to tremble. "I thought as much."

Looking at Gasper, he spoke barely above a whisper. "Secretly, I have been doing much research into the life of this man you call Jesus Christ, and I have come to the conclusion that He was who He claimed to be ... the Anointed One, the promised one, Jessie's Righteous Branch."

A tear formed in the wrinkled corner of his eye and trickled down his weathered cheek. "Our fathers rejected him and we have suffered severely for it. When they said, 'his blood be upon us,' they meant it."

Taking the elderly man's hand, Gasper gave it a gentle squeeze. "But sir, that's what we all need ... His atonement, His blood covering us. We may have rejected Him, nevertheless, God has not rejected us. Our transgression in rejecting the Messiah brought salvation to the entire world. However, when we turn and repent of our transgression, He will abundantly pardon. It is as if God removed the natural branch from the olive tree in order to graft in an unnatural branch, the gentiles, thus making Israel jealous. So then, when we recognize our failure and return to Him, He will graft us back in and restore to us the mercies of David."

Tears welled in the old man's eyes and he tugged the edge of the sheet to his face to wipe them aside. "Behold,

Heshem's ways are past finding out. What must I do to receive these mercies you speak so freely of?"

Gasper spoke from memory. "The word is nigh, even in your mouth, that if you will confess and believe that God has raised Jesus, the anointed one, from the dead, you will be saved."

The rabbi's grip tightened on Gasper's hand as he turned his heart toward the light of the glorious gospel. As he prayed, the deep lines on his countenance softened and a broad smile stretched across his face. "Bless God, I feel like a new man."

Looking down, Gasper and Simon rejoiced.

"My friend," Simon said, "you are a new man."

It didn't take a messenger from Heaven to communicate the good news that another lost sheep of Israel had been found. The Good Shepherd Himself had long sought this wayward Jew and gently rescued him from the cliffs below. Placing him on His broad shoulders, the Good Shepherd returned to His throne rejoicing. As the announcement spread across the heavenly regions, spontaneous songs erupted and swelled until all the portals reverberated.

Meanwhile, the scene on earth was quite different. Those demonic forces responsible for the rabbi's blindness recoiled at the glorious light and sprang back into the shadows from where they came. In their place, rows of glistening angels formed a protective barrier around the hospital room. Even more significant was the movement of God's Spirit as He took up residence in the elderly man's heart. After doing a thorough cleaning, He dusted off the throne upon which Rubin once sat and took

His seat.

"There now, let's get started. We've got a lot of work to do," the new master of Rubin's life said. Then He began illuminating Rubin's heart. Starting with Moses and the prophets, He began to expound the scriptures of things concerning Himself.

Chapter Thirty-Three

The following morning, Pastor Wyatt's cell phone rang. It was Josh Mattingly, the young man who led the prayer and praise gathering around the flag pole at the local high school.

"Hello, Josh. How's it going?"

Josh cleared his throat. "Fine Pastor Wyatt. Sorry to call you so early, but I wanted to catch you before you headed to the office."

"I was just leaving, how can I help you?"

"Well, I was at the Prayer Meeting last night and thought you did a good job explaining a difficult issue."

Pastor Wyatt smiled at his assessment of his Bible study. "That pretty much sums it up. To be honest, this whole thing had me up all night."

"Yes, sir. I figured as much. Look, my fellow classmates talked about it after the service, and we'd like you to come to the prayer gathering this morning."

Scott didn't feel like facing anyone, let alone a group of inquisitive teens. What he really wanted was to find a hole and climb in and pull it closed. But the urgency in Josh's voice told him that wasn't an option. *Be instant in season and out of season. Be ready to give an answer to everyone who asks you for a reason of the hope you have with meekness and fear.* "You got that right, Lord," Scott whispered softly.

"I hope you're not wanting me to share some scripture, and say an encouraging word, because right now, I'm not feeling very reassured."

"No, that won't be necessary. We just wanted you to come so we could pray for you and show our support. It seems we Christians are under spiritual attack. A lot of my friends are really upset too. This is the time when we need to draw closer to each other rather than pull apart."

Scott's esteem of the young man spiked. Feeling encouraged, and shamed for so quickly giving up, he released a heavy sigh. "I would be happy to join you. Do I need to check in with the school office?"

"Yes, sir, but the principal is real supportive of us. He might even join us if he knew you were coming."

"Wait a minute. You won't get in any kind of trouble for inviting your preacher to the pole, will you?"

Josh laughed. "Nah, this is before school officially starts, and I have written permission from the Secretary of Education to meet publicly at the pole. Who I invite is my business."

Josh's assertiveness reminded him of his early days in the ministry … before the rigors and realities of ministry took over. For a moment, he tried to remember what it was like to be so naive, so tender hearted, so vulnerable. He took a halting breath and let it out slowly. *If only I had chosen a different calling.* Calling. The word seemed to have echoed from the distant past. *I am called. I didn't choose, I simply obeyed.* Conviction, followed the gentle wooing of the Spirit, and Scott caught himself repenting as Josh waited.

"I'll take your word on that, but if things go south, I want to share a cell with you. We could sing our way out of jail like Paul and Silas. See you in a few minutes," Scott said with a chuckle.

Angela leaned against the counter sipping hot chocolate from a large mug. "What was that all about?"

Scott slipped his phone into his belt clip. "That was Josh Mattingly. He invited me to the prayer and praise gathering around the flag pole this morning."

"Is that legal?" the pleats on her forehead gathering.

Scott paused mid-stride. "Josh says the principal would be there, so I guess if it's okay with him, it's okay with me."

Grabbing her coat, Angela set her mug on the counter. "I'm coming too. If they're going to throw you in jail, they'll have to throw me also."

Scott leaned down and tugged her close. "I am so grateful to have you by my side. Let's go and face the firing squad together," he said with a smile.

An early morning cold front had drifted across the region, painting the low-hanging clouds a steel-grey. The north wind cut through the barren trees, whipping leaves and debris in tight circles. Despite the threatening weather, however, an unusually large crowd of students and teachers gathered around the flag pole.

Scott angled his van into a parking slot and shut off the engine. Seeing Josh, Pastor Wyatt helped his wife from the vehicle and greeted him with a manly hug.

"Hey, Josh, I had no idea you had such a large gathering. Maybe I should hire you as our outreach coordinator."

"Josh's face brightened. "That would be cool, but first I still have to finish high school and college."

Scott patted him on his broad shoulder. "That's all right … maybe we could work something out for summers."

As they drew near, the principal broke from a cluster of teachers, his face a wash of concern. Taking Scott's hand, he shook it vigorously. "Thanks Pastor for coming out. I got to tell ya, we have a lot of really scared people. What can you tell us to set our minds at ease?"

Scott forced down a hard swallow. Josh had assured him he'd not be expected to say anything, just be encouraged by the youthful prayers. As Scott wavered, the principal tugged him to the center of the group nearest the pole.

"Look, I know this is highly unusual for a preacher to speak on school property these days, but this is before school officially begins. So, you have my personal assurance you will not be charged with violating the separation law. Go ahead and say whatever God has put on your heart to the group."

His heart sputtering, Scott checked his watch. "How long do I have?"

The principal checked his watch as well. "We've been having a little trouble with that dang bell system. Sometimes it works and sometimes it doesn't. Go ahead and speak until I give you the signal to stop."

Scott felt tanked. This mid-trib, pre-millennial controversy had him tied in knots. He knew what he believed, what he'd been taught. The words King Agrippa said, "much study has made you mad," rang in his hears. This mid-trib issue was driving him nuts. Taking a shaky breath, he glanced at his wife. Their adoption was within weeks of being consummated. It was his earnest prayer for the Lord to come soon, yet, he was torn. He wanted desperately to hold the newborn child the adoption agency promised him and Angela. If the Lord came today ... he shuddered at his lack of faith.

Turning to II Thessalonians 2, he began to read. "Now concerning the coming of our Lord Jesus Christ, and being gathered unto Him don't let your mind be shaken, or be worried as if spoken to by a spirit, or by someone's words, or even by a letter from us. The day of Christ is at hand. Let no one deceive you, for that day will not come, without first there being a decline, and then the man of lawlessness will be ..." His shoulders slumped. He tried to continue, but the next word lodged in his throat like a piece of dried bread.

"I can't—" his admission lead to a torrent of tears. "Forgive me," he sputtered.

Immediately, Angela and a host of teens along with the principal gathered close and began to pray. It was like a wounded man being carried on a stretcher to a triage unit. All he could do was to let himself be carried by others.

Josh's voice rose above the others, and Scott felt his strength returning.

Standing nearby, Prince Selaphiel drew closer and touched Angela Wyatt's flagging spirit. There was too much at stake to fail now. He whispered a word of wisdom in her ear, and she opened her Bible.

Standing, she spoke in a clear voice. "If you continue reading, you will see that the mystery of iniquity is already at work. But he who restrains will continue to restrain until he is removed. And then the man of sin will be revealed. Folks, we're not there yet. This show of solidarity tells me we are not declining, we are advancing. And that man over there in the Middle-East will be exposed as a fraud, so take heart, believers. The Lord hasn't come yet."

The school bell sounded causing several girls to jump, then red faced, they started to giggle. Wiping tears, Scott watched the students and teachers hustle to class. Movement caught his attention as the principle extended his hand. "Thank you both for sharing God's word with us. An expectant believer makes the best Christian, whether you are young or old."

Nodding, Scott smiled. "Thank you for allowing this gathering. Keep praying and watching."

Angela squeezed her husband's hand and together, left the school parking lot. "That was really good, Angela. I needed that."

"The Lord gave me that word. Now go back to your office and study. I can't wait until Sunday to hear what you have to say."

Scott released a tense breath. "Neither can I."

Prince Selaphiel saluted his commander as he retook his place. He and a host of his mightiest warriors had fended off the legions of demons allowing the prayers of the believers to penetrate the portals of Heaven. He had strengthened the pastor's faith, but the battle wasn't over. It always amazed him how and why the Almighty entrusted such critical matters as world evangelism to frail human beings. *How could redeemed sinners, living in depraved, carnal, dying bodies be trusted to carry on such a monumental task?* Prince Selaphiel rubbed the back of his neck. If this wasn't a demonstration of God's faith in His creation, nothing was.

"Prince Selaphiel," Prince Argos said, "I want you and your cohort to stand guard over Pastor Wyatt. The Spirit of God will lead him into all truth, but he must not be allowed to slip into another bout with despair like he did at the pole. He nearly gave up his confidence. I know for a fact that his Lord has prayed for him that his faith wouldn't fail, yet the enemy is at work. He knows if he can destroy this man's faith, others will fall like dominos."

"You can depend on me, my lord," Selaphiel said. Clutching the hilt of his blazing sword and raising it heavenward, a bolt of lightning sprang from the blade and scattered across the sky. Then, he and his forces thundered in the direction of the church.

Time was of the essence.

Chapter Thirty-Four

Wearing a black formfitting shirt and slacks, Jacque St. John stumbled backward out of the ring. The phone call he'd received from his team outside the Institute in Antiquities left him in a foul mood, causing him to lose focus. He'd already had the wind knocked out of him by his sparring partner, now he was losing the match. It was time for him to put all that pent up anger to good use. He had to regain his momentum.

With much effort, he focused his energy on his Tao Chi sparring partner. The shorter man dressed similarly, waited for Jacque to return to the ring before resuming his training. Venting his anger, Jacque threw himself into a flurry of blows and kicks, knocking his opponent from the ring, but he wasn't finished. Two other men stood by as additional trainers, and he lashed out at them. Within a minute, three men lay unconscious on the gym floor.

"Give me a phone," he barked.

Fearing the same treatment, Duncan handed Jacque a cell phone, then quickly backed away.

Still seething, St. John dialed the UN building and spoke to the head of security. "I think there was an intruder inside my office, a man named Gasper. He must be stopped." He paused for a question. "No, I don't know how he got there. All I know is, I got a call from one of my men in Israel and he reported hearing a conversation between a man named Saul and one named Gasper. I don't know if he is still there or not, but if he is there, hold him until I arrive. I want to personally interrogate him."

After ending the call, he dialed another number and waited until a thick male voice answered on the third ring. Dispensing with the usual cordialities, he spoke through clenched teeth. "I've got a location. It is in the Gaza Strip, in an abandoned airport which goes by the name Khan Yunis Airfield. I want those traitors taken out. Once you have secured the site, call me." He finished his call and he tossed the phone back to Duncan.

Gasper had only been gone for a few minutes before the UN security team stormed through the glass doors and rushed the secretarial room frightening the cleaning crew. Guns drawn, they began to search each room, systematically looking for any unauthorized personnel.

Fortunately, Amber had found her way out of the building using the Secretary General's private exit. Back in the parking deck, she dashed to her car and left. A moment later, another team flooded the area and sealed all the exits. Their search would reveal nothing.

Knowing her apartment would be under surveillance as well as her cell phone, she found the first coffee shop with Wi-Fi and logged onto one of their computers. It only took an hour for her to assemble her team and make the arrangements for an early morning flight. If all went as planned, she and her media team would be in Rome by noon.

Meanwhile the security team continued a room to

room search. After scouring the entire building and not finding anyone, the lead officer made the call. "Sir, we searched everywhere and came up empty. We are going through surveillance tapes now and will keep you posted, but I think he got away."

A string of profanities spewed from St. John's mouth. After venting, he calmed his voice. "All right, but if you find him, remember, I want to interrogate him before you hand him over to the police."

Next, he turned to his chief of staff. "I want a direct flight to Israel. Tell the pilot of United Nations One to submit a flight plan and assemble my security team and staff. We are going to Israel," he said with urgency.

"But sir, you're not expected for another two days," his shaken chief of staff said.

"I am now, and where is Miss Kline?" he hollered as he headed to the shower room.

"She called earlier in the day. You were in the ring with your sparring partner, and I didn't think you wanted to be disturbed, but she said to—"

His eyes ablaze, he turned to Duncan. "Give me the blasted phone, you fool."

A few moments later, the phone rang and Amber picked it up.

"Yes, sir?"

"Where in blazes are you?" he demanded.

Keeping her voice level, she answered in lines she'd rehearsed, over and over in anticipation of his call. "Mr. Secretary General, I am following your orders. My team and I have just departed for the Vatican. We should be there by noon. As soon as we clear customs, I'll confer with the Pope, then on to Israel. We should be arriving sometime around mid-morning, the following day. From there we'll go to the King David Hotel and begin making the final arrangement for the arriving entourages."

Her nervous chatter continued unabated while St. John fumed.

I didn't send you to the Vatican, nor did I send you to Israel. You were supposed to fly with me, so I could keep an eye on you. It looks like we won't be getting married, after all.

It was fortunate for him, he'd developed many contacts … some good … some not so good. Through his association with the Order of Hospitallers, he'd been able to place some of those individuals into key positions within every government of every country. Always willing to do his bidding, these people had systematically removed any opposition to his permanent appointment as Secretary General. It was to one of these clandestine operatives within the Vatican his next call went.

"Very well, Miss Kline. Carry on and give my regards to the Pope."

After ending the call, he had one more to make before departing. He picked up his sat-phone and punched in the number.

"Please authenticate," he waited for the recipient to recite a series of letters and numbers, which matched the ones on his computer screen.

Once it was confirmed who he was speaking with, St. John began, "I need you to do a little work for me." He paused long enough for his contact to give him his full attention. "Don't worry, you'll be well compensated, but the job must look like a mechanical failure. Am I clear?"

"Very clear. When?"

"Do it tonight." After giving his operative the specifics, he ended the call without saying, good-bye.

"Shall I intervene?" Prince Azrael asked his commander.

Gabriel stroked his chin a moment. "No, not this time. It is for us to stand back and let the Almighty do his holy work. If and when we are needed, He will summons us. Until then, we watch and learn. You would be amazed at the intricacies of the Master's plan. How He brings all things together after the counsel of His own will is a marvelous thing to see. And to think, we get to serve such a wise, all knowing King."

The two angels, though separated in rank, and position, stood in unified wonder and worshiped their creator.

Chapter Thirty-Five

Streaking across the moonless sky at thirty-six thousand feet above the earth's surface, the sleek black fuselage went undetected by any and all eyes. Inside, six men wearing high altitude, rapid descent gear made the last minute preparations before starting their mission. Suddenly, a red light flashed and the men stood. A pair of bay doors opened at the rear of the plane, and the men took their positions. Seconds ticked, then froze as the light flashed from red to green. The team's commander gave the signal and led his men to the threshold and leaped into the night.

Their point of descent was well outside the invisible line between Israeli airspace and international waters. As the six commandos made their rapid descent, no one but them and one other man knew of their mission. As silent as eagles, six parachutes popped open slowing the men's fall, allowing them to touch down on terra firma unharmed. The moment they landed, they began releasing their gear and stowing it beneath the Joshua trees. In the distance, a row of vacant airplane hangars and a strip of asphalt awaited their arrival. With precision, they lined up in single file and moved as a unit.

Like phantoms of the night, they appeared from the thin fog wearing body armor, night-vision gear and carrying M16s mounted with silencers. The four men guarding the perimeter of the hangar stood in the cross-hairs and would soon fall. The lead commando whispered the signal and four soft pops dissipated into the night air. A moment later, four men crumpled to the ground leaving the building unprotected.

Using wire cutters, they easily sliced through the chain linked fence and moved quickly into position. Once they were sure the guards were dead, the team leader signaled for the men to move to phase two. Silent as death, the team slipped inside the hangar. Taking their positions, they eliminated the three man standing guard around the tarp covered Ark. The remaining targets were asleep in the concrete offices and would be next.

Hearing a wisp of movement, Colt roused from his sleep and poked his head over the ledge which surrounded the second floor. Seeing the men in black moving with precision, he gulped a breath and hoped they didn't see him. Lowering himself to a prone position, he inched back as far as he could, being careful not to make a sound.

All at once, the room beneath him shook from the blast of a flash bang grenade followed by a series of soft pops. Then silence.

Still holding his breath, Colt counted the seconds. *Who were these killers? Were they there to rescue him? Or was this the work of a rival seeking to take the tarp covered object? Whoever it was, knew how to kill and wouldn't stop until everyone was eliminated, including him.*

For the next thirty minutes, the team of operatives dragged eighteen bodies into the center of the hangar and placed them in body bags. Once they confirmed Saul Mueller, and Mohan were among the dead, the team commander lifted a sat-phone to his ear and waited for it to sync with the phone half-way around the world.

"We got them, sir," he said succinctly.

He paused to listen.

"No sir, there was no young boy."

He waited.

"Yes, sir, we've secured the site and will prepare for your arrival ... thank you, sir. See you soon."

After ending the connection, he assembled his team. "Okay men, listen up. I want this mess cleaned up, the bodies stacked over there," he pointed to an unoccupied corner, "And if you see a young boy around here, kill him. Understood?"

A crisp unison, "Yes sir," echoed throughout the hangar.

By now, Colt's blood had turned to ice. His breathing shallowed and he began to sweat profusely. He needed to call Gasper or Mr. Levi, but with no cell phone, that was out of the question. He wished he could blink in and out like Gasper, but being only a wise man in training, he doubted he could do more than get himself caught.

The team leader continued. "At exactly eighteen hundred hours the UN Secretary General, Mr. Jacque de Molay St. John will arrive with his personal security detail. They will assist in securing the perimeter to keep the media from getting too close. Once we are certain everything is in place, he will address the world. In the meantime, I want this place swept for bombs, listening devices and anything else that could potentially derail this event. Do you understand?"

Another unified, "Sir, yes, sir" shook the building.

Fearing detection, Colt hunkered lower. All at once, a familiar clatter caught his attention as one of the soldiers kicked a wooden pole sending it skittering across the floor. Another man stopped it with his foot and lifted it. Thinking it to be a homemade javelin, he hoisted back and pitched it in the direction of the second floor above the offices. The staff sailed straight and true in Colt's direction and stuck in a pile of insulation. Satisfied he'd hit his mark, the soldier high-fived the other man and the two began their duties.

Still breathing in short gulps, Colt felt like a burden had just been lifted from his shoulders. If he could master the art of blinking, he could enter the offices undetected, find a cell phone and return to his hiding place where he could make a call. Much depended on his success, and he wished Sasha were at his side.

Once the men and their commander had cleared the immediate area, they began a sweep of the perimeter. With it being a moonless night, the dry air quickly gave up its heat and temperatures tumbled into the teens. As the men moved about, great puffs of condensation trailed them like phantoms.

As soon as the last man left the hangar, Colt saw his chance. After practicing and succeeding to blink across the hangar to his first hiding place and back again, he had gained enough confidence to try a more risky move.

Concentrate, he told himself.

Sucking in a steadying breath, he thought about the lower level and closed his eyes. A moment later, he opened them and found herself in a small, poorly lit room. *I dare not turn on the light.* Instead, he waited for his eyes to adjust. When they did, he saw what he was looking for ... Saul's phone. With trembling fingers, he picked up the phone, but it slipped, and it clattered to the floor. Fearing the worst, Colt scooped it up and held his breath, waiting. If someone came through the door, he wondered if he'd have enough sense to blink to a safe place.

No one came.

Hand to his chest, he waited until his heart calmed enough for him to think about his hiding place one floor above him. Pinching his eyes closed, he imagined himself sitting upstairs. An instant later, he was back in his hiding place with the cell phone in his hand. Wiping the sweat from his eyes, he tried to remember the number he'd heard Gasper repeat one time.

Fortunately, he had a pretty good memory for numbers, and the call went through the first try, but after ten rings, it went to the answering machine. Keeping his voice as low as possible and still be heard, he said, "Mr. Levi, this is Colt. I'm in an airplane hangar somewhere in Gaza. The place is crawling with heavily armed men, and they are ordered to shoot anyone who comes near the place. They are guarding a golden thing with wings and are expecting some man named St. John. If you get this, you need to—"

The answering machine ran out of time and clicked off. Frustrated, he slid the phone in his pocket, but not before lowering the ring tone to vibrate. *No sense giving away my position with a dumb wrong number.* Satisfied he'd done all he could do, he snuggled deeper, closed his eyes and fell asleep.

All at once, he and Sasha were skipping hand in hand

across a wheat field. A smile pinched the corners of his lips as his sleep deepened.

###

A swirl of gold dust stirred as Prince Azrael retook his place in formation with his legion. It had only taken him a few minutes, and he was back before his commander missed him, or so he thought.

"Prince Azrael." Prince Gabriel's voice carried to the back of the line where he stood. An impish twinkle sparked in his ever blue eyes.

"Yes, my lord?"

"Please step forward."

A few chuckles from his companions bubbled up and spread like wind-blown leaves.

Prince Azrael tucked his chin and moved to the head of the line. "You wanted to see me, my lord?"

Prince Gabriel, a burly angel with broad shoulders and golden hair held in place with a silver band, crossed his arms over his chest. "Is that a tear in your cape?"

Another round of snickers scattered across the lines of warriors.

Glancing down, Azrael noticed his misdemeanor. "Sorry, my lord. I must have torn it on my last foray."

"Yes, I can see. But was that last *foray*, as you called it, one that I sanctioned?"

Azrael felt his face heat. "Uh, let's see. You did tell me to shadow Gasper and the young boy and keep them from getting into trouble."

Gabriel stroked his cleft-chin. "That I did, but I don't remember giving you permission to alter the laws of physics, now did I?"

Lifting his chest, and squaring his shoulders, Prince

Azrael gave a sideways glance at the angelic hosts to his rear. "Well, if you are referring to my helping that staff to fly twice as far as it should have, then yes ... guilty as charged. I must add in my defense, I made a perfect bull's eye in that roll of insulation."

Barely able to contain his own laughter, Gabriel squared his stance, locked his hands behind his back. "I would have expected no less from you. Carry on."

As he turned to go, his commander cleared his throat. "Oh, and get that tear repaired right away. I wouldn't want you to be caught out of uniform on your next foray."

Prince Azrael gave his commander a slight bow and fluttered off in the direction of the heavenly seamstress."

Chapter Thirty-Six

While he slept, Sasha's smiling face mesmerized Colt's attention. With his hand reaching out, he tried to grasp hers, but it kept eluding him. Frustrated, he lunged, nearly knocking over a nearby crate. A moment before it clattered to the floor, he jolted awake and grabbed it. It teetered, then steadied. Taking a quick glance over the ledge to see if anyone heard the commotion, Colt settled back. Fortunately, the building was empty, and he was safe for the moment. It was then he realized the phone he'd taken was vibrating.

Not sure if he should answer it, he waited for several rings. Then he realized it was Simon's number. He must have gotten the message. Pressing the green button, he whispered. "Hello?"

"Colt, is that you?"

It was Gasper.

"Yes." He tried to keep his voice down, but hearing Gasper nearly made him shout.

"Where are you? Are you safe? Can I come and get you?"

Gasper's questions flew at him quicker than he could answer them.

"I don't know where I am, somewhere in Gaza and no, I'm not safe. The men who set the fire are the same men who stole the Ark, but now they're all dead."

"Dead?" Gasper interrupted, his voice, a decibel higher.

"Yeah, some military guys came and killed them all. They even killed Mr. Saul. I'm scared." His voice broke.

"Can you tell me anything more about your location?"

Colt sniffed back a sob. "Yeah, it's a big airplane hangar—"

Suddenly, someone jerked the phone from Colt's hand. It tumbled to the floor and was crushed under the heel of a hooded man.

Glancing up, Colt stared into the eyes of a hired killer.

"Who were you talking to?" the man demanded.

Shaken and biting back a cry, Colt stood speechless.

"Who?" His repeated demand brought tears to Colt's eyes.

No one had ever screamed at him, not like that. His father on his worst day had never raised his voice to him. Now the man was screaming obscenities at him. It was all he could do to keep from wetting his britches.

"I want to go home," he sputtered. "I want my mom."

It was true, but it seemed at that moment, neither was going to happen.

Grabbing him by the arm, the man yanked him forward toward the ledge. "Come with me," he hollered.

Colt tripped over his own feet and splattered on the rough surface. Gravel cut into his palms and knees.

"Ouch!"

"Get up, kid."

As he pushed himself up, his fingers touched the rod. In an instant, they closed around it.

Focus.

But before he could think of a specific place, the man jerked him up and tossed him over the ledge. It was fortunate for Colt another man stood at the bottom of the ladder waiting.

"Catch," the first man hollered, just as Colt landed into the second man's arms.

The sudden jolt nearly knocked the wind from his lungs, and he lost his grip on the staff. It sprang from his hand and landed on a stack of body bags.

Something moved.

No one noticed.

Half walking, half being carried, Colt stumbled into the office where the assault team leader sat.

"Stand," he demanded.

Colt pushed himself up on quaking legs.

The man eyed him wearily. "So this is the kid we've been looking for. Where'd ya find him?"

The soldier smirked." About ten feet above you. He'd been hiding right in plain sight. I caught him on this." He tossed what was left of the cell phone on the desk.

"Who was he talking to?"

"Don't know, maybe his momma."

The commando leader glared at him. "You call the police, kid? Because if you did, so help me ..."

Whatever threat he was about to make was interrupted as the low roar of a jet engine grew louder.

"Lock him up someplace safe. I'll deal with him later."

Overhead, a Boeing 737 with UN painted on its fuselage and tail fin began circling the airfield. On either side were two US made, Israeli F-15E Strike Eagles flying security. Jacque St. John had arrived earlier than expected, and the commando leader still had a few details to attend to.

Chapter Thirty-Seven

It had been nearly two months since Gasper's departure. Not being used to moving her clock back one hour for the semi-annual time change, Felicia found her days shorter and the nights even longer. Her heart grew weary. She knew she was madly in love with him and was pretty sure he loved her. But the few calls she'd received from him, however, were hurried, and she began to wonder.

Having survived the *Fiddler on the Roof,* her days of working with the cast and crew came to an end. No more drama for a while, or so she thought.

As she sped along the highway on a late Saturday afternoon, a set of blue lights appeared in her rear-view mirror. As usual, whenever she saw a policeman, an icy finger wormed its way through her stomach. She knew her Visa had expired, but she had held out hope that Gasper would return and would solve her problem with a marriage proposal, but with him out of the country, that notion had been put on hold. Now she faced a crisis.

She slowed and pulled to the shoulder of the road expecting a stern rebuke for her heavy foot. Seeing him approach, she rolled down her window. "Officer, I can explain," she said through tearful eyes, an act she'd perfected over the years.

"Explain what, that you were traveling thirty-five

miles over the speed limit? And you being a teacher," his tone turned mocking. "What kind of example is that?"

"Yes, sir ... I was distracted." It was a poor excuse, one that elicited a 'you're not kidding me,' expression from the officer.

"Wait here while I check on a few things." Turning, he trudged back to his service vehicle.

Felicia waited with mixed emotions. Partly wishing Gasper was with her, partly too embarrassed to admit it was thoughts of him, which made her speed.

The officer took his time in processing her information causing her heart to palpitate all the more. Catching a glimpse of the officer in her mirror, she saw him talking on his phone and typing things into his on-board computer.

Finally, he pulled himself from his patrol car, hiked up his britches and approached her vehicle. "Miss Beauchamp, are you aware you're here in the US illegally?"

Felicia took a forced swallow. She knew the consequences of lying to an officer would be worse than the truth. Nodding she offered a weak smile. "Yes, but I can—"

The officer straightened and hooked his thumbs in his belt. "Miss Beauchamp, I'm going to have to ask you to step from your car and follow me."

"Why? Where are you taking me?" her voice wavered.

"Miss Beauchamp, your name has appeared on the watch list. The Immigration and Checkpoint Authority wants you brought in for questioning. From there, you will probably be deported."

Her eyes watered. She could hardly believe her ears. "Deported! Isn't that a bit severe?"

The officer clutched the handle and opened the door. "Ma'am, I'm just doing my job. So if you will please, step out of your vehicle and follow me."

"But what about *my* job, my car, *my* belongings? I have responsibilities. I can't just disappear without letting my boss, and landlord know."

Between her tears and her logic, the officer slowed his pace. "Okay, I'm giving you twenty-four hours to make arrangements. But after that, I will expect you to honor your word and report to the US Citizenship and Immigration Services down in Atlanta tomorrow."

Wiping tears from her eyes, Felicia barely noticed a van following her all the way to her home. Oblivious to any danger, she trudged to her apartment wracking her brain for an excuse which would explain her oversight. *How am I going to explain this to the principal, to my students ... to Gasper?*

Suddenly, a deep yearning engulfed her, and she slumped to the couch. "Oh, Lord. I need your help," she cried out in her pain.

While waiting for an answer, she had an idea. *Call Jacob Myers.* Though not an immigration attorney, he might have some advice. Fingers shaking, she dialed his number and sent up a quick prayer. She didn't need this drama. She needed to be here for her students ... for Gasper.

"Mr. Myers?" she said between hiccupping breaths. "This is Felicia Beauchamp—"

"Oh, Miss Beauchamp, nice to hear from you. Have you heard from—"

She cut him off. "Sir, I'm in a bit of trouble, and I was wondering if you could advise me."

Jacob's tone grew somber. "Miss Beauchamp, what kind of trouble?" It was not the first time someone called him and said the same thing. Over the years, he'd helped a lot of people with their troubles. As a successful lawyer, he'd established himself as someone people could depend upon when they got into a scrape with the law.

Biting the edge of her thumbnail, she explained her situation as succinctly as possible.

After a moment, Jacob addressed the issue head on. "Well, not being an immigration lawyer, I can only advise you to report to the USICS and let them sort it out. I'm guessing it's all a big mistake. From the little I know, if you haven't exceeded the 180-day grace period, you might get away with a slap on the wrist."

"But what about my apartment, my job? I've even been watching Melchior's dog while he's been gone." Throat thickening with emotion, another round of tears attacked her eyes.

"Look, Miss Beauchamp … Felicia, don't worry about those things. Cindy and I will take up the slack. You just worry about following the officer's orders. I don't want you to get into any more difficulty than you already are."

His calming tone brought Felicia's blood pressure down a few notches. Glancing in the mirror, she noticed a fresh set of hives creeping up her neck and fanned herself. "All right, thank you."

It took Felicia only a few minutes to gather her most treasured belongings, hoping she'd be able to return to normal life soon. But just in case they deported her, she was prepared.

"Shall we pick her up?" the surveillance team leader asked his supervisor.

The two member team of skilled operatives had been tracking her ever since the police call went in. They'd been tasked with following Miss Beauchamp, and now that she was home in her apartment, it would be a simple thing to do a snatch and grab. The team leader waited for an answer.

The supervisor had a direct line of communication with St. John. Ever since Gasper's name had come up on the computer and subsequently in association with Simon Levi, anyone he spoke with came under suspicion. The O'Dell's also fell under the same scrutiny, but were quickly dropped from the watch list. Felicia, on the other hand, had the value of being used as leverage if Gasper posed a threat.

"Yes, but make it look routine. I want you waiting for her when she leaves the USICS. As soon as you acquire the subject, I want her subdued and brought to the UN complex where she will be interrogated."

"What if she tries to make a break for it tonight?"

"You can't let that happen." The supervisor snapped back. "If she tries anything, think outside the box."

The connection went silent, and the two men began their long boring vigil.

Standing directly in front of the van and in a guarding position between the two men and his charge, was Prince Uriel, protector of the saints. Down through the ages, he had been responsible for saving countless lives; those who the Almighty, in His providence, deemed worthy of rescue. Still others He'd taken home according to His sovereign will. Since Felicia's work was not completed, it was Uriel's responsibility to see to it that no evil befall her. Moving closer, he shielded Felicia's every move, keeping a wall of protection between her and the two hired guns at all times.

Chapter Thirty-Eight

The aircraft in which Amber and her media team sat was adequately equipped with a wet bar and on-board movies ... none of which interested Amber. She was on a mission. Despite the extended flight across the Atlantic and then across the Mediterranean, she had to stay focused.

She and her advanced team spent the previous day speaking with the Pope and other heads of state making arrangements for the summit. Now she was on her way to meet with leaders in the Israeli government to prepare for the event of the century.

While her eleven member team enjoyed wine and cheese and reclined in posh leather seats, she worked the phone cajoling reluctant bureaucrats to support the unity effort, at least until she could expose her boss. Then with the media in a frenzy, she would let the other shoe drop.

Finally, after hours of labor, she congratulated herself. She had succeeded where others had failed. After handling dozens of calls from all over the world, she had cobbled together a strong show of support for St. John's summit.

Her phone vibrated and she looked at the caller ID. "Mr. St. John, what does he want now?" she muttered.

"Hello?"

"So you did it," he said without a greeting. "You managed to pull together all the moving parts. I'm proud of you, Miss Kline."

His call to congratulate her, however, was laced with jaded praise. *How did he know what I've been doing? Is he still inside my head?*

Amber tried to maintain an even tone; the kind St. John would expect from someone he'd hypnotized. "Yes, sir. I only seek to please."

"And that little matter of my family?" he asked cryptically.

"Hmm, your family. Oh, of course, you're speaking of your father. Such a great man. Sorry I'd not had the privilege of meeting him. It would have been a thrill to do an exclusive—"

"Yes, yes, and about the other matter?"

Amber stared blankly out the window. She knew he was fishing. Lying to him would be easy, but with his enhanced ability to read minds, it could be a slippery slope. "If you are referring to all that research I wasted my time on, you know, the Knights of something, and the Order of Hospitality, well ... you'll be delighted to know, that's gone, deleted, shredded."

She could hear the relief in St. John's voice. "Miss Kline, you don't know the load you've lifted from my shoulders. If that kind of distorted propaganda fell into the hands of the wrong people, well, it could derail my plans for world peace. After all, isn't that what we're all after?"

"Just happy to serve." She forced the words out. "Is there anything else you want to cover?"

St. John paused for a minute. "When do you expect

the press to arrive?"

"I expect advanced security teams and the media to arrive within twenty-four hours. Why?" She bit her lip. A hypnotized person doesn't ask questions. Chiding herself for making such a blunder, she waited ... hoping he missed it ...

He didn't.

St. John released a wicked chuckle. "That's what I expected you to say. Miss Kline, I'm not as stupid as you think. I know perfectly well you didn't destroy all the information concerning my background. As a matter of fact, you have arranged to have me embarrassed and humiliated the moment I step off my plane. And the media would be there to capture it all on live video." He released a mirthless laugh. "But I have beaten you at your own game. By now, the men who stole the Ark are dead, and all your media buddies will be the moment they set foot on the tarmac."

Amber's stomach knotted, and she crossed her arms over her midsection. The ulcer she denied having, made its presence known. "And what about your press detail and me? We're just about to land."

"No, Miss Kline, you're not about to land ... you're pilot is about to ditch in the Mediterranean Sea. So I guess this is good-bye."

The connection went dead. A moment later, the aircraft shuttered and dropped.

Chapter Thirty-Nine

The Boeing 737 Captain Rodney Dunbar piloted shook violently followed by a series of beeps.

Dunbar, an eighteen-year veteran of the Gulf War and every conflict since, had experienced nearly every kind of in-flight emergency a plane could offer, but this was something new.

He flipped off the autopilot and gripped the yoke, while his co-pilot began checking the flight manual to determine what the problem was.

"Sir, have you seen the oil pressure gauge?"

Dunbar glanced at it as he too grappled with the yoke. "Yes, at this rate, we won't be able to go much further before one of our engines seizes."

"And it's too far to return to Rome, isn't it?"

"Yes, and with that storm front closing in on Tel Aviv, we can't afford to go into a holding pattern."

"If there is a secondary airfield, should I contact Israeli air-traffic control to divert us."

Dunbar thought a moment. "Yes, there is a small airfield in the Gaza Strip. It isn't much, just a short tarmac."

All at once, their headphones sprang to life. "This is BGA Israel, please be advised you are entering Israeli Airspace. Please identify yourselves.

The pilot toggled his microphone. "BGA, this is

UNHAS Miami, Charlie, Baker Five Six Three Hotel, request VFR traffic advisories."

"We have you on our VFR, be advised you are approaching a severe storm system, over."

"Copy that BGA Israel, we have a problem. We are rapidly losing oil pressure. Request permission to land at the closest non-commercial airport, over."

"UNHAS Miami Charlie, Baker Five Six Three Hotel, this is BGA Israel, recommend landing at Khan Yunis Airfield, over?"

"Copy that BGA Israel, are we cleared for an emergency landing, over?"

"Miami Charlie, Baker Five Six Three Hotel, be advised the airfield is not in use. You're on your own. Godspeed, over and out."

The pilot, nosed the ailing Boeing 737 south around the edge of the cloud bank, adjusted his trim and leveled off. All at once, his port side engine seized. The plane shuttered and began to lose speed. As the nose of the plane dipped, Captain Dunbar struggled with the yoke to keep the aircraft level. A moment later, the starboard engine flamed out.

"We're going down," the co-pilot said.

"Let's put her in a glide pattern. Dump all the fuel, and correct the trim. Maybe we can make it a few more miles before we go for a swim."

Pressing the intercom button, Dunbar spoke in an even tone. "This is your captain. I am sorry to inform you we are having some difficulty with our engines. We have been cleared to make an emergency landing at an alternative airport. In the meantime, please be sure your seat restraints are on and follow your stewardess' instructions."

As the plane descended, an updraft from the storm which pummeled the Judean coast, caught hold of the wings, lifting it several hundred feet. It was as frightening as riding a roller-coaster, and much deadlier. Most of the occupants in the cabin had time to buckle their seatbelts. Those who didn't were thrown around like rag dolls leaving several badly injured. Amber suffered a laceration to her forehead ... the result of flying debris. Others didn't fare as well.

"Captain," his co-pilot said, pointing at a dark strip of land.

Dunbar glanced up from the spinning dials long enough to see what his co-pilot pointed at. In the distance, the Gaza coastline looked like a narrow slit of land, but the closer they came, it became clear, it was a sandy beach.

"Can we make it?"

"I don't know. That last gust of wind helped us, but without another one, we'll probably miss it by a few hundred feet. It'll be too far to swim."

As he spoke, his port side engine sputtered to life. The renewed thrust gave the struggling aircraft the boost it needed. Gripping the yoke, Dunbar pulled back.

"Set the landing gear," he ordered.

"For a soft landing?"

"Yes, with the rain, the sand might be firm enough to handle it."

The co-pilot followed his command and waited for the red light to turn green, indicating that it was fully deployed and locked.

"This is taking too long. We may have to make

another pass."

"We don't have the altitude, give another fifteen seconds. If they don't lock, we may have to do a belly landing."

After an excruciating twelve seconds the red light turned green just as they passed the breakers. As the light aircraft touched down on the sandy beach, it cut deep gouges in the virgin seascape. Seeing a rock outcropping several hundred feet ahead, the pilot applied the brake while the co-pilot reversed the engines thrust.

With the aircraft still bouncing, Captain Dunbar was barely able to control its direction. Finally, the aircraft responded and Dunbar nosed the plane past the rocks and brought it to a gentle stop.

Relieved, the co-pilot leaned back. "Thank you Lord."

Dunbar cocked an eye. "I didn't know you were a praying man."

"I'd be a fool to fly with you and not be," he chuckled. "Let's check on our passengers," he said, not knowing how much his prayers had attributed in saving the lives of his pilot and passengers.

Captain Dunbar glanced skyward as another jetliner hugged the horizon on approach to the Khan Yunis Airfield. *For it being an abandoned airfield, it certainly has a lot of activity.* Releasing his seat restraint, he pushed himself to the cabin where he found several members of the UN Secretary General's advanced media team struggling to free themselves from the wreckage.

Grabbing the door release, he yanked it open. Immediately, an inflatable slide deployed and he began to assist his passengers out the door. Once the last of them had escaped, he helped his co-pilot out and then jumped. He slid down and hit the bottom where several grateful passengers assisted him to his feet.

"All passengers and crew are accounted for, Captain," the co-pilot announced.

"Roger that."

"Where are we?" Amber asked.

Captain Dunbar shifted to face his anxious passengers. "We are in the Gaza Strip not far from the Khan Yunis Airfield."

As he spoke, several jeeps with 50 caliber machine guns mounted behind the driver, approached at a high speed. Captain Dunbar stepped in front of the others and held up his hands in surrender. He hoped his black skin would work to his advantage.

The jeeps skidded to a halt, their gunners training the barrels of their weapons on the group as a man jumped out and approached them. He appeared to be the local militia's commander. Taking a glance at the large UN stenciled on the tail fin of the plane, his countenance changed.

"I see you have misjudged the distance to the landing strip, Captain."

Chagrined, Captain Dunbar smiled sheepishly. "We had engine trouble. We're lucky to have made it this far."

The militia commander offered Dunbar a sloppy salute, to which Dunbar returned smartly.

"Engine trouble notwithstanding, welcome to the Gaza Strip. I understand my country has been chosen by Allah, peace be upon him, to host a monumental announcement. Are you part of the UN Secretary

General's entourage?" his tone was welcoming, much to Amber's relief.

"Yes, we are the advanced media team. We have no weapons, as you can see, but we do have several injured. Can you assist us?"

The solidly build man approached the captain and extended his hand. "Yes, we will be happy to help you in any way we can." His lips parted, revealing a set of pearly white teeth.

By the time they'd finished treating the injured, two other jeeps had joined them. The commander of the militia split the passengers and crew into four groups.

"I will take you to Khan Yunis Airfield where you will honor my country for being a peace-loving nation."

Dunbar eyed the machine guns and wondered at the truthfulness of his statement, but didn't express his thoughts. He was glad to be alive, but had a bone to pick with St. John. *Was he responsible for sabotaging my aircraft?*

Time would tell.

Chapter Forty

It had been an excruciating wait. Since Simon and I returned from the hospital, he had been called to meet with the authorities to explain why the sprinkler system didn't work. In addition, the insurance companies representing the precious artifacts were beginning to ask questions. Questions Simon couldn't answer. Revelations of fake specimens and replicas instead of the authentic pieces were coming to the surface, and he was faced with the reality that he might go to jail for insurance fraud.

In addition, we hadn't heard from Abdullah for days. It seemed everything had ground to a halt while the world spun out of control. Even my repeated calls to Felicia had gone unanswered, and my confidence began to flag.

The next morning, however, our fortunes began to change with the arrival of Abdullah, who showed up on Simon's doorstep with a dozen heavily armed men.

Simon stood, unspeaking. Apparently, he had never seen so many paramilitary soldiers lined up in front of him. Neither had I, come to think of it. I was gratified, however, that they were not pointing their weapons at us.

"What took you so long?" Simon asked, trying to keep his frustration in check.

Abdullah smiled. "These things take time, my friend. You can't assemble an army overnight. You have to choose the right men for the job and let me tell you ...

these are the right men."

I took a quick assessment of his troops. This was indeed a formidable group of men. A deep sense of gratitude and awe formed in my chest as I realized these men were willing to lay down their lives for a cause I didn't even understand. My only hope was that they understood and were ready to face the consequences of their decision.

"We need to get going?" Simon stated.

"Why? What's happened since we last spoke?" Abdullah asked.

"Last night, Gasper got a message from Colt, the young man under his charge. He said he was somewhere in Gaza ... said he was hiding in an airplane hangar, but that it was crawling with armed men. Then the phone suddenly went dead, and I can only assume he's been caught."

Abdullah knuckled his hips and squared himself in front of his men. Rigid lines formed on their faces. These were men experienced at dealing out death and destruction. They feared neither men nor spirit; these were the children of the Lehi Group, a paramilitary group committed to an independent State of Israel. Their ancestors had, at one time, aligned themselves with Stalin and the Bolsheviks in order to throw off British rule throughout Palestine, now they fought Palestinian and Syrian incursions.

Stepping into the cab of his truck, Abdullah prepared to lead his men into harm's way. After getting into one of the heavily armed vehicles, I strapped in. "I'm glad to finally be on the move, but I wish I had my staff."

Simon nodded. "That would come in handy right

now, but we'll just have to depend upon those men and their skill."

Laying my hand on his arm, I held his gaze. "Simon, just remember, some men trust in chariots, and some men trust in horses: but we will trust the name of the Lord our God."

As we moved out, a vast number of angelic warriors surrounded the two-vehicle caravan as it rumbled in the direction of the Gaza Strip. For these men to enter this territory was paramount to an act of war. Fortunately, Abdullah knew all the back trails and avoided the usual delays and questions at the border crossing.

Ahead of the caravan flew Prince Gabriel whose gossamer wings were beating at a blinding speed. Nodding to his second in command, he signaled for him to open a corridor for the caravan and hold back the dark forces which pressed in against them. Unseen by their human charges, the angels of light cut a swath wide enough for Abdullah and his men to pass unhindered. Their wings overlapped forming an impregnable shield, while above them an additional layer of shining beings hovered with drawn swords. It took the caravan only ninety minutes to reach the Khan Yunis Airfield, but by then, Amber and those escorting her team had already arrived.

Chapter Forty-One

S aul Mueller's eyes popped open as a jolt of energy surged through his body. The last thing he remembered was a hooded man pointing an assault rifle at him and feeling his chest collapse with the force of a bullet. Agonizing pain radiated through him as the scalding bullet ripped through his body, then blackness. The next thing he knew, he was standing amidst flames. His parched throat cried out for just a drop of water … none came. All around him, the wail of lost souls and the anguished screams of the condemned echoed in his ears. One voice, in particular, rose above the cacophony … it was his own.

Lifting his eyes, he saw in the distance a mighty tree. On either side of the tree flowed streams of fresh, cool water. The branches of the tree spread as far as the horizon … among its leaves hung fruit of every kind, and beneath its shadow sat Father Abraham. The patriarch of old appeared to be in the prime of life as he reclined on a soft cushion while youthful servants waited on his every want.

"Father Abraham," Saul cried out.

He turned to face him; Saul saw a deep sadness in his eyes for the plight of his distant kin. "Yes, my son?"

"Could you dip your finger in water and touch my tongue, for I am tormented in this flame?"

His face softened. "My son, you spent your days chasing the vanities of life. Your heart was filled with bitterness, anger, and revenge. You had no time for God. Now, you are receiving the reward of a wasted life."

"But My Father, no one told me about the right way. My parents, my siblings … they all were wiped away from me by the Nazis. I grew up as an orphan. I had no one to point me to the light."

Thunder rippled from a distant mountain and Abraham stood and approached the gulf which separated him from the abyss. "This is most unusual, I must say, but God has heard your petition. He has granted a moment of grace. See that you don't waste it."

Gasping for air, Saul whipped out his service knife and began to slice through the canvas bag which entombed him. As the hole opened, fresh air filled his lungs. Pushing his head out, he looked around. Bright sunlight temporarily blinded him, but his eyes soon adjusted. *Was I dreaming I was in Hell? Am I dreaming now?*

Outside, a large aircraft sat near the mouth of the hangar. A set of stairs had been rolled in place, and scores of suited men poured from the side of the plane. He knew immediately who they were and what their purpose was. It didn't take him long to figure out Jacque St. John sent the assailants to kill him and his men before he arrived. Now he was there to claim his prize. *So much for my plan.* Looking at the knife in his hand, he considered dashing from the shadows and plunging it into St. John's chest. It would be an act of desperation and probably fail, but that was all he could think of doing.

The men entering the hangar were the UN Secretary

General's personal security detail. They set up a protective perimeter and waited for the Secretary to descend the stairs.

Shading his eyes against the glare, Saul watched St. John step to the exit. His white suit glistened in the Middle Eastern sun as he surveyed the situation. After adjusting his Gucci sunglasses, he began a slow, deliberate descent as if he owned the world.

Still questioning how he'd survived the bullet wound, Saul examined his body. No wound, no bullet hole, and then he remembered ... he was wearing a Kevlar vest. He glanced to the body bags next to him. His entire team lay in similar bags ... unmoving, apparently they weren't. Then he saw it ... Gasper's staff. *It couldn't be.*

After freeing himself from the bag enclosing him, he stood and moved to a shadowed corner. Hearing voices inside the office, he clung as close to the wall as he could. If he made the wrong move, he knew he'd be placed in another body bag. This time, he wouldn't be leaving. His plan to expose St. John had fallen apart. Now all he wanted to do was execute the man whose father was responsible for killing his family. *But how?* The man was encircled with body guards.

Heavy footsteps preceded a large man as he exited the office. He marched directly toward Mr. St. John, and the two began to talk. Seeing his chance to find a better hiding place and get his hands on a weapon, Saul sprang into the office. No sooner had he entered, than he heard someone's sharp intake.

Glancing to the side, he saw a young boy. "No, you couldn't be," he said in surprise.

"I couldn't be what?" Colt muttered.

"You couldn't be the boy my men were searching for ... could you?"

Colt nodded. "And you are Mr. Saul, the man who set the Institute in Antiquities on fire and stole that Ark thingy."

Saul couldn't help but smile. "Yes, guilty as charged, but I did it—" stopping mid-sentence. His reasons didn't seem to hold up now ... not to a young boy. "Let's just say, I was trying to do the right thing, but I went about it all wrong." The words, *'you have been granted grace,'* echoed in his ears.

His explanation seemed to satisfy the boy.

"My name is Colt O'Dell. I was the shepherd boy in the live nativity scene. We met in that cave where they are storing the stuff for the temple."

"I remember you. You have a quick tongue."

Colt bit his lip. "Well, your men almost got me killed."

Saul looked at the sweaty faced boy and suddenly felt the weight of his guilt. Many years ago, he had a young son about Colt's age. If it weren't for his pride, his stubbornness, his obsession with his career, he would still have a home, a wife, a son. That dream, however, was shattered when he signed the divorce papers. Now, all he had to live for was revenge, and even that seemed hollow.

He had been given a second chance at life, and he was not going to squander it chasing an illusion.

Looking at Colt, he pulled his knife from its sheath. "Reach out your hands."

His face contorted into a question, but Colt complied. "What are you doing?"

"I'm getting you out of here."

"Where can we go? The place is crawling with men with guns." Colt said.

Saul thought about the van his men had used, but quickly ruled it out. They'd be cut down before they got halfway there. "You know they shot me and left me for dead, but I think Gasper's staff brought me back to life."

Colt's eyes rounded. "It did?"

"Yes, but as I was waking up, I saw a vision. I saw a man on a cross. He looked down at me with such compassion, I'd never seen before."

Colt nodded. "Did He say anything to you?"

Saul shifted to look Colt in the eyes. "As a matter of fact, He did. He said, 'Father, forgive him for he doesn't know what he is doing.'"

Smiling, Colt said, "That was Jesus. He was dying for your sins ... for mine."

The statement caught Saul off guard. He had always rejected the notion that Jesus Christ could be real. His people had never accepted the story of Calvary, let alone the empty tomb. Yet, he distinctly remembered seeing the man on the cross standing in front of an empty tomb with the Roman centurions lying prostrate on the ground. Again, the risen Savior looked at him with compassion and said, 'I am He that lives, and was dead; and, behold, I am alive for evermore, Amen; and have the keys of hell and of death.' In my mind, I saw myself bow alongside the centurions."

What does that mean?"

Colt glanced at the door, then back to Saul. "It means God has given you another chance. He has granted you grace to believe. Now will you?"

Without hesitation, Saul fell to his knees and in an act

which shook him to the core, opened his hardened heart to the Savior. "Jesus, I receive You," he said through trembling lips.

Unseen, but more real than the physical, Jesus extended His arms and welcomed his child home.

Standing on unsteady legs, Saul spoke in a thick voice. "I have never experienced such love." He wiped the tears from his face.

"What are you going to do about it?"

The question stunned Saul. This boy kept pressing him to think outside his comfort zone. His forehead wrinkling, he looked at Colt. "What do you mean?"

"I mean, are you going to tell someone about accepting Jesus as your Messiah? That's what the Bible tells us to do."

Saul thought a moment. Feeling renewed in his spirit, he had to agree. He wanted to tell someone. Who better than the man he'd hated for as long as he could remember? "I must tell Jacque that I forgive him. I've been carrying anger and hatred for him too long."

As he stepped toward the door, Colt called out to him, "Mr. Saul, have you seen Gasper's staff?"

The question sparked an idea. "Yes, it's just outside this building. Why?"

Not speaking, Colt bounded out the door. A second later, he returned triumphantly with the staff and a broad smile.

Saul's heart slammed against his chest. "What were you thinking? You could have gotten us killed," he said through pinched lips.

"We might need this before it's all over."

Saul swiped his hand over his brow. "What good is

that stick against all those guns?"

Colt fingered the staff. "You've seen what this can do. This is more than just a long staff, it was the very staff Moses used to part the Red Sea," his voice rang with confidence.

As he spoke, two columns of vehicles approached the hanger from opposite directions.

Chapter Forty-Two

Standing on the tarmac, Jacque de Molay St. John watched the two columns of vehicles approach. *This is not good,* the voice inside his head said. Jacque St. John felt an icy hand grip his chest. *No, but I can handle this, just give me a little more time.* His mental protestations had little effect on the spirit driving him. *Give me a chance to destroy these intruders, then we can—*

No more talk Slave. Do I have to remind you who I am and what I want?

Jacque felt a wave of shiver flesh crawl over his skin, but stayed calm. *No, master. I am your servant to do your bidding is my only desire.*

Good, I desire a blood sacrifice ... lots of blood. If I don't get enough ... I will require yours.

The mental conversation went unheard by Jacque's men as they formed a protective barrier around him. It was obvious; however, they were not prepared for the show of force offered by Abdullah's Lehi group and the local PLO militia.

As the two groups neared each other, it also became clear neither group trusted the other. If someone didn't step forward fast, it would turn into a bloodbath. The leader of the militia lifted his hand, and the jeep formation stopped fifty feet from the hangar's entrance.

Abdullah's Lehi group fanned out to form a semicircle with St. John at the focal point.

"Miss Kline," Captain Dunbar whispered. "Do you have a camera crew?"

"Yes, why?"

"Get out of the vehicles and set up as many cameras as possible, but stay low. I don't want you to get your head shot off. You're about to witness a world-class story or the beginning of World War Three."

Taking his cue, she and her media team quickly set up a satellite dish and synced it to a satellite hovering three hundred miles in geosynchronous orbit above the earth. Within minutes, she was live and speaking with her news director, Mr. Womack, who had chosen to remain in New York City.

"This is Amber Kline with CCN news coming to you live from Gaza to bring you this historic event. UN Secretary General, Jacque de Molay St. John is about to make an announcement of global proportions, but there is a problem. There are two groups of heavily armed men who have taken up positions in and around the airplane hangar where the Secretary General has chosen to make this historic announcement. We are not clear what their grievance is, but it is certain, if this situation isn't defused quickly, we might see the beginning of World War Three." Amber's voice was a sea of calm, despite the building storm all around her.

Womack cut in with a flurry of questions, all of which Amber deftly ignored.

"We have also recently uncovered information about Mr. St. John, which could jeopardize his claim to the position he now holds. Sources tell us that he is the son of a Nazi war-crimes sympathizer, and a member of a secret society called The Order of Hospitallers. This radical organization is committed to Israel's destruction. I am going to try to get closer to see whether the Secretary General will respond to these allegations."

As she and the camera crew broke from behind the parked jeeps, she was immediately met with St. John's security detail. Their guns aimed and ready to shoot the first person who stepped any closer.

"Mr. St. John, I would like to thank you for warning my pilot of the possible danger we were facing with our engines. Would you like to comment on that?" Amber called over the shouts of his protective detail.

He ignored her question.

"Mr. Secretary General, would you like to comment on the allegations of your ties to the Hospitallers?" she called.

As the scene unfolded in front of the hangar, I caught a glimpse of movement deep inside the hangar. Colt darted from an office door, grabbed a long pole and returned before anyone else noticed. A moment later, Saul emerged from the office followed by Colt.

I couldn't believe my eyes. *What was Colt doing with Saul Mueller? Was he a hostage? Was Saul going to use him as leverage? Had Mueller convinced Colt to join his ill-conceived plan?* Holding my gaze, I nodded to Simon.

"Look, it's Colt," I whispered through tight lips. "I'm going after him." I took a step but Simon and Abdullah grabbed me by the arms to keep me from rushing to Colt's side.

"Hold still," Abdullah said in a firm tone, "you could

have gotten us all killed. My men can handle the PLO, but you must stay back."

I struggled against their grip as the three groups of armed men stared at each other, daring the other to make the first move.

Stepping forward, St. John spoke in a clear tone. "Come no closer. What you see behind me is the most powerful weapon in the world, and I alone hold the keys to its power. I, the Secretary General of the World, demand you to lay down your weapons, or I will unleash it. When I am finished there won't be one of you left standing before me. Yea, nothing will stand before me. I am the ruler of this world, and I demand complete obedience. Now let everyone bow their knee to me."

All at once, my eyes were opened, and I saw into the spirit world. Jacque St. John stood in the inky shadow of a large dragon. Its flashing eyes roved the area. Angry puffs of red smoke emitted from its nostrils with every breath. Having one clawed foot deeply embedded in St. John's skull, the beast maintained control of his movements like he was a marionette. The evil presence reminded me of what I had seen in the Temple of Endor, only larger.

Not far from where he stood was the Ark. It was surrounded by a host of shining beings. Their swords were drawn and flamed like torches. Their eyes blazed like diamonds, their wings fluttered, but failed to stir the air. Astonished, I held my breath while time stood still. *Were these beings here to protect the Ark of God? Would they strike us all dead for looking upon it?* The sudden realization that we stood on the brink of a massive spiritual war struck me with the force of a raging bull. I feared for the believers as well as the unbelievers.

"Jack," Saul's voice sailed through the wire-tight atmosphere catching everyone's attention, including mine.

The UN Secretary General pivoted on his heels. It was obvious no one had ever called him that before.

"Jack the Molay, or should I say, Jack the mole. Yes, the mole. You have finally come out of your hiding place. You disgrace your ancestors. You're no St. John. That name belongs to the noble Order of St. John of Jerusalem; a Christian community dedicated to the benefit of the Jewish state. You've done nothing but steal their wealth, and now you claim to own their most precious treasure. How dare you."

Squaring his shoulders, St. John faced off with his adversary. "I have every right to claim it. I discovered its whereabouts and hired you to dig it up."

"Yes, and then you sent a team of murderers to kill my men and me," he hollered loud enough for Amber to record.

"Mr. Secretary, is it true you sent men here to kill Mr. Mueller?"

Again, he ignored Amber's question.

"You traitor," St. John bellowed, clearly losing control of the situation.

"Traitor, it was your family who sided with the Nazi's and condemned my family to death. You are no friend of Israel neither are you a friend of the people of this world. But I have a message for you. In Jesus' name, I forgive you."

In a rage, Jacque St. John charged Saul, who stood with his arms extended. St. John plowed into the defenseless man, knocking him to the concrete. Saul regained his footing and held out his hands in surrender. "Stop this madness. You are only going to get someone killed. I said I forgive you. I have no more quarrel with you."

Screaming obscenities, Jacque pivoted and landed a solid kick to Saul's midsection, doubling him over. Then he spun and delivered a deadly kick to the wounded man's neck.

Saul collapsed, not moving while the world and I watched in horror. Then, to my amazement, the angel of the Lord appeared next to Saul's broken body and knelt. As gentle as a nurse, the theophany lifted Saul's spirit from his body, together they ascended heavenward. *Was that what it was like to die?* I wondered.

My thoughts were interrupted as Colt dropped the rod he'd been carrying and ran to Saul's crumpled body. "You killed him, you murderer," he hollered with a ragged voice.

Chapter Forty-Three

After seeing my rod fall, I began to move to the left. A moment later, I disappeared in the shadow of the building.

Seizing the opportunity, St. John grabbed the boy and yanked him to his feet. "Everyone stand back."

Then he tugged the corner of the tarp and let it fall to the ground. Immediately, the sun-rays danced off the golden wings of the two cherubim. "Behold, the awesome power of the Ark. It is greater than anything the world possesses. With it, I can annihilate any nation that refuses to embrace me as their Lord. Did you get that, Miss Kline?"

The camera crew inched forward despite the armed guards.

With every eye riveted on the Ark of God, I grabbed my staff with two hands, and advanced several steps. In an instant, some of St. John's protective detail formed a barrier between him and me. Overhead, one of the angels signaled to me, indicating what I should do next. Using the end of my staff like a broom, I wiped the floor clean, sending the men sprawling a dozen feet away. The angel nodded approvingly.

"You," St. John raged. Still holding Colt, he ran toward me like a wild man. "Come no closer."

I stood my ground and raised the tip of my staff.

"Drop the boy." I demanded.

St. John skidded to a stop, pulled a gun from an unseen holster and pointed it at Colt's head.

"Drop the staff and back away or the boy dies."

The angel signaled for me to obey. Feeling the wind drain from my lungs, I wavered. *How could I face the O'Dells if I let this man kill Colt ... how could I face myself?* Slowly, I bent my knees and laid the staff down. In an instant, three burly guards grabbed me and threw me to the concrete floor. My cheek struck the hard surface sending bolts of lightning across my sight. The irony taste of blood stung my tongue and I felt light headed. Forcing my mind to focus, I blinked away the spider webs.

As the men pinned me down, I watched the movements of the angel who first signaled to me. He showed no fear in the face of the black creature; rather, it seemed the demon that held St. John in its clutches couldn't see the smaller angel. How all this happened without anyone else's notice was beyond me, but it gave me a sense of peace.

A satisfied smirk stretched across St. John's face. For a moment, it appeared he'd won, but I knew differently. Tossing Colt to the hard surface, he stepped in front of the Ark of God. The black spirit which possessed him, spoke through St. John's voice.

"I am the God of this world, and this is my throne. You will either submit to my authority, or you will be crushed under my heel. Bow." His voice resonated throughout the cavernous building, shaking it until the glass shattered.

I couldn't believe my eyes, or my ears. The clatter of

weapons hitting the floor echoed as each member of the Lehi group, the PLO and his security detail bent their knees. Further back, I saw Amber's news crew panning the camera across the scene.

She appeared to be as awestruck at the sight as the rest of us. "Mr. Secretary, would you give me a few minutes to answer my questions?"

Heads turned.

The momentary distraction was all Colt needed to grab my staff. Standing with his feet apart, he pointed it at St. John and shoved as if he were pushing a large object.

A bolt of energy leaped from the staff sending the man sprawling backward. The dragon-like demon controlling St. John bellowed and raged at the young boy who stood between him and his prize. Lifting St. John to his feet, he dragged him closer to the Ark. By now, St. John's pristine white suit had been smudged with oil, but he ignored it.

Colt must have seen the demon too, as he shoved again, flinging St. John against the stack of fuel drums knocking them over. Within minutes, the floor slicked with a dark substance.

"I'll get you for this." He screamed and raised his gun.

A host of unseen angels formed a barrier blocking the bullet that was sure to blaze from the weapon. He fired, but to my surprise, the bullet fell harmlessly to the floor sending sparks dangerously close to the spreading fuel.

Standing his ground, Colt swung the end of the staff toward the Ark. St. John rose and flailed about like a fish on the end of a fishing pole. Then he dropped the tip of the rod, and St. John landed hard next to the Ark.

"I'll show you," he raged. Before anyone could stop him, he stretched out his hands and grabbed Balthazar's and Melchior's staves, which now hung on either side of the Ark of the Covenant.

The angel signaled for us to duck. Colt and I did so without hesitation.

Deep within the throne room of Heaven, a spark ignited, then flashed into a flame. The flame grew into a blaze which quickly raged into an uncontrollable, unquenchable inferno. It leaped across the divide between Heaven and earth like a wildfire. The world watched in breathless wonder as the conflagration from God's throne cut across a cloudless sky, and struck St. John in full force. His body arced as if electrified. His eyes bulged, his hair ignited in flames. He screamed in agony. A moment later ... he was dead.

Somewhere in the blackness of the abyss, a tiny voice spoke. From deep within the dark chambers of Hades a voice echoed across the far reaches of Hell. The shriveled soul of Jacque de Molay St. John cried out in agony, in pain, in his rebellion ... "Jesus is Lord."

At the same instant, St. John's hands touched the rods, a burst of light brighter than the sun blazed from the Ark like an electromagnetic pulse. Everything electrical immediately shut down; the cameras, the microphones, the engines of all the vehicles.

Seeing the UN Secretary General fall down dead, his security detail snatched up their weapons and began firing erratically. Caught in the crossfire between the

Lehi group, the PLO and the security detail, Colt scampered toward me still clutching my staff.

By the time he reached me, two of the three men holding me, lay dead. The angelic beings had shielded me from the withering assault.

"Mr. Gasper, catch," he said, tossing me the staff.

I caught it in one hand and focused just as Colt leaped into my arms. The next moment we were standing outside of the hangar as gunfire shook the structure. Hunkering down so as to not get hit with a stray bullet, we waited with patient anticipation for the shooting to stop. I feared for my friends and prayed somehow they survived the mayhem.

Finally, the gunfire subsided. As we emerged from around the corner of the building the first thing I noticed was the absence of the giant demon.

It was gone.

In its place, a host of angels filled the expanse ... and they were singing. Though I couldn't understand them, I knew it must have been a song of victory, for I too felt triumphant. I was also relieved to see Simon and Miss Kline. They, along with the Lehi group survived the massacre. Captain Dunbar and his co-pilot were also among the living and were helping the news crew drag themselves from the carnage.

"Did you get that on film?" I asked, struggling to breathe amidst the acrid smoke.

Amber nodded. "Mr. Gasper." Her outburst caused many heads to turn. "How did you get here?"

I shrugged, but that didn't stop her from rushing me and throwing her arms around me. Struggling to extricate myself from her embrace, I held her at arms-length. "It's complicated," I said as Colt eyed the woman with suspicion. "I'll explain later," I whispered.

He shoved his hands in his pockets and tried to act like he hadn't seen, but I knew he did. If word got back to Felicia that this gorgeous woman was fawning all over me, I would have a lot of explaining to do. "Did you record what happened?" I repeated, trying to change the focus.

"Yes, thanks to my good old-fashioned Kodak, I got it all, at least the still images. I'll never forget the sight as long as I live. Thank you for saving my life." She tried to grab me again.

Holding my hands in surrender, I said, "No, Miss Kline, this young man is the hero. Were it not for him, we all would be dead."

She turned to face him and in an instant, scooped him in her arms. "Oh, thank you, thank you."

Colt's face reddened and he tried to speak.

Giving him a knowing smile, I jammed my hands in my pockets. "It'll be our little secret," I said holding his surprised gaze. He nodded as she released her hold on him.

Squaring his shoulders, he said, "We pledge our lives and our sacred honor to each other, and choose to follow where the God of Heaven leads us that we may fulfill His will. So say we all."

My chest swelled with pride, and I clutched his hand in a manly grip. "So say we all."

Chapter Forty-Four

As I assessed our situation, I realized we couldn't stay there much longer. With the rapidly pooling engine fuel spreading across the floor, I knew it would only be a matter of time before the entire facility blew up.

Looking around, I saw the captain of the airplane which brought Amber and her media team. He was safe and unharmed.

"Captain Dunbar, do you think you can get that plane in the air?"

The captain glanced at the danger gathering behind me, lifted his cap and ran his hand over his close-cropped hair. "If those tanks don't blow first and the plane's electrical system is still intact, I should be able. I just hope that electrical shock didn't fry the electronics, but I'm willing to give it a try."

"Good, get that plane as far from the hangar as possible and be ready to take-off the moment I get back."

He glanced at the aircraft, then back to me. "Where are you going?"

I stepped toward the Ark of God. "Don't ask, just get the plane ready."

Grabbing the tarp, Simon and I threw it over the winged trophy. "What are you going to do with it now?" Simon asked as he finished tucking the corner.

"You and I are going to take this somewhere safe. Somewhere no one will find it until God is ready."

"But—"

"No buts, the timing isn't right. Now grab those rods, this place could blow any minute."

Clearly shaken, he resisted. "Gasper, that's suicide."

I ignored his protests. "Simon, it's suicide if we stand here discussing the matter. Your last name is Levi isn't it? That means you're a Levite. You have every right to carry the Ark of God. Now grab them and lift."

Simon ran his hand over his face and wiped his slick hands on his pants. "Whatever you say."

His fingers clutched the rods, and he released a nervous breath. "Hey, I'm alive."

"Of course you're alive, you schlep. Now grab ahold." As I closed my eyes and prepared to vanish, Colt leaped on my back.

"You're not going anywhere without me. We go where the God of Heaven leads us."

His determination caused me to smile. "So say we all. Hold on." Then I closed my eyes and focused.

A moment later, we appeared on a rugged path halfway up a jagged mountain.

"I know this place," Mr. Levi said surveying the scene. "This is none other than the Mountain of God ... Mount Sinai. This is the place where God came down and gave us His commandments."

I glanced around. "Yes, and the instructions for the Tabernacle and its furniture," I added.

Simon shielded his eyes against the blazing sun. "I have been here once before, a long time ago, but the

Saudis ran us off before we could do any excavating."

"Well, we don't have any time for that."

Incredulous, Simon asked, "Then why are we here?"

Huffing from exertion under Colt's weight and the pull of the Ark, I paused and set my end down. Pointing up range, I said, "See that opening? That's Elijah's cave. It's the place where he hid from Jezebel and the place where he heard the still small voice of God."

Simon peered upward toward the small opening. "Yes, I see it."

"I do too," Colt said, pointing excitedly at the dark opening in the side of the mountain. "I hope there are no bats in there. I hate bats."

"Now you're sounding like me," I said, patting the boy on his shoulder. "Let's go and find out." Grabbing the rods, we began a slow march up the rocky path with Colt trailing behind.

After thirty minutes of climbing, they reached the mouth of the cave. We stopped to catch our breath and Colt handed me a bottle of water he'd taken before we left. After taking several long pulls, I wiped off the top and handed it to Simon. He finished it off in four swigs and handed the empty bottle to Colt.

"Sorry for drinking it all. I was just so thirsty."

Colt produced a second bottle and twisted off the cap. "That's okay, I brought along another."

Simon and I exchanged surprised looks. "The kid's got moxie," Simon said with a wry smile.

We stood on the cliff for a moment admiring the vista. "And to think, Moses once stood right here. Just look at that view." I said, inhaling the thin air.

After a few more minutes, Colt stepped closer and

peered into the cave. "It looks spooky."

Hand to my chest, I knelt and followed his gaze. "It's just big enough for us to get in. Let's hope we can get the Ark in without it bumping against the walls." As I spoke, my voice faded into the darkness.

Simon barely had time to catch his breath before I tugged him forward, but I was anxious to get out of sight as quickly as possible. Once inside the cooler air prickled my skin. "That's better. Let's see how far we can go."

Using the end of my staff which glowed like a lantern, Colt guided us deeper.

"I want to take this to the heart of the mountain and leave it there. It is too powerful to fall into the hands of the wrong people. Just look at what trouble that man, St. John caused. He had the world believing him to be the savoir of the world." As I spoke, a low rumble shook the ground beneath my feet. Memories of the Witch's Cave flashed across my memory causing me to stumble backward.

"I don't like the sound of that," Colt said, his eyes rounding. "It reminds me of—"

"Don't say it. This is a holy mountain. We'll be safe, just keep going." My confidence waned, but I knew this was the right thing to do.

Glancing around, I saw evidence that the furry creatures had lived there, but I saw none of them at the time. What I did see was the remains of several smaller animals. Their bones had been picked clean. It was obvious we were not the first to visit this cave in recent times. That thought concerned me. *What if someone stumbled onto our secret? What if, like the Dead Sea Scrolls, some inquisitive goat herder got nosy and discovered the Ark's hiding place ... what then?* I shuttered at the thought that Israel's treasure would fall into the hands of the wrong person, again. Shaking off my concerns, I pushed on.

The further we went, the louder the rumbling became. It was like the earth welcomed a long-awaited friend. Finally, we reached the deepest chamber. Were it not for the light from my staff, we would have wandered in darkness for hours. But now we had reached the end of our journey.

"What are we going to do now?" Simon asked, huffing from exertion.

Turning, I took a few steps back. "We are going to leave the Ark until God sees fit to reveal it."

"But the temple, the sacrifices, Israel itself—"

"I know Simon. The Ark of God at one time held the center of Israel's attention, but we as New Testament believers have something better. The Ark was the place where the atonement was made."

"Yes, on the Day of Atonement."

"Right, but Christ, as our sin-bearer, didn't enter into the earthly Holy of Holies made with human hands, but into the one in heaven and appeared in the presence of God on our behalf. And it wasn't done as it was on earth, where the high priest had to repeat the sacrifice year after year. But he offered His own blood once for all thus ending the dispensation of Law, and canceling its penalty of sin by his own sacrifice. Just as it is appointed for a man to die once, so Christ offered Himself once for all. So actually, as much as I appreciate the Ark and all it represents, to be perfectly honest with you, it isn't necessary, not any longer."

Simon considered my words for a moment. Then, with slow deliberation, began to nod his head. "Yes, it all makes sense. I can see it now. The Law and Commandments were just guideposts ... pointing us to the Messiah, Christ the anointed One."

Suddenly, the earth shook throwing us to the uneven floor. Fearing the worst, I called over the roar, "We have to get out of here. This place is about to cave in."

"But what about the Ark?" Simon pleaded. "It will be destroyed."

"Leave it. Get out of here. God has protected it for the last two thousand years. He will continue to do so, now run."

A deafening roar filled the cavern. Causing me to hold my hands over my ears and run. By now, Colt and I had backed out of the chamber. The earth shook violently, and large rocks began to fall causing us to duck for cover.

"Get going, Colt." I called over the rumbling.

"No, Mr. Gasper, I'm not leaving you." He grabbed me by the hand and tugged.

Suddenly, the ceiling collapsed separating us from Mr. Levi. The air became unbreathable and the light dimmed to a dusty brown.

"Simon." My pleas were drowned out in the cacophony.

Rocks continued to tumble, forcing me back. "Simon, can you hear me?"

Simon's muffled cry was barely audible. "I'm okay, I can hear you, but it's dark."

Trying desperately to remove the rocks, Colt and I began to dig through the rubble, but another collapse sent us scrambling to safety.

"Simon, can you hear me?"

"Yes, but you must get to safety. Leave me. I'd rather die with the Ark of God than live with its secret."

"Nooo!" Colt hollered, tears soaking his muddy face.

I threw my arms around him and held him close to keep him from getting injured. It was true … we were never going to dig him out. It must have been God's plan from the beginning. Either way, we had to get out. Clutching my staff in one hand and Colt in the other, we struggled over fallen boulders and gaping crevices back to the mouth of the cave. As we cleared it, the earth again shook; sealing the cave like a tomb.

Slumping down, Colt began to cry. "I keep losing friends. Balthazar, Melchior, Sasha, now Mr. Levi."

It broke my heart to hear the boy's cry. I too had lost much, but I had also gained much more. I found my grandfather, saved the Ark of God from falling into the hands of evil men, and rescued Colt. Kneeling next to him, I looked him in the eyes. "Colt, your mom and dad would be so proud of you. Your courage saved dozens of people's lives, and I am proud of you. Now you must be brave. You have a life ahead of you filled with new friends, new adventures, and new challenges. And you have me ... so say we all?"

Colt swiped his sleeve across his soaked eyes smearing it with sandy mud. "So say we all," his boyish voice cracked with emotion.

Deep inside the chamber, Simon leaned against the pile of rocks, which blocked his escape. This was now to be his resting place, his tomb, the door to eternity. At first, he feared, but then the chamber blazed with light.

Shielding his eyes with his forearm, Simon shrank back, fearing for his life.

"Simon, Simon, I am Prince Azrael. Fear not."

The light faded to a dim glow as the angel knelt down and helped the quaking man to a rock to sit upon. Feeling strengthened by the angel's touch, Simon tried to relax.

"I see you have brought the Ark of God to its new resting place." Prince Azrael said as he peered at the treasure.

Unsure whether he was dreaming or dying, Simon asked, "Am I being punished?"

"No, no, Simon, on the contrary, you have done well. The Almighty has not seen fit to allow the Temple's completion and without this," he dipped his head toward the Ark, "the temple will not be complete."

"But I thought the man of sin had come and led Israel into a false peace."

"Indeed, there are many who will come in that day saying I am he. Others will say he is here, or he is there, but believe them not. As the All-Knowing One said to Daniel the Beloved, many shall run to and fro, and knowledge shall be increased. Many shall be purified and made white and tried, but the wicked shall do wickedly, and none of the wicked shall understand; however, the wise will understand. Blessed is he who waits. But go thy way, you shall rest and stand in your place in the end of day."

Azrael's words brought peace to Simon's anxious heart. Leaning back, he said, "One thing I desire of the Lord, that I may dwell in the house of the Lord all the days of my life, to behold the beauty of the Lord, and to enquire in His temple. I have sought for this treasure all my adult life, and now I have come to realize it was all in vain." Tears welled in his eyes and he began to sob.

Again, the angel's touch warmed his broken spirit and Simon took a halting breath. "It just occurred to me, God doesn't dwell in temples made with hands. He desires my body to be a living temple, my heart to be the altar and my life to be spent in His service." Cradling his chin in his hands, Simon sighed heavily. "What a wasted life."

"No, Simon your life has not been wasted. Misspent maybe, but certainly not wasted."

"All I ever wanted to do was reclaim Israel's rich heritage."

"That is a good desire, and you have. Behold ..." Azrael lifted the corner of the tarp, and a golden light filled the chamber.

Simon's eyes danced with joy as the blazing light enshrouded him. As he exhaled for the last time, he inhaled celestial air. Hand in hand with his Savior, he skipped down the streets of glory, kicking up small swirls of gold dust.

Chapter Forty-Five

While we were gone the fuel reached a bare electrical wire. Within minutes, the fuel caught fire and spread to the drums. The blast leveled the hangar and would have obliterated the airplane, the Ark and everyone within a quarter mile of the place. Had Captain Dunbar not followed my instructions, many lives would have been lost. Fortunately, he and the others had retrieved St. John's body before moving the aircraft a safe distance from the hanger.

Knowing how dangerous it would be to return to the burning hangar, I wisely decided to reappear some distance away from the potential danger. It was a good thing I did.

In the distance, I could hear the jet engines purring in the background as Captain Dunbar, and the others waited for our return. As abruptly as we disappeared, Colt and I reappeared and stepped around the backside of the airplane. We were met with worried expressions.

"Where did you go? We thought you were blown up in the explosion. And where is your friend ... Mr. Levi?" Abdullah asked.

I glanced over my shoulder and then back. "We needed to take the Ark somewhere safe for the time being and he decided to stay with it for a while longer and guard it. You know how those Jews are ... very passionate."

Abdullah patted my shoulder. "Aren't we all, my friend, aren't we all."

After waiting for Colt to ascend the stairs, I turned to my friend. "Aren't you coming?"

Abdullah shook his head. "No, someone has to stay and pull the stairs back. Anyway, where would I go? I have a family to care for, a temple to build. You know how we Palestinians are ... very passionate ... about my faith, that is."

"You're not going to immigrate to America?"

The big Palestinian glanced at his men and back to me. "Maybe, it's in God's hands."

Once inside the aircraft, the exhausted passengers strapped themselves in and prepared for the long flight home. Within minutes, the Boeing 737 with UN markings on its tail-fin was airborne. Captain Dunbar barely had time to get the wheels up when a pair of Israeli fighter jets closed in around him. With the border between his aircraft and international waters being twelve miles ahead, he hoped he could stall them. By now, his aircraft had reached five hundred miles an hour and was racing against time. At that speed, we could be out of their jurisdiction in less than five minutes.

"This is Commander Benjamin Levi with the Israeli Air force, please identify yourself."

Dunbar gave his co-pilot a nervous glance. "Commander Levi, this is Captain Dunbar. We are flying under UN colors. We request permission to leave Israeli airspace."

Four minutes, thirty seconds.

"Commander Dunbar, we have no flight plan for a departing aircraft flying in UN colors. Please return to Tel Aviv International Airport for landing instructions."

Three minutes, ten seconds.

"This is Captain Dunbar. Please be advised, this is a humanitarian flight sanctioned by the UN. We have the Secretary General on board and are en-route to New York, La Guardia International Airport. We request permission to leave your airspace."

Two minutes, five seconds.

The jets backed away and assumed an attack formation.

"Captain Dunbar. You have not received permission to leave our airspace. If you do not reduce your air speed and make an immediate right turn, we will be forced to shoot you down."

One minute, thirty seconds.

As the exchange between the commander of the Israeli fighter jet and Captain Dunbar continued, I and the other passengers craned our necks to catch a glimpse of the jets up close. They were impressive to say the least, but I knew they were not there to be admired. They were there to enforce international law, which we were about to break.

I stepped to the galley outside the cockpit, but a moment before I knocked, movement caught my attention, arresting my hand. As gentle as a dove, an angel appeared just out of sight of the passengers. He gave me a respectful bow.

"Hail, greatly beloved one."

I took a hard swallow. "Who are you and what are you doing on this plane?"

The angel seemed amused at my sudden outburst.

"My name is Prince Azrael, I have been following your movements from the day you stepped into Israel. It was I who caused the stack of limestones to topple over. I have been standing guard over young Colt as well. Now I have come to give you a special message."

I eyed him with suspicion. From what I knew, God communicated with his servants through His Word, and the Holy Spirit. Getting a special message from an angel was the basis for many cults. Weary, I crossed my arms over my chest. "I must warn you, God's word commands us not to believe an angel if what he says contradicts God's word."

Prince Azrael nodded. A broad smile parted his lips. "That's not exactly how it goes, but I get it. Let me assure you, I am just a ministering spirit, sent here to minister to the heirs of salvation."

Relieved, I softened my stance. "I saw you in the hangar, didn't I?"

The angel nodded. "Yes, that was me."

"You did a pretty good job taking care of the big black demon. Weren't you the least bit frightened?"

Prince Azrael shook his head. "Satan's forces are defeated foes. We battle from a position of victory. He was never a real threat to you or your young charge."

I could barely believe my ears. I was actually having a conversation with an angel. "So what message do you have, my ministering friend?"

"You will arrive at your destination safely."

Stroking my chin, I eyed him with interest. "Not bad,

but I've read better from a Fortune Cookie."

Prince Azrael's eyebrows hiked up. "Okay, let me be more specific, but you're about to leave my jurisdiction, and I'm running out of time." Glancing around as if he were a junior boy about to play a prank on some unsuspecting girl, he tried again, "Those pilots will not shoot you down."

"Too vague," I said.

Frustrated, the angel furrowed his brow and pinched his lips together. "Okay, okay, but you're pushing me. "That pilot, the one flying the lead jet? He is Jacob and Simon Levi's nephew. If you mention you know the Levis, he might let you go."

"Might? That's kinda thin, don't you think?"

The angel stole a glance over his shoulder. "All right, but you can't tell him where you got this information. Promise?"

I formed the Boy Scout's sign. "I promise."

The angel cleared his throat. Why, I didn't know. "Commander Benjamin Levi's wife, oh, what's her name?" scratching his head, he paused to think, while the seconds ticked by. "Oh yes, her name is Leah. She is going to have twins next year. Tell him that, it will buy you enough time."

I was incredulous. "Enough time? For what?"

Glancing over his shoulder, he squinted and nodded. "Oops, I must be on my way."

He was gone in an instant, and I sucked in a sharp breath. Still shaken by my encounter, I knocked lightly on the cockpit door.

"It's Gasper, let me in," I said through strained lips.

"Unlock the door," I heard Dunbar tell his co-pilot.

As I stepped inside the tight space, I heard the tail end of an intense conversation. "This is Commander Levi, I have authorization to shoot you down if you don't respond to my order."

Leaning forward, I got Captain Dunbar's attention. "Could I speak to the commander of the Israeli jet tracking us?"

"Why?"

"I gotta hunch, please, if you will indulge me."

"This is very unorthodox, you know."

I nodded. "Yes, but if you don't, we might be swimming back to the United States ... I have to try."

Captain Dunbar handed the microphone to me, then flipped the switch, so he could hear. "Go ahead."

Palms slick with anxiety, I toggled the microphone. "Commander Levi, this is Gasper, advisor to kings, potentates and men seeking truth. Are you a truth seeker?"

After a moment's pause, he responded. "Yes, but you must turn that aircraft around, immediately."

"Yes, of course, you wouldn't happen to be Jacob and Simon Levi's nephew, would you?"

Seconds ticked. I crossed my fingers, which I almost never did, but I was getting desperate.

"Yes, why?"

I smiled "Your uncles are fine men. Simon actually is responsible for locating your country's national treasure. We just left him. He and the Ark of God are safe."

One minute and counting.

"That is wonderful to know, but I have my orders. Now turn that aircraft around," the commander responded.

Fifteen seconds ticked by.

My mind raced. I had to play my last card. "Your wife Leah, will have twins next year."

Silence filled the connection as another fifteen seconds eeked by.

"How did you know my wife's name?" And how do you know we will have twins?"

"Commander, I am a wise man, and have knowledge of the future. Now I implore you, let us pass." My comment reminded me of my encounter with the Witch of Endor so many years ago. I just hoped the outcome would be better.

"Look, I appreciate your prophesy, but I need you to slow your air speed and turn right, or I will be forced to fire upon you. Please respond."

We were down to fifteen seconds, and out of options.

"Those Israeli pilots aren't fooling around. They're going to fire upon us," the co-pilot sputtered.

Captain Dunbar's shoulders sagged. "Your stalling tactic didn't work, Mr. Gasper. We had less than a mile to go, but with the kind of weaponry those Israeli jets are carrying, they could easily shoot us down in seconds. Time has run out."

Five seconds.

Gripping my staff, I looked at the captain. "Sir, get ready for the ride of your life." Then I focused and blinked.

Chapter Forty-Six

Static filled the onboard speakers, then cleared. "This is La Guardia's air-traffic control. You have entered US airspace, please respond."

Captain Dunbar and his co-pilot gaped at me. "What just happened?"

I handed him the microphone. "Let's just say you had a strong tailwind. Shall I prepare the passengers for landing?"

He glanced at his co-pilot who wore a broad grin. Hands raised, he said, "Don't ask me, I'm just here for the ride."

Dunbar pushed his cap back and scratched his forehead. "Go ahead, but later, I need to talk to you about a few things."

By the time we landed, a gaggle of media personnel had gathered at the gate to welcome us. Cameras flashed, and recording devices rolled as members of all the major news outlets vied for position. As scores of questions flew at us, Amber, in her usual calm demeanor, stepped to the bank of microphones and addressed the crowd.

"My name is Amber Kline, the UN Secretary General's press secretary. As you know, the Secretary General went to Israel for a summit meeting with many of the world's major religions. It was his vision to unite them in one common purpose … to eliminate the differences which have caused so much strife in the world. Having discovered Israel's Ark of the Covenant, it was his plan to establish a new covenant based on peace and mutual respect for all peoples.

But as he stepped forward to proclaim the beginning of the golden age, he came in contact with an unground electrical wire. Sadly, he suffered a massive jolt of electricity and died instantly. He was a great man, and we will all mourn his passing."

"That's not exactly how it happened," Colt whispered. Standing in the back of the group of passengers who'd made the miraculous journey, he eyed Amber as she continued with the press conference.

"I know," I replied, "but people wouldn't believe the truth if she told them. They were convinced he was the savior of the world."

Amber's explanation wasn't the best, but since the shock wave knocked out all recording devices, it was her word against the few of us who survived, and we weren't talking.

After a chorus of questions, she continued. "Yes, there was an electric shock wave which temporally knocked out our communication. And yes, I have a photograph of Israel's national treasure which I will make available as soon as I get the film developed."

More questions.

"No, Israel's Ark will not be put on display. You have to understand, at that time, we were facing several groups of armed militants all vying for power. The moment Mr. St. John died, we were attacked. My team and I took cover as the gunfire broke out all around us. When the fighting subsided, the Ark was gone. Someone must have taken it moments before the building we were in exploded. I'm confident the Israelis will find and reclaim it, but for the time being, it remains lost to the world along with a great leader."

As she spoke, she allowed a single tear to form in the corner of her eye and trickle down her cheek. Slowly and with great drama, she swiped it aside. Taking a shaky breath, she continued. "It was all we could do to get out of the Gaza Strip before another war broke out."

A dozen hands shot up followed by questions about the Ark, the future of the Unity Accord, peace, war and more. Amber fielded them like a pro. "I'll take one more question," she finally said.

"What about the Secretary General's body? Were you able to recover it?" a reporter asked.

"That's two." She offered the camera her best smile. "Yes, Mr. Jacque de Molay St. John's body was recovered. While I can't speak for the General Assembly, I'm sure there will be a state funeral in which the world will be able to express their condolences. As for me and those of us who survived the ordeal, I can say his life was an inspiration to us all."

More questions.

Turning, she strode in our direction, while calls for Captain Dunbar to address the crowd of news hungry reporters continued.

"An inspiration to us all?" I questioned.

"That's the best I could come up with. Besides, what was I to say? The man was a shyster?"

I had to agree. Sometimes the truth was better left unsaid.

"I want to thank you for all you did?" She said as we

escaped down a deserted corridor.

Feeling my face redden I offered her a pathetic, "Awe, twas nothing' ma'am."

Colt rolled his eyes.

"How can I ever make it up to you? You saved our lives back there." As she spoke, she edged closer.

Colt, clearly not comfortable with her advances, stepped next to me. "My father, can we go home now, pleeeze!" An impish twinkle danced in his eyes, and I knew what he was up to.

My mind raced for a quick come back. I didn't need her accolades. I just wanted to get home, and I knew Colt did too. Then I had an idea. "You know that picture of the Ark you took?"

Stepping back. "Yes, why?"

"Remember Mr. Abdullah Hasad, the man who led the Lehi group?" I asked.

Again, she answered with a questioning look.

"The Israeli government promised him, that if he could help them find the Ark, they would help him immigrate to the United States. Could you use your position with the UN to influence the Israelis and the Palestinians to honor their commitment?"

Amber bit the corner of her thumbnail. "I have an idea." Turning, she began a determined stride back the way we came.

"Where are you going?" I called after her.

"I have a plane to catch. I'm flying back to Israel, there's a man named Abdullah Hasad, I want to interview." She smiled and waved as she turned the corner.

I felt a tug on my sleeve and glanced down. It was

Colt. "Do you think we'll ever see Mr. Hasad again?"

Walking along the concourse, I thought a minute. "You never know. Nothing so far has turned out like we'd planned. It wouldn't surprise me if one day very soon, he and his family showed up in Georgia."

"You mean, Georgia, as in 'Georgia, Georgia, the whole night through, just an old sweet song keeps Georgia on my mind.'"

By the time he'd finished we were standing outside North Hamilton Bible Church humming the lines of the old song. I inhaled the fresh, clean Georgia mountain air, savoring the moment. "It smells like home."

Colt's nose wrinkled. "Home? I thought India was your home."

Looking at his upturned face, I shook my head and patted the lad on the shoulder. "No, not any more. I may have grown up in India, but this is home now. No more world traveling, blinking here and there. I plan on settling down, marrying Felicia, if she'll have me, raise a family and help my community."

As we stood outside the church, Colt turned serious. "I saw them." His flat tone and cryptic statement left me wondering.

"Saw who?"

He tipped his face upward as if counting the stars. "The angels, thousands of them."

"You did? Where?"

He gave a boyish shrug. "I don't know ... in the airplane hangar, all around us when we were leaving Israel, even now. They're everywhere."

Feeling conspicuous, I glanced around. I saw no one, but felt a presence like none other. "You have a rare sense of the spiritual. I knew they were with us in the battles, but I never actually saw them. Then again, there was that time in the airplane hangar, and in the aircraft's galley—"

Colt's face beamed.

"What?" It was like he knew something I didn't.

"They're talking about you."

He could hear them? How could he? I stood in amazement. "Whoa, what are they saying?" I stuttered.

He shifted his gaze and broke into a belly laugh. Between gulps of air, he tried to speak. Finally, he gained control and said, "I was just pulling your leg."

I felt my face redden and looked at my leg, then back at Colt. "I didn't ... oh, I get it." But he didn't fool me. I knew he'd overheard the angels speaking. They must have said something he wasn't supposed to hear, I guessed. "Let's start the next chapter of our lives, shall we?"

He nodded and blinked.

Chapter Forty-Seven

For the people of North Hamilton Bible Church, Christmas was a blur. The usual pageantry surrounding the Christmas season didn't hold the ambiance of the past. With their attention riveted on the controversy over Christ's Second coming, they paid little attention to His first coming. And rather than having large crowds of onlookers for their Live Nativity, many nights they closed down early due to lack of interest. It seemed the entire world waited to learn the outcome of the summit meeting in Israel.

News of St. John's demise had not yet reached the small community of North Hamilton, and Pastor Wyatt arrived early Sunday morning to put the final touches on a message he believed would be his last. As Pastor Wyatt got out of his car and made his way to the office, a gaggle of reporters stood nearby ready to snatch any comment he might give them.

"Pastor Wyatt, have you heard the news about the Secretary General?"

"Can you comment about the latest developments on the Middle-East?"

Ignoring their questions, he hurried past them and entered his office through a side door. As he walked by the copy machine, he noticed a couple sheets of paper he'd overlooked when he left the previous day. He lifted them from the tray and began to read the lines.

Forty-five minutes later, the auditorium was abuzz with activity. Ushers hurriedly placed folding chairs down the aisles and across the back of the auditorium to accommodate the swelling crowd, Glenn and Karen squeezed in and found three seats next to the pastor's wife close to the front. The lines around Angela's eyes spoke of the strain she felt over the last three or four days.

Karen gave her a warm hug. "We have been praying for you guys. I know it must be hard."

Angela sniffed back a tear. "You have no idea. Scott has been bombarded with phone calls from pastors from all over the country, and angry church members. They feel betrayed. Some are even talking about—" her throat closed with emotion.

"Glenn leaned over. "Why are people so quick to judge? Pastor Wyatt is only trying to rightly divide God's Word."

Angela nodded and put on a brave smile. "That's just it; people have been slicing and dicing the Word of God for centuries; all to justify their private interpretation. By the time they get done, the true meaning of what God said is lost and we are left wondering who is right."

Glenn leaned closer. "Let God be true and every man a liar. That's what I have to say." His comment, though true, didn't calm Angela's jitters.

"By the way, has anyone seen or heard from Felicia?" Karen asked, glancing around the auditorium. "I've been trying to reach out to her since yesterday and this morning and haven't been able to get an answer."

Jacob, who was sitting directly behind Karen, leaned forward. "I can answer that. She's run into a bit of trouble with her Visa. She had to make a quick trip to Atlanta to get it straightened out."

As the music started, the women exchanged worried looks. Then they settled back and sat stone-faced in support of their pastor, husband and friend.

Taking his place behind the podium, Pastor Wyatt began in a solemn tone. "This morning I want to share with you the result of my spiritual journey into end time prophecy. Let me begin by saying, no two theologians agree on most points. If you get three preachers in the same room, you will have four opinions when it comes to the future." A series of chuckles broke the tense moment.

Using his laptop, he began to enumerate the most readily accepted views. "From my study of I Corinthians, and I Thessalonians and even Revelation 4, I believe that the church will be removed from this earth before the Tribulation begins." A scattering of sighs wafted through the auditorium.

"But now, we have a problem. According to scripture, the Antichrist will lead the nation of Israel to sign a peace agreement which will last seven years. This will not only usher in a period of great environmental catastrophes, but also God's divine judgment. At the same time, or at least during the first half of the seven-year treaty, Israel will have world favor and will be granted permission to rebuild the temple. We are seeing this unfold right before our eyes. So I have to ask myself. Am I wrong? Have I misinterpreted scripture all these years? Have I been teaching heresy since becoming a minister of the gospel?"

As he posed the questions, different individuals called out, "No!"

Scott flipped his Bible open to a passage he'd prepared to read. Reading I Thessalonians from his Plain English Bible, he began, "Now about the days and times, it isn't necessary for me to write to you because you know that the day of the Lord will come as a thief, at night. And while peace and safety are commonly accepted, suddenly destruction will come just as an expectant woman's birth pains do, and they will not escape. Nevertheless, you are not to be deceived that this day should surprise you."

Turning to a secondary passage, he continued, "In I Corinthians 15:51 and 52, the Word of God says, 'Look, I tell you a mystery. We will not all sleep, or die, but we will all be changed. We will be changed in an instant, like the twinkle of an eye, at the last trumpet sound. For the trumpet will sound with a loud blast, and the dead will rise up first as immortals, and we will be changed."

Pausing, he scanned the group for his wife's smiling face. Seeing her glistening eyes, he winked and continued. "I read these first to lay a foundation. We learn from these that Jesus' return is imminent, meaning … it could happen at any time. Next, it is unexpected. And third, it will happen in an instant. But we still don't know if that will happen before or after the tribulation begins." He paused to let his words sink in.

"After doing much study and comparison between the primary views Bible students have taken on this point, I believe I have good news for you. We are cautioned in I Thessalonians not to be deceived. So what are we to think about this man named Jacque de Molay St. John? Is he the Antichrist or just another despot seeking power?" He waited, no one answered. "Okay, let's examine one other passage which gives us great hope. In II Thessalonians 2:2-4, the King James Version stated it so beautifully this way. 'That ye be not soon shaken in mind, or be troubled, neither by spirit, nor by word, nor by letter as from us, as that the day of Christ is at hand. Let no man deceive you by any means: for that day shall not come, except there first come a falling away, and that man of sin be revealed, the son of perdition; who opposeth and exalteth himself above all that is called God, or that is worshiped; so that he as God setteth in the temple of God, showing himself that he is God.'"

Pulling a folded sheet of paper from the fly cover of his Bible, he flattened it out. "Yesterday, I received this fax from Bro. Gasper, but I just discovered it this morning." He waved it for all to see. "It is very revealing. It seems Mr. St. John is not exactly who he says he is. The evidence I am holding in my hand reveals this man's shady past, and his associations put a big question mark over his motives toward the state of Israel. So what am I saying? I am saying, this guy isn't the Antichrist. He's just another power-hungry politician. That's what Paul was telling us, not to be deceived by the news of the day. Jesus will come first, then the man of sin will be revealed. After that, he will lead Israel to sign a seven-year peace treaty."

Encouraged, by the church's "amens", Pastor Wyatt pressed on. "Secondly, he led Israel to sign an agreement called the Unity Accord. I might add this accord does not mention anything about seven years. That being said, it does grant Israel permission to rebuild the temple in exchange for them giving away a large portion of their land."

Glenn's hand shot up causing scores of eyes to turn his direction. "Plus, we are still here."

Another round of nervous laughter broke the wire-tight atmosphere.

"Yes, that is true. So, let's examine the scripture and see what God says on the topic." For the next forty-five minutes, Pastor Wyatt listed scripture in their respective contexts and gave the historical background to each point. He saved his most powerful passage for last. As the morning came to a close, he read from I Thessalonians 1:10. "'And to wait for his Son from heaven, whom he raised from the dead, even Jesus, which delivered us from the wrath to come.' Skipping down to chapter 5:9, he read 'For God has not appointed us to wrath,' that is the wrath to come, but to obtain salvation by our Lord Jesus Christ.'

In the Book of the Revelation, 4:1, 'After this I looked and behold, a door was opened in heaven: and the first voice which I heard was like a trumpet talking with me; which said, Come up here.' From that point forward, we don't read about the church until the Marriage Supper of the Lamb. After that, the church, robed in white and sitting on white horses, will follow their conquering King as he returns to earth to set up his kingdom.

I direct your attention to one other passage. It's found in Second Thessalonians 2:6-8. 'And now who restrains that he might be revealed in his time. For the mystery of iniquity is already at work: only he who restrains will do so until he is taken out of the way. And then shall that wicked one be revealed whom the Lord shall consume with the spirit of his mouth, and shall destroy with the brightness of his coming.'

Brothers and sisters, what we have witnessed is, you might call, a near miss. Not all the pieces of the puzzle were in place for it to be the middle of the tribulation. The Rapture hasn't occurred. We didn't miss it. The Tribulation hasn't started. This man, Jacque de Molay St. John was just another impostor like so many deceivers who've come in the past and will come in the future. My admonition to you is, be ready, be watching and be witnessing."

The congregation stood and began to sing in spontaneous celebration. After weeks of emotional and spiritual testing, the people of North Hamilton Bible Church were finally ready to celebrate the Christmas season.

As they filed from the sanctuary, a flurry of activity interrupted the flow of people. Ripples of laughter sprang from the foyer as the congregation gathered around a couple of people.

Chapter Forty-Eight

S tanding in the church foyer, Colt and I peered through the glass windows into the auditorium at a full house. Pastor Wyatt held court behind the plexiglass pulpit with a number of Bible passages on the big screens. As he brought his sermon to a close, the congregation sprang to their feet, and began to sing the Doxology. Then they broke out in thunderous applaud. The moment was so palpable we couldn't help but join in. Singing at the top of our lungs, we smiled and hugged.

"Looks like we got here right on time," Colt said, his face beaming with joy. "I can't wait to see mom and dad."

As the music faded, the church people continued to hug each other passionately. Holding hands, they formed small circles and began to dance and sing. It was a celebration like none other.

We remained in the foyer, not wanting to intrude in their joy, knowing the moment they saw us, their attention would immediately be diverted from celebrating the Lord's victory to us. After several minutes, however, the singing subsided and the people began to file out. Suddenly, a face appeared in the crowd.

"Colt!" Karen O'Dell's voice rang out across the foyer.

Hearing her call his name, I glanced up and saw

Glenn and Karen pushing through the crowd with the pastor and his wife close behind. Karen scooped Colt up in her arms and began swinging him in circles, much to the delight of the onlookers.

Suddenly, we were encircled with a host of people patting our backs and shaking our hands. The welcome seemed to go on forever. My cheeks ached from smiling, and my hand was worn out from shaking hands. The one moment which brought a dark cloud was when someone asked where Balthazar and Melchior were. I hated to break the bad news at such a joyous occasion, but the truth be known, they were heroes and needed to be celebrated as such. I inhaled and looked at Colt for support.

"Balthazar and Melchior gave their lives defending Colt and me. We were attacked by a force of overwhelming strength. I received a severe wound and was bleeding badly. Melchior used the last of his energy to heal me. Balthazar demonstrated extreme courage when facing a demon from Hell itself. It was he who stood between me and death and gave his life in service of his Lord."

As the crowd of well-wishers grew silent, Colt took to the center of the foyer. "Mr. Balthazar and Mr. Melchior were the bravest and wisest men on earth. Without their courage, I would not be here, so let's celebrate their lives not mourn their passing."

At that, the people began another round of singing, albeit muted. As the singing subsided, we began to unpack the story of our most recent journey. I personally enjoyed Colt's rendition better than mine. His details of what took place in the airplane hangar chilled me. He had come so close to being killed. Then I remembered his statement about seeing the angels, and I knew he was never in real danger. He was as safe as an insect in a roll of carpet, or something like that.

In the excitement of the moment, it suddenly dawned on me; there was one face I had not seen. "Where is Felicia?" I asked, scanning the crowd.

Glenn and Karen exchanged worried glances. "I guess you haven't heard."

"Heard? Heard what Glenn? I just got here, and you might say, I've been a bit out of touch." My mind raced. *What could have become of Felicia? Had something tragic taken place and they didn't want to be the bearers of bad news at such a joyous occasion? Had she found another man?* I braced myself for the worse ... yet hoped for the best.

"I can address that." It was Jacob Myers. The crowd parted and he stood, hands in his pockets, looking concerned. "Yesterday, I got a call from Miss Beauchamp. She, as you know, is a foreign exchange teacher from France."

I indicated this was old news.

"Well, it seems she overstayed her Visa and got caught. I recommended she consult an immigration attorney, but first she needed to report to the USICS down in Atlanta as soon as possible."

My heart raced at hearing I might lose her. Yet I knew it was all in God's hands. If I was willing to go half way around the world to stop an awful deed from taking place, I was certainly willing to go to France to solidify what I knew in my heart ... that I loved Felicia and wanted to spend the rest of my life with her.

"Do you have the address of the USICS?"

Cindy, who had followed the conversation intently, spoke up. "Yes, I just googled it and wrote it on this …" She handed me a tithe envelope with an address hastily scribbled on the back of it.

"Do you need a ride to Atlanta?" Jacob asked.

I glanced at Colt. He winked and I knew what he was thinking, but disappearing in front of all these people would certainly raise a lot of questions, ones I'd rather not have to answer … at least not now. "Yes, I think I'd like that. On the way to Atlanta, I can tell you about your uncle. He was a great man."

Concern darkened Jacob's face as all of us stepped from the auditorium. "Except for making arrangements to send you guys to Israel, Simon and I haven't spoken since I trusted Christ as my Savior. You see, he and I have not been on speaking terms."

I nodded, Simon had confided in me and said as much. "You will be happy to know Melchior led him to the foot of the cross, and he was gloriously saved. The changes in his life were remarkable."

Tears welled in Jacob's eyes. "It has been my prayer since my conversion that he, and all Israel would come to the knowledge of their Messiah."

Patting him on the back, I smiled. "Keep praying."

Chapter Forty-Nine

Felicia hated missing church, especially at such a pivotal time. She had as many questions as everyone else and wanted to know where the pastor stood on the issue of Christ's return and the Rapture. *I guess I'll just have to watch the podcast later today,* she mused.

Not being experienced at driving through heavy traffic, she was relieved it was Sunday, and the roads were somewhat clearer. Having to navigate through two mazes, however, left her head swirling. Finally, she found the Office of Immigration and Checkpoints and parked. To her shock, she saw a line of people as varied as the rainbow extending out the door and down the sidewalk. Discouraged, she slumped to a nearby bench. "This is going to take forever," she muttered to herself.

All at once, an elderly woman from somewhere south of the border took a seat next to her. "You would think they were conducting Mass inside, by the length of the line."

Felicia gave the woman a weary smile. "It looks more like a mass exodus, if you asked me." As she spoke the dam behind her eyes broke and tears flooded her eyes.

"I'll bet you wouldn't be so upset were it not for a young man in your life."

"Is it that obvious?"

Patting Felicia's hand, the women continued, "I was young once." As she spoke, a knowing twinkle sparkled in her eyes. "Tell ya what, follow your heart, it will never fail you." Straightening, she began to hum lightly.

"What is that song you are humming?" Felicia couldn't help her curiosity.

Smiling, the woman grew quiet and said.

"When a man wants to get a gal's affection,
He must get her to glance in his direction.
And then if he is smart, he will try to win her heart.
That's the only way to get a gal's affection.
If a lass wants to catch a man's attention,
She may use her wit to conceal her intention.
And once she has him lookin',
She can lure him with her cookin'.
If a lass wants to catch a man's attention."

Felicia chuckled at the woman's limerick. "Hmm, I'll keep that in mind if I ever get a chance to get my man's attention, so far, it seems I haven't been able to do that. At least not for long." she sighed heavily.

Felicia knew the longer she delayed the more her chances of not getting into the office grew. Taking a frustrated breath, she thanked the woman and stepped in line. When she glanced back to thank the woman, she was gone.

Focusing ahead, she was surprised at how quickly the line moved and within an hour, she was inside the building. She pulled a number from a dispenser and found her wait time to be approximately ten minutes. When it was called, she approached the glass window and handed the woman her Visa.

"I see you have overstayed your time in our country

by 178 days," her voice barely audible over the room noise.

"Yes, ma'am. I'm a teacher and was busy—"

The woman cut her off with a cold glare. "You were an exchange teacher, and you should have known better. Two more days and you would have been penalized. As it is, you can ask for an extension or apply for permanent citizenship, but you will need to leave the country for a few days and then return in order to do so."

Still fuming over her own stupidity, she asked, "How long before I can reapply?"

The woman thought a moment. "As I said, a few days, maybe a week. I have arranged to have you placed on a flight later today, so if you will kindly follow the officer, he has a van waiting to take you to Atlanta-Hartsfield Jackson International airport."

"But what about my car? I can't just leave it here."

The woman waved the next applicant forward. "It will be taken to impound. If and when you return, you can claim it using the information I handed you."

Felicia glanced at the folded papers the woman gave her. Turning, she grabbed what few personal belongings she'd brought and started for the door. Blinded by tears, to the danger that awaited her, she trudged across the lobby. As two men in dark suits closed in behind her, she dropped her purse, spilling its contents. The men held their positions while she knelt down.

This was not the place for a scene.

Heart aching and her vision blurred, Felicia stuffed the items in her purse and took another step. All at once a tall man stepped in front of her causing her to slam into him.

"Excusez-Moi." Her constricted throat barely allowed the words to escape.

"Vous etes excuse … you are excused." The man's French was impeccable.

She sniffed back a sob, and caught a familiar scent. Eyes glistening, she looked up, and found herself staring into Gasper's eyes.

In an instant, she squealed his name threw her arms around his neck. The next thing she knew, he had tipped her chin upward and warmed her lips with his.

Felicia's response communicated more than words could say, and she knew she had found her soulmate. Not wanting to release him, she held him close allowing the warmth from his body to radiate through her blouse, and into her throbbing heart.

"Oh, Gasper, how did you know where to find me?" She finally asked between halting sobs.

Gasper pulled back and looked into her eyes. "Jacob Myers told me all about your situation and brought me here. But even if he hadn't, I would have followed you to the ends of the earth."

His response brought on another round of kisses. "Gasper, how would you like to meet my parents?"

He held her gaze for a moment. "I'm not expected back at school for another week. So I think that is an excellent idea ... let's go."

After finding Jacob, they returned to his car and headed to the airport. They had a plane to catch, and a future to face together.

"What should we do, we can't just let her and that guy named Gasper slip through our fingers, can we?" Asked one of the two men who were assigned to snatch Felicia.

The lead operative glanced at his partner. "With the Secretary General no longer alive, that woman is no longer our problem. Let's get outta here before someone spots us."

As they sprinted for the van, a demure woman from somewhere south of the border emerged from around a large bush. "Going somewhere, gentlemen?" and then she let out a heart stopping scream.

Her cries for help brought a swift response as the police swarmed the two fleeing men. Within seconds, they were cuffed and the contents of their pockets emptied; guns, false identities, foreign currency et.al.

Satisfied his mission was completed ... Prince Uriel stepped back around the large bush. *That's what they get for messing with my charges,* he smiled and disappeared.

Chapter Fifty

In the weeks following the UN Secretary's demise, the earth shook with violent conflicts both in the physical and spiritual realms. As news of Jacque de Molay St. John's death spread, long held rivalries within the UN and around the world broke out. Radical Muslims, who felt disenfranchised in the peace process, began a fresh wave of attacks in major cities throughout Europe and the United States. Russia and China began to move against their neighbors threatening the fragile peace the world enjoyed during the Christmas season. It seemed the New Year would start with the world facing its darkest days.

Within the spirit realm, the scene was not much different, with one exception. The Almighty had not lost control of His kingdom. Everything was happening according to His sovereign, determinate will. Michael the Archangel's armies had been dispatched to hold back the dark forces controlling principalities, powers and wickedness in high places over the Middle-Eastern realms, while Prince Argos maintained control of the eastern regions of America.

After waiting several weeks for an answer, Prince Azrael broke through the cloudless sky and approached his commander.

"What say you, Prince Azrael? Has the tide of war

turned in our direction?"

Azrael dusted off some soot which he'd acquired while battling a particularly evil foe before breaking through to deliver his message. After straightening his robe and adjusting his sword, he squared his shoulders and spoke. "My Prince, I apologize for the delay, but I was held back for three weeks by the Prince of Europe. Thanks to Prince Raphael, I was able to break through. The answer to your question is yes. The tide has turned. The President of the United States, along with Prime Minister David ben Isakson have been in constant contact with the leaders of the PLO and worked out an agreement. All of the signers of the Unity Accord agreed to maintain its terms until a more permanent arrangement could be formed."

Prince Gabriel shifted his stance and eyed his emissary. "Hmm, I see," his resonant tone reverberated across the ethereal plains. "And have you any information as to what that agreement will entail?"

An impish twinkle danced in Prince Azrael's eyes. "You know as well as I, it is not for us to know the times or the seasons, which the Father has put in His own power."

Gabriel stretched out his hand and brushed some dirt from his messenger's shoulder and smiled. "Yes, I know. I was just wondering if you may have ... heard something."

"No, my lord ... only that all is well in the kingdom of earth as it is in Heaven."

Prince Gabriel nodded. "Thank you, Azrael, now return and strengthen the brethren."

As Prince Azrael turned to leave, Prince Gabriel

cleared his throat stopping his underling mid-stride. "And what is that in your back pocket?"

Azrael turned sheepishly and faced his commander amidst snickers from a group of towering mighty warriors. His face turning a slight shade of red as he pulled a roll of papers out from under his robe, he handed them to Prince Gabriel.

Scanning them, he handed them back. "I see you have taken it upon yourself to advance Mr. Abdullah and his family's departure from Israel."

Hands held in surrender, Prince Azrael took a step back. "Well, he was responsible, in a way, for the recovery of the Ark of God, and he helped bring his brother to justice. It's the least the State of Israel could do for him. And yes, I know he is a Palestinian, but he holds a dual citizenship which allowed him to work on the temple site. The Palestinians bureaucracy needed a little nudge for them to honor their promise. I'm simply moving the process along." His answer seemed to pacify his commander.

Stroking his chin, Gabriel nodded his head. "Yes, I see. And where, pray tell, is he and his family immigrating?"

Prince Azrael rolled the papers and stuffed them under his robe. "I hear North Hamilton, Georgia, is a great place to raise a family."

Smiling, the mighty angel couldn't help but ask, "You mean, 'Georgia—'" the words of the song barely left his lips before the angelic choir standing behind them broke out in song.

As the famous tune faded Prince Azrael's face grew sober. "My lord, was it necessary to bury the Ark?

Couldn't you have just left the cave open?"

Prince Gabriel tucked his chin and locked his fingers behind his back. "I knew Mr. Levi could not live with himself knowing the Ark was just miles from the Temple. He would have eventually let its location be known. It was the only way."

Nodding, Prince Azrael held his commander's gaze.

Finally, Gabriel broke the moment. "It was a kind thing you did; appearing to him and guiding him to Heaven's door. I am putting you in for a commendation."

The diminutive angel's face brightened. "A commendation? For what?"

Patting him on the back, Prince Gabriel spoke for all to hear. "For taking the initiative and going above and beyond your assignment."

Prince Azrael's chest swelled. "Thank you, my lord. I was just following your example and that of the Almighty's royal Son."

Chapter Fifty-One

After returning from meeting Felicia's parents and obtaining their blessing, she and I began to make wedding plans. It was bitter-sweet knowing Balthasar and Melchior would not be in attendance, but knowing they were in a better place.

In the months following our return, Colt and I sat for more interviews than we could count. It seemed he had captured the imagination of the media and public and had become the poster-child for fire-safety. I was very proud of the way he deflected praise; giving glory to God for protecting him through the fire in the Institute in Antiquities, and the events which unfolded following the Ark's discovery.

I, on the other hand, couldn't shake the feeling of loss over the deaths of my friends, Balthazar and Melchior. I found the only remedy was to focus on building a relationship with Felicia, and teaching and instructing Colt in the ways of wisdom. I hoped my days of adventure were over, with one exception … marrying Felicia. Getting to know her better and trying to understand the way she thought was probably the biggest adventure of my life.

She, however, had taken a deep interest in cooking, which I thought was curious. Before my departure, she showed little interest in the culinary arts, now all she did was cook.

One day, as Felicia and I exited the church after a pre-marital counseling session with Pastor Wyatt, we met Glenn, Karen and Colt O'Dell. They had arrived to begin work on this year's new project, a live Easter pageant complete with Roman soldiers and music. Felicia and I were heading the drama while the O'Dell's handled the staging and props. I, of course, had the lead solo part, playing Jesus. It was a daunting assignment, and I prayed I could do it justice.

"Glenn, you certainly know how to make Easter special," I observed.

Glenn ran his hand through his hair and nodded. "Since my near-death experience, Easter has become my favorite time of the year. You should see the yard display I'm planning."

Karen's knee-jerk response caused him to double over in laughter.

Hands held in surrender, he said, "Just kidding. I'm focusing all my attention on making the live Easter pageant the biggest event in the county."

I couldn't hide my mirth. Ever since getting out of the hospital, he was a new man. I especially enjoyed seeing the dramatic transformation take place in his life. To think about it, we all had seen a dramatic change since those early days in the O'Dell's attic.

Having saved Ashton from the White Witch, seeing Samantha come to know Christ as Savior along with her parents, Jacob and Cindy Myers ... it seemed a lifetime ago. And then there was that wild trip back to Israel. What a journey. The memories of the Temple of Endor, the fire in the Institute in Antiquities, Simon's conversion, Colt's rescue ... there were so many miracles. But it was worth it, knowing, at least for now, Satan and his dark forces had been defeated. Once again, the power of God and a united praying church had won the day.

While his parents headed down the narrow path leading to the make-believe village, I turned to Colt. "How are you enjoying normal life?"

He must have grown five inches and matured ten years since the first time I met him. There were lines around his eyes and a confidence in his stride I'd not seen in older men, let alone an adolescent. He too had changed ... had grown up. I hoped not too soon or too much. He needed to be a kid again, but having seen so much death and suffering, so much loss ... I wondered.

He looked at me with clear, wide eyes. "I don't think life will ever be normal for me again." Lowering his voice, he whispered, "I still see them."

I had guessed as much. "Are you okay with that? I mean, they aren't bothering you, are they? No bad dreams, no nightmares?"

He shrugged his shoulders in a boyish way. "No, they are my friends."

It worried me that a boy this young enjoyed the presence of invisible friends. I hoped and prayed he would develop normally. Taking a halting breath, I squeezed his shoulder. "You're a good man, Charlie Brown," I kidded.

He smiled at my poor attempt at cheering him up.

As Felicia and I walked to my car, the rumble of a large truck caught our attention, and we looked up. A large U-Haul truck pulled to a stop along the curb, and a man stuck his head out the window. "You guys know of a good church to attend?" a thick, gravely, Middle-Eastern voice asked.

It was Abdullah Hasad.

He and his family had been granted political asylum along with being awarded a sizable sum of money for helping bring Mohan to justice and partly recovering the Ark of God. The fact that the Ark disappeared shortly after being discovered was of little consequence. With Amber Kline's picture in hand, he fulfilled his part of the agreement and forced the Israeli government and the Palestinian Liberation Organization to work together to meet their obligation.

As Abdullah helped his wife and children from the truck, he began to introduce them one by one. "Of course you know Kamil."

We shook hands. He too had grown several inches. His warm brown eyes glowed with excitement.

Continuing, he said, "And this is my wife Sophie."

I nodded respectfully. To my surprise, she extended her hand. I was surprised at her offer, but with a nod from her husband, I accepted the gesture. "Thank you, Mr. Gasper, for helping my husband," she said with enthusiasm.

"Mrs. Hasad, your husband is a hero. His contribution was immeasurable. I owe him my life."

I could see Abdullah's face brighten with pride.

After a moment, he shifted his stance and continued the introductions. "These are my daughters Isabel, Malanie, and Sasha."

Upon hearing the name Sasha, Colt's eyes lit up. "You're Sasha?"

The wide-eyed girl with long dark flowing hair tucked back in a pony-tail nodded sheepishly. "Yes?" she offered him a coy smile.

Glancing at her from head to feet, he blurted, "You remind me of someone I once knew." All at once, he took her by the hand and tugged her forward. Pausing, he looked at Mr. Abdullah. "You don't have a rule about a boy holding hands with a girl before they are betrothed, do you?"

Shock registered on Abdullah's face. "No, but I—"

"Good, I'd like to show Sasha something, if you don't mind."

"Well, I—"

Before he could stop him, Colt pulled the breathless girl in the direction of the Easter village. "Come with me, I have something I'd like to show you." Their giggles followed them around the corner of the building.

As I watched the two young people scamper off, I knew Colt would turn out all right. "Abdullah, I have a feeling he has more in mind than just showing Sasha the Easter village."

Sophie stole a nervous glance at her husband.

"Oh? And what else would be on his mind?" he asked.

I laced my hands behind my back and smiled. "I think he would like to introduce Sasha to his mutter and papa." I didn't say it, but I got the distinct impression that the idea pleased Mr. and Mrs. Hasad. I also guessed Colt had found his soulmate.

After taking the Hasad family to the church office and introducing them to the pastor, I left them to talk, and Felicia and I returned to my car.

Glancing around, I caught movement in the corner of my eye.

Several pairs of glistening wings folded behind a couple of angels, and I knew we were not alone. I peered skyward and winked.

Chapter Fifty-Two

After closing my notebook, I laid my pencil down. It had been years since I'd thought about the Ark and Miss Kline and our wild escape from Israel. The secret Colt and I held had not been violated, the Ark of the Covenant was safe. However, there was one thing that still bothered me. When would God allow the Ark to be rediscovered?

As much as I knew about the future, I knew the Ark would play a major role in it. And I knew the trouble it would cause. Yet it was part of God's plan, and I longed to see that fulfilled. More than that, I longed for the Lord's return.

My years with Felicia had been so wonderful ... I couldn't imagine being separated from her by death. That was one adventure I did not look forward to. And yet, seeing the angel of the Lord gently guide Mr. Saul Mueller across the divide gave me courage.

As Colt eased down next to me, I glanced up. His clear eyes held no secret from me. "Colt, do you still see them? ... the angels?"

He lowered his head and spoke in my ear. Not that I was hard of hearing, but we didn't need inquisitive ears listening in on our conversation. "Yes, from time to time." His boyish voice had deepened into a manly tone; one of authority, of confidence ... of wisdom.

I wasn't surprised. "Have they told you anything?"

His face, once ruddy and flawless, now bore the weight of years. "They said I might have one more journey ahead of me."

"That's kinda vague. I've read better from a Fortune Cookie."

We shared a chuckle, one that harkened back a lighter moment in our common history.

Colt took a deep breath and grew somber. "What if the Ark of God was rediscovered? Do you think God's plan would be hastened or hindered?"

I shook my head. "I don't know."

"I've heard rumors, you know," he said cryptically.

My interest stirred. "Oh? Rumors? Of what?"

"In my travels, I've heard rumors of an ancient people ... and a tree."

My hearted quickened. I too had heard of such a tree, but with my attention being focused on the witch and her accursed medallion, I had no time to chase an old wives-tale. Now I began to wonder.

Colt's interest in biblical archeology was no secret. He had already gone on several digs after obtaining a doctorate in the subject and had made a name for himself in the archeological community.

"I certainly am not up to another quest, if you're asking me to join you."

A gleam danced in Colt's eyes and I knew what he'd say. "You are no older than Balthazar when he set out on the quest to find the Christ child."

"Correction, you must add a couple thousand years to my age. That definitely disqualifies me as a traveling partner," I said, rubbing my aching knees.

"Up to what, Grandfather?" Belle and Mel's heads popped up from behind a bush, their eyes sparkling with interest. Although Felicia and I had no children of our own, I claimed Colt as my son. Having his children call me Grandfather warmed my heart.

"Have you two been eavesdropping on our conversation?"

The two girls pranced up the stairs and squeezed up on my knees. Innocence dripped like honey from their golden hair. "We haven't been dropping any leaves, Grandfather? We just wanted to hear what you were talking about."

I laid aside my notebook and gave Colt a quick wink. Standing, I clutched my faithful staff and took a few steps. They were slower and more painful than I remembered, but then, that was to be expected in a man of my age. "We were just discussing how nice it would be to eat a bowl of homemade peach ice cream. Did you know I grew those peaches right here in Georgia?"

"Georgia?" Mel chimed "as in, 'Georgia, Georgia, the whole night through, just an ole sweet song, keeps Georgia on our minds,'" the twin girls crooned.

Gazing into their angelic faces made my heart stumble the same way it did whenever I looked at Felicia. "I feel sorry for the poor schleps who fall in love with you two girls one day."

The two girls exchanged devilish glances followed by ripples of giggling. "We've decided to marry you and daddy," they said in harmony.

Felicia and Sasha emerged from the kitchen with a tray of bowls, spoons and a keg of ice cream.

"I'm afraid your daddy and grandfather are spoken

for. You'll have to wait and find your own knights in shining armor."

The two girls offered us a chorus of endearing giggles, then began to dance in circles. After a few minutes, Belle skipped over and winked. "When I get married, I want to go on a long journey and find a great treasure."

Lifting her in my arms I stroked her golden hair. "And I look forward to my last journey being skyward where my real treasure awaits me."

Mel shimmied up to us, and Belle wormed from my arms and took her place next to her sister. Lifting their right hands, they formed the girl-scouts sign with their fingers. Squaring their shoulders they began. "We pledge our lives and our sacred honor to each other, and choose to follow where the God of Heaven leads us that we may fulfill His will. So say we all."

Colt and I returned the sign. "So say we all."

Discussion Questions

Which character did you find yourself drawn to?

What flaws in my characters did you see reflected in your own life?

Was there a moment in which you found yourself lost in the story?

In what way did you see a clear connection between the Messiah of in the Psalms and the Lord Jesus Christ's sacrificial death in Calvary?

Have you made Jesus the Lord of your life?

What issues are there in your life in which you need wise counsel?

When God's Word addresses those issues, would you be willing to obey it, even if it was painful?

Do you know someone with whom you could share this

story of hope and redemption?

After reading this story, what singular truth stood out in your mind?

Acknowledgments

Growing up in a home where my mother read stories out loud to me and my four siblings stoked my imagination, so it goes without saying, I love hearing my wife read my stories. She is my Alpha and Beta reader and I thank her for her patience and insight.

I also want to thank Elaine Day for her encouraging comments when she said; "This book has real potential. I really did enjoy reading it and wish you the best!!

The Chase Newton Series
by Bryan M. Powell

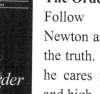

The Order
Follow investigative reporter Chase Newton as he goes undercover in search of the truth. What he finds puts him and those he cares for in mortal danger. Fast-paced and high- energy describes this first of three mystery and action thrillers.

The Oath
The president and vice president have been attacked. The vice president survived, but he is a hunted man. The man who was sworn in is an impostor and Chase must get a DNA from him to prove who the real president is.

The Outsider
After a thousand years of peace, the world is suddenly thrown into chaos as Satan is loosed from his prison. These action-packed stories will hold you breathless and capture your imagination until the exciting conclusion.

The Jared Russell Series
by Bryan M. Powell

Sisters of the Veil
Jared Russell, a former Marine turned architect, must navigate the minefield of hatred and prejudice to find the meaning of love and forgiveness.
ISBN - 978151057994

Power Play - #8 on Amazon Political Fiction
Jared and Fatemah Russell go Beirut, Lebanon, to establish the Harbor House, a refuge for converted Muslims and find themselves caught in a Middle East conflict of global proportions.
ISBN – 9781511402750

The Final Countdown – #25 on Amazon
The clock is ticking and Jared once again finds himself battling against forces beyond his control. Can he and his friends unravel the mystery in time to stop two radical Muslims from perpetrating a horrible crime against our country?
ISBN – 978153297825

Non-Fiction Series
by Bryan M. Powell

Seeing Jesus a Three Dimensional Look at Worship
Seeing Jesus is a thought providing and compelling expose' on what is true worship.
ISBN -9781511540582

Show Us the Father
A thirty-day devotional showing how Jesus demonstrated His Father's character and qualities.
ISBN -9781517633905

Faith, Family, and a Lot of Hard Work
Born the year Stock-Market crashed, Mr. Gillis grew up in South Georgia with a 3rd grade education. After being challenged to get the best job in the company, he worked hard and got a degree from the University of Georgia and Moody Bible Institute in Finance. By mid-life, he owed 14 companies. **ISBN -9781467580182**

About the Author

Novelist Bryan M. Powell is the author of 8 Christian Fiction novels, 2 Inspirational Books and 1 Memoir he co-authored. Working within a Christian ministry for over forty-two years, Bryan is uniquely qualified to write about Christian topics. His novels have been published by Tate Publishing, Lightening Source, Create Space, Kindle Direct Publishing and Vabella Publishing. His novel, The Witch and the Wise Men, held the #23 slot on Amazon's best seller's list and The Lost Medallion hit #22 on Amazon Christian Fantasy.

In addition to his novels, Bryan's short stories and other works appeared in *The North Georgia Writer* (PCWG's publication), *Relief Notes* (A Christian Authors Guild's book, released in 2014), and in the *Georgia Backroads* magazine.

Bryan is a member of the following organizations: American Christian Fiction Writers (ACFW), The Christian Author's Guild (President, 2016), The Paulding County Writers' Guild (PCWG), and the local chapter of ACFW, the New Life Writers Group.

www.facebook.com/authorbryanpowell
www.authorbryanpowell.wordpress.com
authorbryanpowell@reagan.com

Made in the USA
Lexington, KY
12 November 2019